A
Memory

Krishna Narayanan

Vite Publishing, Inc.
North Andover, Massachusetts

A Tender Melody
by Krishna Narayanan

Published by
Vite Publishing
800, Turnpike Street, Suite 300
North Andover, MA, 0 1845, USA.

Order from :
Book Masters, Inc.
30, Amberwood Parkway,
Ashland, OH 44805
order@bookmasters.com

All rights reserved. No part of this book may be reproduced and transmitted in any form or by any means, electronic or mechanical including photo copying, recording or by any information storage and retrieval system, without written permission from the another, except for the inclusion of brief quotations in a review.

Copyright@2006

First Printing 2006

Published in the United States of America

Layout, Compilation and Cover Design
Dr.T.S.Naryana Swamy

Printed by
Orion Printers,
11-6-871,Baig Island, Red Hills,
Hyderabad - 500 004, INDIA.

ISBN : 0-9706541-5-4

Foreword

It is great pleasure and privilege to pen the foreword for the Novel ***'A Tender Melody'*** *and in introducing the young author Krishna Narayanan.*

In his first book titled ***'Wasted Talent',*** *Krishna Narayanan presented the significant events of his life from childhood indirectly giving simple messages on the struggles of life and the secret of succesfully overcoming the struggles.*

In his second book ***'Quest'*** *he, like a mountaineer, highlighted every step he made on an upward journey towards great goals of his life filled with values.*

Standing from the top of a peak, he has allowed his emotional feelings and thoughts of romance and music to flow like a waterfalls and then rise like a fountain on earth with rythm in his Novel ***'A Tender Melody'*** *to be released on the eve of new year 2006.*

The author's deep rooted conviction on the divinity of romance and the sancitity of music is reflected in an effective language with tenderness in the novel. His Novel style is made intersting to the reader by presenting the conversation of characters in direct speech in a drama format. The author's hidden histrionic talents, artistic skills, commitment to human values, aspirations of love and devotion to music are reflected throughout the Novel.

It is a novel with a romantic theme described through tender expressions mixed with musical melody. I am sure that the readers will identify themselves with some character of the novel and enjoy recapitulating their pleasant and unforgettable memories of the past.

Dr. T.S. Narayana Swamy
Media Research Co-ordinator
Tattvaloka *(An International English monthly)*

About the Author

This novel is **Krishna Narayanan's** third book. He has already authored two books; **"Wasted Talent;** *musings of an autistic"* and **"Quest ;** *search for a quality life"*.

He studied calculus to non-linear differential equations in Mathematics and different aspects of Physics including Quantum Physics. He has completed all the course work at home for a B.S.Level Electrical Engineering degree.

He has a special love for English Classics and English language which is reflected in his books.

Classical music is dear to his heart.

Dedication

To my Dad
*My Friend,
Philosopher and
Guide*

Preface

I wrote this novel for fun and joy !

It depicts youth in this modern technology dominated life. That is the busy, fastpaced, stressful business environment. On the other side, is music - deep and soothing. Utmost torn are the key characters of this novel between the two. This is a snapshot of modern life.

I enjoyed writing this tender love story. I hope you love these characters as much as I do !!!

Krishna Narayanan

Chapter - 1

Kumar and Harrish were having lunch at the MIT Student Union Cafeteria in Cambridge Mass, USA. They had formed a strong friendship. Harrish was a tall, handsome, young man with sharp features but a serious-looking intellectual. He was completing his PhD in Economics at Sloan school. Kumar was good-looking, smart, outgoing, glib, talkative and jovial. Kumar was a PhD graduate student in math & computer science.

Kumar started the conversation with a question; "Harrish, how was your trip to India?"

Harrish replied, "I had a great time in India. My mom cooked delicious dishes and I got to hear some divine carnatic music."

Harrish's parents lived in Chennai, India. Harrish's father received his PhD from Stanford University, USA and went back to India to teach in Indian Institute of Technology, Chennai. He was the head of the Computer Science Department there.

Harrish asked, "Kumar, how was your vacation?

Kumar answered, "Well, Harrish – I went back to our home in Atlanta. I just relaxed – I played a lot of tennis with my brother, Rohan"

Kumar's father was the Chairman of Neurology department at Emory University in Atlanta.

Harrish asked, "Kumar, what does your brother do?"

Kumar replied smilingly, "He is in medicine and trying to follow the footsteps of his father."

Harrish smiled and said, "Like father, like son."

Kumar asked, "Harrish, what did carnatic music do for you?"

"Kumar, marvelous music enthralls the mind. My cousin, Geetha, is a connoisseur of carnatic music, an expert. She is an upcoming vocalist too" replied Harrish.

Kumar was curious— "How old is she?"

Harrish replied, "Twenty three; she is dedicated to music."

Kumar asked smilingly, "Is she married?"

"No, she is too involved with her music. Carnatic music can be demanding, deep and tough and it involves dedicated attention."

"Very interesting." commented Kumar.

Harrish continued, "To Geetha, carnatic music is an all consuming passion. It is an ancient art and so many scholars have developed it over several centuries – Ragas capture one's soul."

Kumar enquired, "Harrish, how come Geetha got so interested in Carnatic music?"

Harrish replied with emotion, "It is a long story, Kumar. Her father passed away suddenly when she was ten. That was a devastating blow to her. She listened to popular songs to cheer herself. One day, she heard M.S. Subbhalakshmi's meera bhajans. She was charmed and she began to devote all her time to listening to MS. Slowly, that led to her love of carnatic music.."

Kumar was touched and became thoughtful and then said, "Geetha, indeed is a special person."

Kumar was not too familiar with carnatic music but was more curious about Geetha and hence asked, " Harrish, what is a raga?"

Harrish replied, "Raga is a melody defined by notes Sa, ri, ga, ma, pa, da, ni. Each Raga has a specific rising notes and the same or different falling notes."

Harrish intoned a couple of Ragas.

Kumar was dumbfounded but his interest increased. "How many Ragas does Geetha know?"

"I wouldn't know – may be around three hundred or more."

At this point, Kumar spotted Latha, a fellow doctoral student working on her thesis in mathematics, bringing her food in a tray. He called her name "Latha!"

She turned around and said "Hi, Kumar!"

Kumar asked, "Do you like to join us, Latha? "

Latha said," OK". Latha is a young woman with bright eyes and beautiful features and her intelligence shone through her sparkling eyes. Latha's parents lived in Syracuse. Her father got his PhD in Economics from Harvard University and her mother, through intense self-effort founded and managed a real estate business.

Kumar introduced Harrish to Latha;

"Latha, this is Harrish, my friend, who is doing his PhD. in Economics; Harrish, this is Latha who is my colleague in the math department. Latha, Harrish has just returned from Chennai, and is giving me an insight to South Indian classical music. Latha, do you know anything about Ragas?"

A Tender Melody

Latha looked at Harrish and was quite impressed with his handsome face.

Latha replied, "Oh, yes, I love carnatic music – my favorite is, of course, "Thodi Raga" Harrish said "Thodi is divine."

Kumar was baffled and said, "You guys are going too fast – slow down – explain to me what "Thodi" Raga is?"

Harrish replied, "Thodi is a beautiful and deep raga", He sang the tune in a low voice and Kumar liked the tune and said " That is a nice tune. I need to listen to south Indian music. Can you get me a few cassettes?"

Harrish said, "Of course",

Latha said to Harrish, "Your tune is perfect – you have a good grasp of south Indian music."

Harrish replied politely, "Thanks, my cousin Geetha is doing her PhD in music and I have learnt a lot from her."

Kumar teased, "Oh, she is going to be Dr.Geetha soon."

Latha interrupted, "Why not? Carnatic music demands total dedication. Actually, next week there is a music concert at MIT by Bombay Jayashree"

Harrish commented," Is that so? I want to hear her."

Kumar intervened, "I will also go. Latha, are you going?"

Latha answered "Oh yes, Kumar, I love music"

At that time a young and a beautiful woman came to their table and said in a perfect English accent, "Hi, Latha, I have been looking for you - I tried calling"

Latha replied, " Hi, Veena, what a pleasant surprise! – Would you like to join us for lunch?"

Then Veena came with her tray; Latha introduced Harrish and Kumar to her and then said, "This is Veena, a PhD student in computer science. Veena – are you coming to the music concert next week?" asked Latha.

Veena replied, "Latha, you know, I love carnatic music and I definitely plan to come."

Veena was unusually beautiful; she was also brilliant. Her father was the founder and chairman of a billion dollar high-tech company. Veena was so unassuming that no one would say that she was the daughter of a multi millionaire.

Kumar, the most talkative person in the group, asked Latha. "Hey Latha, I wanted to ask you for a long time – why did you choose math as your major?"

Latha said, "I like math because it is highly stimulating and challenging to the mind. Logic is its basis and is deeply intellectual. I enjoy math."

Harrish watched Latha as she spoke and said, "Me too; math is nurturing to the mind. It deepens the mind."

Kumar added, "Nothing is as deep as math. I like it more than computer science. But I have more job opportunities in computer science."

Kumar turned to Veena and asked, "Veena, do you like computer science"?

Veena replied,"Yes, Kumar, it is a vast field and one can branch into so many different disciplines, like math, linguistics, artificial intelligence etc."

Kumar added, "That is true – it is a diverse field."

Harrish commented, "Almost all fields, nowadays, use computer."

Veena observed, "My love is artificial intelligence. "How can we simulate the human mind on the computer?" is the challenging question."

Kumar responded, "That is fascinating".

At this time, Harrish observed that he had to leave to attend a seminar and everyone left agreeing to meet at the music concert next week. In the evening, Harrish was in a serious, involved mood. He was thinking about Latha; "Her lovely sparkling eyes are captivating" he thought.

"She is attractive and brilliant. We both love carnatic music and math. But she has been born and brought up in USA even though her parents are Indian. I have grown up in India. I am not sure if we are compatible and I am not sure if I can adjust to American culture. Let us wait and see ; it is too early."

Latha thought differently, "I like Kumar's sense of humor and outgoing personality.

But I am impressed with Harrish's love of carnatic music. But, he has grown up in India and there is a cultural gap."

As Latha started to think in this vein, her phone rang and she heard the familiar voice of her mom. "Hi, Latha dear."

"Hi, mom."

Her mom said in a hurried voice - "Hey Latha – I would like to come to MIT campus next week. I have a meeting in Boston. Is that okay?"

"OK, mom. Actually there is a concert by Bombay Jayashree. Please arrange your trip so that you could attend that."

"Great, Latha, my secretary will reserve a room at the Marriott and I will let you know all the details as soon as the trip is firmed up."

"OK, mom, how is dad?"

"He is alright, Latha, but a little sick this morning".

"What did the doctor say, mom?"

"Latha, he said his heart is OK but dad's blood pressure shot up a little. But it is under control now."

"I am sure you are taking good care of him, mom."

"I am trying to, Latha; sometimes, it is very tough."

" Mom, don't get discouraged; you are doing a great job"

Her mom sounded busy and said, "Thanks Latha - will see you next week – take care."

After hanging up the phone, Latha started to think about her mom. Her dad was a top executive in a Fortune 500 company. When Latha was eight years old, he had a major heart attack. That changed their life drastically. Her mom became his nurse at home and also had to manage the home. She worried that her husband might die and she might had to take care of children.

So, she started as an apprentice in the real estate business. She had to learn the hard way the intricacies of the business. She had to work hard and put in long hours. Suddenly, her life became intense and hectic. In a few years, she learnt the business and was successful.

At present, she had a staff of twenty real estate agents and had a flourishing, independent business. Single handedly, she had brought up Latha and her brother, Vijay. Her mom's sacrifice and courage were touching. Her mom's love for the family was deep. Latha loved her mom dearly.

Chapter - 2

The music concert was organized in a large, modern auditorium. The Concert Hall was getting filled up fast. Harrish came in early and sat in the front row.

Latha and her mom came rather early also and Latha proceeded to the front row. Latha was well dressed in a colorful Indian salwar and her mom in a sari. Harrish turned around and spotted Latha. He was at first captivated by her charming personality and the lovely "salwar" dress. He quickly checked himself but not before Latha's mother's alert eyes noticed his fascination of Latha. She also saw his quick self-control. Far innocent was Latha and was oblivious of Harrish's admiration.

When Latha saw Harrish, she introduced her mom to him. She greeted him saying "namasthe" with folded hands. Harrish returned the greeting. Latha's mom, Mrs.Gangadharan, sat next to Harrish and they started a small conversation before the concert.

"Harrish, do you like carnatic music?", asked Mrs.Gangadharan.

"Yes, Mrs. Gangadharan, I like it very much", answered Harrish.

"Harrish, where and how did you get your interest?"

"My mom loves carnatic music and she sings at home. I got my interest from her. Later on, my cousin, Geetha went deeply went into music and that accentuated my interest."

"Harrish, I used to sing also and that is how Latha became interested. However, I am rather busy now. I still love that music."

Latha interrupted this conversation and introduced to her mom to Veena who had just arrived. Mrs. Gangadharan greeted her and hugged her.

Kumar arrived and was pleased to meet Latha's mom.

The concert started. Bombay Jayashree sang in a neoclassical style and hence attractive to young students. The hall was full. Her music touches the soul and is deep and melodious. During the concert, Mrs.Gangadharan turned to Harrish. "Harrish, do you know this ragam? – I forgot the name".

Harrish replied "Nalinakanti".

Mrs.Gangadharan replied "Thanks – Now I remember. It is so melodious."

Harrish agreed. Mrs. Gangadharan was impressed with Harrish's grasp of carnatic music. At the end of the concert, the audience gave a warm applause to Bombay Jayashree.

Mrs. Gangadharan invited Harrish, Kumar and Veena to join Latha and her for dinner. She took them in her rented car to a nice restaurant. They seated themselves around a round table with Latha to the right of her mom and Veena to Mrs.Gangadharan's left. Kumar sat next to Veena and Harrish next to Kumar. As it was a round table, Harrish was next to Latha. He could not help but notice her. She was indeed attractive.

Kumar asked Mrs. Gangadharan, "Mrs. Gangadharan, what song did you like best?"

Mrs.Gangadharan replied, "Thodi ragam song" "Koluva maraghatha".

Veena chipped in "Me too".

Latha said, "Sarvam Brahmamayam – it was melodious".

Mrs.Gangadharan asked, "Harrish, what song did you like best?".

Harrish answered, "Thodi also- it was a grand song "Koluva maragatha". "Sarvam Brahmamayam" is my next favorite".

Kumar joked "Hey, Harrish, are you trying to get Latha's attention by adding the second choice?"

Latha laughed at the joke as she was an ABI (American born Indian) but Harrish was a little embarrassed and blushed a little.

Veena noticed it and so did Mrs.Gangadharan, but Latha did not. Mrs.Gangadharan came quickly to Harrish's rescue, "Kumar, please don't tease him".

Kumar remarked, "I am just joking. Look, Latha is laughing."

Mrs. Gangadharan said, "He is from India and not fully used to such jokes."

Kumar smilingly replied, " Mrs. Gangadharan, he has to get used to such jokes".

The conversation was interrupted as the waiter came to take orders.

They ordered Nan, malai kofta, mutter paneer, shahi paneer, and jal fareezhi and shared them. As they were enjoying the food, Kumar who was next to Veena asked her, " Veena, where do your parents live?"

"San Francisco."

"That must be fun., Veena"

"Yes, Kumar, I love it." said Veena

Asked Mrs.Gangadharan, "Veena, what work do your parents do?"

Veena answered, "My dad has a passion for high speed computers. San Francisco is the Mecca for high tech inventors. My dad started a high Tech company twenty four years ago."

Kumar enquired, "Is that Gigabit Inc.?"

Veena said in surprise, "Yes, Kumar, how did you guess that?"

"I am in computer science, Veena. Did you forget that? Gigabit is a pace setter in ultra high speed computers".

When Veena and Kumar started to get deep into computers, Latha interjected –"You guys are talking shop. Please do that later." Veena and Kumar apologized.

Veena stated, "By the way, my dad, Dr.Ravi, is coming here next week to give a talk on High speed computers."

Kumar said, "He got his PhD from MIT. I am sure his talk would be well attended. I will definitely come."

Harrish and Latha both agreed in chorus, that they would come to that talk. They agreed that they would all meet outside the auditorium after the talk. Mrs.Gangadharan said, "I would like to attend too but I am not sure that I could make it". After dinner, they all went back to the campus.

When they arrived at the campus, Latha and her mom went to her mom's room in the hotel. Mom remarked, "Latha, today is the day your dad had his heart attack fifteen years ago."

Latha said, "Mom, what a terrible day it was."

Mom said, "Life takes on suddenly unexpected turns, Latha"

"Why, mom?" asked Latha.

"Latha, one theory is that it is "prarabdham" *i.e.,* the net culmination of one's past actions. In each previous life, we have done actions for which the results may come in a later birth. This might explain a lot of events in life."

Latha questioned, "Mom, how do we know— what we did?"

"Latha, we don't. But, we can guess from the results."

"But, it appears so random" said Latha.

"True, because, we don't know the past. Whichever way we look, life has these sudden twists and turns."

"Mom, we can spend hours on this topic. How is dad?"

"He is OK; active and reasonably healthy. Latha, did you notice Harrish admiring you?"

"Mom, really——I didn't –How do you know?"

"Latha, you just know from the way he looked at you—not only in the auditorium but also during dinner. Remember, he was seated next to you."

" Well. Mom, we have not talked about marriage etc"

" Latha, you were very much into studies"

"Mom, still am—I really want to finish my PhD—and then think about these issues"

"Latha, What are you looking for?"

"Mom, off the cuff,—probably someone well versed in both cultures—smart, good looking and all the good stuff."

"Latha, where would Harrish fit into this?"

"Mom, that is an unfair question—you just told me—I need to know more about him. It will take time. I am not in a hurry—I am busy, busy."

"Okay, Latha, I got it. Let us wait and see."

When Veena went to her room, she thought of the dinner, "It was a wonderful evening and an excellent group of people. I like Latha and her mom. Kumar is smart and jovial. Harrish is serious and thoughtful. He loves carnatic music. He is handsome and likeable. But, is he attracted to Latha? Why? Does she like him? She did not give any encouragement."

Kumar thought in a different vein; "Harrish seems attracted to Latha so quickly. He hardly knows her. She is totally unaware of his interest. Veena is brilliant and pretty—she is indeed attractive."

When Harrish reached his room, he started to wonder, " What is going on? I seem to be drawn to Latha. Why? Veena is more beautiful and equally classy. Why is this attraction? She has little interest—strange—I need to think deeply later—I am a little busy now."

Chapter - 3

Harrish was pouring over issues of the Sunday New York Times and the Wall Street Journal for a summer job. One advertisement caught his eye. It said, "Wanted a PhD student in economics to research for a book on India - USA trade enhancement and strategies for business development – call Dr.Raman."

Harrish called Dr.Raman immediately. Harrish's intense interest in Indo-US business development coupled with his desire to start a business in India and USA impressed Dr. Raman. Harrish had the right credentials with a graduate study at

Delhi School of economics and now a PhD student at MIT- Sloan school. Therefore, Dr. Raman invited him to come and visit him.

Next day, Harrish flew to Syracuse to meet Dr.Raman. He prepared well for this meeting. He had worked one summer in the Export promotion center in Delhi; there, he wrote an outstanding paper for which he received," President of India's Gold Medal." He brought that paper and the Gold Medal with him. He also took a copy of his PhD thesis in preparation on US international trade.

Harrish took a cab from the airport to Dr.Raman's house. The house was a sprawling twelve room colonial house with a beautiful and well-maintained garden. Harrish rang the doorbell.

A woman opened the door. Both the lady and Harrish were speechless.

Lady said, "Harrish".

Harrish exclaimed, "Mrs.Gangadharan".

It took a few minutes for the shock to die down; at that time, Dr.Raman came. He was in his fifties, tall, lean with grey hair. He looked an erudite scholar. He was astonished that Mrs.Gangadharan knew Harrish. He asked enquiringly,

"Chitra, do you know each other?"

" Honey, this is Harrish, who is Latha's friend. I met him in MIT a week ago", answered Mrs.Gangadharan.

Harrish added, "I did not know that this is Latha's house."

Dr.Raman sheepishly said, "Oh! I used the name Raman because I did not want too many people to know that I am writing this book at this time. If I had advertised as Dr.Gangadharan, you probably would have connected to Latha as I am in Syracuse."

"Yes, I would have" replied Harrish.

"What a twist! However, I am glad to see you, Harrish, especially as Latha's friend. Please come in. Would you like a cup of coffee?" asked Mrs.Gangadharan.

Harrish assented and they all chatted laughingly over a cup of coffee. Mrs. Gangadharan asked Harrish to stay for lunch and said, "I am going to office now and would be back at 1 PM."

Harrish and Dr.Gangadharan spent the morning discussing the book. Dr.Gangadharan was deeply impressed with Harrish and his being a friend of Latha clinched the deal.

A Tender Melody

To Harrish, Dr.Gangadharan appeared brilliant, thoughtful in his speech and outstanding in his manners.

Mrs.Gangadharan and they sat together for lunch. Right at that time, the doorbell rang. Mrs.Gangadharan opened the door and there was a big surprise. Latha was standing at the door. Mrs. Gangadharan hugged her in delight and said in an excited voice,"What a surprise?"

"Yes, mom! I wanted to do something unexpected! Where is dad?" said Latha.

"Latha, we are just planning to have lunch – I hope you have not had your lunch, come and join us."

Latha did not wait for her mom to finish but was already rushing to the dining room to meet her dad. There she was surprised to see Harrish seriously chatting with her dad.

She exclaimed "Harrish!"

Harrish was totally taken aback.

Her dad intervened and said,

"Latha, Harrish applied for my summer job and I had used the name "Raman" So, he had no idea that this is your home"

Latha added," Well! Now I understand – Harrish is doing economics PhD with an excellent background about India – but what a bolt out of the blue!"

Mrs.Gangadharan came in and remarked,

"Latha, I was so speechless to see Harrish this morning"

Harrish added "Me too!"

They all had a good laugh and sat for lunch. They were cheerfully chitchatting and eating lunch. Latha noticed that her mom was especially kind and attentive to Harrish. Her dad seemed to like Harrish enormously. At this point, she suddenly remembered what her mom had told her. Her mom saw Harrish look at her admiringly in the Jayshree concert at MIT. This visit would bring Harrish more often to her house. She liked Harrish but not romantically. Hence, these visits may embarrass her and she was not sure what she should do. These thoughts clouded her face.

Harrish watched her face and noticed her thoughtfulness. He was puzzled; he became pensive "something is wrong" he mused, " She must be worried about something related to my visit". Then it dawned on him,"maybe, she is worried about my liking her when she is not; these visits may put her in a predicament."

Far cornered was he. He loved the job but he might lose Latha forever.

At the end of lunch, Dr.Gangadharan and Harrish spent an hour completing their discussion on the book.

Latha, then, as a courtesy, offered to drive Harrish to the airport. Harrish readily accepted it because he wanted to talk to her to allay her fears. As soon as they got into the car, Harrish said to Latha, "Latha, I want to talk to you. I could even take a later flight. Could we go to an ice-cream parlor since we both love ice-cream?"

Latha agreed and she took him to a nice ice-cream restaurant. Harrish ordered pineapple sundae and Latha, hot fudge sundae. The ice cream was delicious and it relaxed them both.

Harrish started,"Latha, I saw your face was rather clouded during lunch time. I felt that it had something to do with my visit. As you know, I came not knowing that it is your home. I love the job your dad has assigned me. However, I am in a delicate territory here – either your mom or Kumar might have told you that I have a liking for you. You may feel embarrassed that I might be here often. Am I correct?"

Latha colored a little and said softly, "Yes, Harrish".

Harrish added," Please do not worry. I came here only for the summer job. You need not concern yourself about me. I would just stick to the job. I promise you that"

Latha added, "You see, Harrish, I am now focused on completing my PhD. This is not against you, in particular."

"Latha, I understand. You are involved deeply in your PhD and you do not want to be distracted. I can appreciate it." replied Harrish kindly.

Latha felt much relaxed after this conversation and her spirits were high and jovial. Harrish and Latha then chatted freely about Veena, Kumar, Dr.Ravi's forthcoming visit, her parents etc. and were in good cheer. The conversation drifted to carnatic music, which they both loved.

Latha said, "Harrish, do you know Sanjay Subramanian may be giving a concert in Boston next month"

Harrish replied, "Great! I like his energy and love for carnatic music. I have heard him often in Chennai."

Latha remarked, "Sometimes, Harrish, I want to go to Chennai in December to attend all these music concerts"

"Well, Latha; my mom goes to a lot of concerts in December. You could stay in our house and she would take you around. She is a good hostess also."

Latha said smilingly "Harrish, I might take up on that offer".

Harrish replied quietly, "Latha, please let me know when you want to go."

Latha answered, "Harrish, I have my PhD to finish - may be after a year."

Latha dropped off Harrish at the airport and came home in a cheerful mood. Harrish, on the other hand, was not that happy. He felt that Latha had zero interest in him. Moreover, he had to be careful not to embarrass her. In addition, he would be seeing her often and he should not display any emotion. He thought, "This is going to be a self inflicted pain. But, I have to rise to the occasion and keep my long term goal in mind"

When Latha came home, her mom was astonished to see her in a good mood and she remarked, " Latha, you seem to be in happy mood."

"Yes, mom. Harrish noticed during lunch that I was somewhat concerned about his visits. He is quite sensitive."

"What was your concern, Latha?"

"Well, mom, you told me that Harrish seemed interested in me. I was worried that these trips may prove embarrassing to me."

"What did Harrish say?" asked a concerned mom.

"Mom, he assured me that these visits would be strictly professional. That makes me relaxed."

"Latha, what is your opinion of Harrish?"

"Harrish is smart and sensitive; he is tall and handsome. But, I want to focus on my PhD now"

Latha's mom knew that Latha is strong willed and so she kept quiet and said nothing.

Latha added, " Mom, by the way, Harrish invited me to stay with his mom to see Chennai and attend music concerts. But, I told him that I might be quite busy for a year"

Mom saw a small opportunity here and said, "Latha, you could do math during day time and go to concerts in the evening. You love carnatic music. The vacation would relax you and actually stimulate your mind."

Latha saw logic in her mom's words. She had been working very hard and could use a vacation. The idea of listening to several top-notch music concerts in a couple of weeks thrilled her.

"Mom; you have a point there. Let me think and then discuss it with Harrish."

Chapter - 4

Harrish, who returned from Syracuse a couple of days ago, got ready to attend Dr.Ravi's talk. Dr.Ravi, a well-known expert on high-speed computers, ran his billion-dollar company very profitably through the vicissitudes of the economy. He is a much-sought-after speaker but extremely busy. His last talk at MIT was five years ago. Hence, Kumar expected a large turnout and he felt many top executives from high tech companies around 128 would attend the talk.

Kumar and Harrish came almost 20 minutes before the talk and found the auditorium almost full already. Luckily, Kumar and Harrish found good seats in the third row. Veena and Latha were coming to the front row as Veena had prearranged seats in the front row. They spotted Kumar and Harrish and they waved their hands. Both Veena and Latha were well dressed and were beautiful. Latha flew back to MIT from Syracuse just to hear the talk.

Dr.Ravi and the MIT President arrived a few minutes before 4 PM and shook hands with some of the dignitaries in the front row. At 4 PM, MIT President introduced Dr.Ravi as one of the role models for aspiring students. When Dr.Ravi rose to speak, he was given a standing ovation. Veena was proud of her father; Kumar, Harrish, and Latha were thrilled by the achievement of a person from India. Dr.Ravi gave an inspiring talk on the challenges facing high speed computing. He again got standing ovation at the end of the talk.

As prearranged, Kumar and Harrish came out first and waited for Veena and Latha. Harrish said to Kumar, "What an audience! Some top executives from leading computer companies were there"

Kumar added, "Harrish, have you noticed some outstanding professors in the audience? They do not normally attend such talks."

"The auditorium was filled to capacity. Students were even standing." commented Harrish.

At this point, they saw Veena and Latha coming towards them.

Kumar said, "Veena, that was a great talk."

Harrish added, "Veena, I enjoyed it and I was proud."

Dr.Ravi spotted Veena and came towards them. Veena introduced her friends, "Dad this is Latha in math, this is Harrish in Economics, this is Kumar in computer science, all doing their PhDs."

Dr.Ravi warmly shook their hands. Veena said, "Dad, you are in a hurry. We will meet you for dinner."

Dr.Ravi said goodbye and left with other dignitaries. Veena had gotten a promise from him to spend the evening quietly with her friends.

Veena remarked to her friends, "We will all meet at 7.30 in Bombay palace. I need to drag my father from meetings. Latha, may be, you could help me. Kumar and Harrish, we will meet you at the restaurant."

Latha, Veena and Dr.Ravi arrived on time at the restaurant. Harrish and Kumar came a few minutes later thinking that Dr.Ravi would be late. They were surprised to find Veena and others.

Veena said, "Kumar, we were here on time".

Kumar smilingly replied, "What a surprise!" They all laughed.

Dr.Ravi had a long relaxed coversation with them about their future careers. Latha wanted to do research in mathematics; Harrish wanted to start a software company and Kumar was interested in developing a new venture in High Speed Routers.

After dinner, Veena dropped off Kumar and Latha in her dad's rented car at the campus and Harrish, as a courtesy accompanied Dr. Ravi to his hotel. Veena and Harrish walked back to the campus.

Harrish started the conversation,

"Veena, that was an excellent dinner and lively discussion with your dad."

"Thanks, Harrish. By the way, you said you are starting a new software venture with your friend, Aravind who is in Stanford. Where do you plan to start—in Boston or near Stanford?"

"Veena, San Francisco, for sure. I love the warm climate and the high-tech atmosphere in Palo Alto."

"Harrish, I agree—I love San Francisco too. When would you be finishing your PhD?"

"Could be in six months, Veena"

"Harrish, are you that far along?"

"Yes, Veena—I am close to finishing"

"That is great. I just passed my qualifying exam. I have to pick a thesis topic."

"Congratulations, Veena. Completing the qualifying is tough—you would be a little bit more relaxed now."

"I hope so, Harrish. By the way, do you sing carnatic music?"

"No, Veena—that is one of my regrets"

"Me too— my mom is excellent. I was too busy to learn from her."

They reached the campus and went their separate ways after saying goodbyes.

Kumar started thinking about his summer job. He felt he wanted to start his own company. Nevertheless, Dr.Ravi's offer during dinner of a summer job at Gigabit was great and the lure of Gigabit was too powerful to resist. He very much wanted practical training, especially in the marketing area. It is a new field for him and so he wrote to Dr.Ravi requesting an assignment in the marketing department of high-speed routers. Dr.Ravi thought it was quite appropriate and invited him for an interview. Kumar decided to go and informed Veena about his plans.

Two weeks later, he left for San Francisco. At the San Francisco airport he walked through the exit ramp from the plane, he entered the security gate area. To his infinite amazement, he saw Veena waiting for him. She was well dressed and looked elegant and very charming. He was in total shock. At MIT, he did not take that much interest in her. Now, she looked very attractive and charming to him.

Kumar gave her a big smile and she returned it.

Kumar said, "What a surprise, Veena! "

Veena smiled and said, "Yes, Kumar—I came here a few days ago quite suddenly to see my mom who was very ill. She is much better now and hence, I thought of meeting you here."

Kumar replied cheerfully, "I am so happy you came. This is my first visit to San Francisco. You could be so helpful. How is your mom now?"

A Tender Melody

"Much better, Kumar—thanks—do you have baggage?"

"Yes, Veena— I need to go to baggage claim area."

Veena took Kumar to the baggage claim area. While waiting, they chitchatted about his plans for the day.

Kumar asked, "Veena, where is Gigabit Inc?"

"It is in Palo Alto, Kumar, where Stanford University is. Our home is close by too."

"Stanford area is the high tech Mecca in California. Outstanding are the companies around Stanford".

"Yes, HP is there also. By the way, do you want to see San Francisco or Stanford?"

Kumar replied, "Veena, Stanford is my preference; I am curious about the High Tech business complex."

Veena said, "That is fine, Kumar— we will drive through San Francisco; you can see the telegraph hill and I will also show you the Golden Gate Bridge"

"Great, Veena "

"Kumar, my dad invites you for dinner tonight at home."

"Thanks Veena – I would be so delighted to meet him. Tomorrow he is very busy and I am only meeting key people in the marketing department."

"Kumar, let me go and bring the car. You can wait outside near the gate. I would be here in about ten minutes."

Kumar brought the baggage out and saw Veena driving a stylish sports car——Porsche.

He got into the car and said, "It is a lovely car, Veena"

"Thanks, Kumar. It is my brother's. Kumar, did you have lunch?

"Veena, not a good one. I hate plane food."

"Kumar, do you like Mexican food?"

"Yes—Veena— now I am really hungry."

"Me too—Kumar. I had only a light breakfast. I know a small but elegant Mexican restaurant close by. We will stop there."

Soon they went into a modern, attractive Mexican restaurant. After they ordered food, Veena asked, "Kumar, have you talked to Harrish lately?"

"No – Veena – both of us have been extremely busy"

"Well – I talked to Latha yesterday. She called when she heard about my mom's illness"

"How is Latha? I have not seen much of her either."

"There is a reason for it. She went home suddenly three weeks ago.

"Could you guess whom she met there?"

"No, Veena"

"In her Syracuse home, she saw Harrish having lunch."

"Wow! That is a big surprise – how come?"

"Harrish had gone there for an interview with her father without knowing it was Latha's home. Her father had used a different name. When Latha's mom opened the door, they were both stunned. They had a good laugh afterwards."

Kumar exclaimed "What a hilarious story!"

Nevertheless, a thought flashed through Kumar's mind and with a serious face, he asked Veena,

"Veena, how well do you know Latha?"

"Quite well, Kumar— we have known each other for three years – quite intimately in the last one year."

Delicious Mexican food arrived at this point and as they were both hungry, they started eating.

Then, Veena asked with curiosity;

"Kumar, why did you ask me how well do I know Latha?"

Kumar said seriously;

"Veena, what I am going to tell you is delicate. That is why."

"Now I understand, Kumar"

Kumar then said in a low tone, " Veena, Harrish likes Latha and this summer assignment would bring them closer. I think Latha is neutral and hence this might be embarrassing to her."

Veena said calmly, "Kumar, Latha talked about it "

Kumar asked with concern, " What did she say, Veena?"

A Tender Melody — *a difficult situation or state*   19

"Latha told me that Harrish noticed her predicament and brought out that issue openly. He promised her that his visit would be strictly professional. That relieved and relaxed her"

Kumar said with satisfaction, " Veena, Harrish has shown great sensitivity and has handled a delicate issue with a touch of elegance"

"In fact, Kumar, Latha is so impressed with Harrish that she might take up his offer to stay in his parent's home in Chennai in December"

"That would be great, Veena"

Now, Veena became quite serious, looked at Kumar, and asked with concern,

"Kumar, could I ask you a question?"

Kumar felt her concerned look and replied softly;

"Veena, please go ahead. If I know, I would answer"

Veena addressed him with an undertone of irritation;

"Thanks, Kumar. My question is in a way simple. Harrish appears smart and intelligent. He should know that Latha's interest is at best lukewarm. Why is he persisting?"

Kumar was somewhat taken aback by this sharp question and the undertone of irritation. He thought for a minute and answered quietly; *not clearly expressed*

" Veena, you are right. Harrish is thoughtful by nature. However, in this case, everything is new to him; he has not been that interested in any one before— moreover, he is extremely busy with his thesis, summer job etc. He is vaguely aware of her lack of interest and has told me so. I think he is letting his optimism rule here."

Veena did not let go but persisted;

"Kumar, do you really understand it?"

Kumar was baffled by her question but defended Harrish since he liked him;

"Veena, all of this has taken place in less than a month or so—please give more time——especially when feelings are involved, time is important. Moreover, Latha could change her mind."

Veena appreciated Kumar's defense of his friend but did not agree with him. However, "Latha could change her mind" was a distant possibility. Hence, she let it go.

The lunch was over soon and they departed for Golden Gate Bridge. As they entered the bridge, Kumar was impressed with its spectacular view.

Veena pointed out;

"Kumar, this is one of the longest suspension bridges in the world."

Kumar replied, " Really, Veena—it is breathtaking—when was it built? Do you know?"

Veena answered, "May be, around 1937."

Kumar loved the drive through the bridge and the magnificent view of the Golden Gate and San Francisco Bay.

Veena asked, "Kumar, could we now proceed to Stanford—about one hour ride?"

Kumar agreed and when they entered the campus, Kumar saw it was a sprawling, spacious university with beautiful Spanish style buildings. The tall Hoover Institution building impressed Kumar.

After seeing the Stanford campus, Veena dropped Kumar at his hotel and Kumar promised to come for dinner at 8 PM. He rested a bit, took shower and rented a car.

He drove to Veena's house and as he approached it, he saw an elegant California Ranch situated on top of a hill, tastefully lighted. Kumar parked the car, walked to the house and rang the doorbell.

Veena opened the door. She was dressed in a beautiful sari and looked gorgeous. Her beauty surprised Kumar. At MIT campus, she was just another fellow graduate student. Now, she was an attractive woman.

Kumar said smilingly, "Hi, Veena"

Veena returned the smile and at that time, Dr.Ravi came in and extended his hand to Kumar and said, "Hi, Kumar; welcome to San Francisco."

Kumar shook his hand and replied,

"Hi, Dr.Ravi. I am glad to be here. Dr.Ravi, it was a big surprise that Veena came to the airport and it made the trip so much better."

"Yes, Kumar— she came here to see her mother who suddenly got very sick. Her temperature shot up to 105⁰F. We were all scared. Nevertheless, luckily, it turned out to be a special virus infection that abated readily. She is amazingly fine, now."

Now, Mrs. Aruna Ravi came in. She was dressed in an elegant sari and looked a little tired but quite healthy. She was in her fifties but attractive. She smiled at Kumar and with folded hands said "Namasthe".

A Tender Melody

Kumar returned the smile and the "Namasthe" greetings.

Mrs. Ravi asked Kumar, "Kumar, could I get you something to drink?"

"Mrs. Ravi, I am glad your health is better—any fruit juice would be fine."

They then sat down in the living room and Dr. Ravi introduced Kumar to his youngest son, Ashok, who is finishing high school that year. Ashok was excellent in Tennis. Therefore, the conversation gravitated to Tennis.

They ate dinner in the spacious, well-decorated dining room; the south Indian cuisine was very tasty to Kumar.

Their conversation drifted to carnatic music. Kumar said to Mrs. Ravi, "Latha's mom, you and my mom should meet. All of you love carnatic music."

"May be we should. I would try to call them and arrange such a meeting."

Kumar said, "My mom practices almost every day."

Mrs. Ravi replied, "Me too; moreover, I go to Chennai every December to hear music concerts."

"My mom also visits Chennai every December. Well——both of you should meet. Why don't I call my mom now?"

Saying that, Kumar impulsively called her mom immediately. Fortunately, his mom answered;

" Mom, I am with Dr. and Mrs. Ravi. I just found out that both you and Mrs. Ravi love carnatic music. I thought you could say hello to each other"

Mrs. Ram said, " Kumar dear, I would love to".

Kumar gave his cell phone to Mrs. Ravi. Mrs. Ravi said" Hello, Mrs. Ram"

Mrs. Ram answered " Hi, please call me Radha."

"Radha, I am Aruna—Radha, it might be rather late for you. I could call you tomorrow morning—we could discuss then our common interest."

At this time, Dr. Ravi signaled to Aruna and she said, "Radha, if your husband is there, Dr. Ravi would like to greet him"

"Aruna, great idea—he is right here."

Dr. Ravi and Dr. Ram exchanged pleasantries and agreed to meet soon.

The conversation, though brief, brought the two families together.

They heard a click on the front door and soon Veena's older brother came in. He shook Kumar's hand saying, "I am Chandran, Veena's brother, in third year medical school."

Kumar said "Nice meeting you, Chandran."

"You know, Kumar, I love neurology and I am applying to Emory University for a sub internship program this summer."

"Kumar, is your father Dr.Ram at Emory?"

"Yes, Chandran."

"Kumar, I saw his name on the web of Emory Medical School, Neurology Department. He has a great reputation and has an illustrious research background. I might go to Atlanta next month."

"Well, Chandran, if I were free, I would meet you there. If not, my brother will see you."

"Ok, thanks, Kumar" replied Chandran.

While eating the dessert, they had a lively conversation. As Kumar was tired after the long flight, he took leave rather early.

Next day, after the interview, late in the evening, Kumar left San Francisco for Boston.

On the flight, he thought about Veena. "Veena is an attractive smart woman. Utmost polite and courteous is she. She fascinates me. However, I want to start a company. I want to wait."

As he thought more, he remembered the luncheon conversation the day before,

"Boy, Veena is a little frustrated with Harrish—why this irritation? —She hardly knows Harrish. Does she like Latha so much that she could not tolerate any slight embarrassment to her? This is rather strange —I need to think about this aspect of Veena. Poor Harrish—Latha has little interest—now Veena is a little upset with him"

After some time, Kumar again thought of Veena—" Yes, I feel a certain attraction towards her. But, unlike Harrish, I want to be cautious"

Veena thought of Kumar;

"What a lovely person is Kumar! He is jovial and witty. I really enjoyed his visit. Boy, he really likes Harrish and defends him totally. But, Harrish is a different story!"

She respected Harrish but was irritated a little with him.

Chapter - 5

Harrish came to Syracuse two weeks later to get his new job started. When he rang the doorbell, Latha opened the door. She gave him a big smile and said "hello". Harrish was happy to see her but was cautious. He smiled back somewhat reservedly and said, "Hi, Latha."

"Harrish – My parents have an engagement during lunch. Hence, I am taking you out for lunch. There is an outstanding Indian restaurant. However, we have to reserve seats; it gets very crowded sometimes. Can I go ahead and reserve?"

Harrish replied "Fine Latha. That would be lovely".

So saying, Harrish went upstairs to meet Latha's father to start his job. He was rather abrupt but Latha understood it as his effort at being "cool to her". She appreciated his sincere attempt. Quite pleased was she.

Harrish was happy about the lunch but decided to focus on the job. He firmly made a resolution not to bother Latha.

At twelve thirty, Harrish came down and as he was coming down, he saw Mrs. Gangadharan and said very warmly, "Hi! Mrs. Gangadharan, how are you?"

She replied smilingly, "Fine, Harrish! Latha and you are going to lunch. We have a luncheon engagement."

"Yes – I Understand - Latha told me about it in the morning."

Latha walked in and soon Latha and Harrish set out for the restaurant. At the restaurant, after being seated, Latha said to Harrish,

"Harrish, I discussed with my mom your offer to stay in your parent's home and attend music concerts in Chennai during December music season. She said "Why not go this year since you love music." The more I thought about it, the more I like it. So I would like to go, if the offer still stands."

Harrish replied,

"Great, Latha! I will write to my mom today and I am sure she would welcome you. My sister is almost your age; a little younger, may be. They both would love to have you."

"Wonderful Harrish! Please write to them."

"Yes. I will, Latha. I heard from Kumar that his mother goes to Chennai every year to attend music concerts in December."

"Is that so, Harrish? Veena told me that her mother goes to Chennai also every year during music season."

"Latha, may be we should all meet in USA before going to India".

Latha replied, "Harrish, that is an excellent suggestion. Let us talk to Kumar and Veena and arrange a music- get-together. I think Kumar's and Veena's moms could sing. We could plan this at MIT next week when all of us would be back."

"Okay, Latha - Let us meet next week at the MIT student union cafeteria. Would you please organize it?"

"Yes, Harrish, I will".

Latha asked, " Harrish, do you know Kumar had flown to San Francisco?"

"No, Latha, I don't. I have been extremely busy with my thesis and the summer job. I do know that he wanted to try a summer assignment in Gigabit".

Latha brought Harrish uptodate on Kumar's visit to San Francisco.

After lunch, Latha dropped off Harrish at the airport. In the plane, Harrish thought,

"Latha is polite, courteous and charming. However, she is not showing much interest in me. She loves to go to Chennai for music and not for knowing my parents. I simply have to accept her lack of interest for now. But, she could change her mind."

Latha was driving back to her home and thought of Harris, "Harrish is a great guy – savvy, intelligent, laconic but articulate when need arises, caring and a gentleman in every sense of the word. Nevertheless, I could only think of him as a friend. Let us wait and see"

Latha returned to MIT next week and so did Veena. Latha arranged a meeting in the cafeteria about the Carnatic-Music-Day. The four had not met as a group for a long time and hence they were happy to see each other.

Kumar arrived first and got himself a cup of coffee. He sat in a table of four and in a minute, Latha arrived. Kumar cheerfully said;

"Latha, I have not seen you in years."

Latha was happy to see Kumar and replied smilingly;

"Hi! Kumar— how was your trip to San Francisco?"

When Kumar was ready to answer that question, Veena arrived. Veena and Latha hugged each other and Latha asked eagerly,

"Veena how is your mom?"

"Latha, she is fine—thanks. Kumar saw her in San Francisco". Saying that, she looked at Kumar and said "Hi" warmly to him.

Kumar commented, " Latha, she is much better but still not back in full health."

At this time, Harrish came with a cup of tea and looked at Veena first and asked;

"Hi, Veena, how is your mom?"

Veena said with a smile, "Harrish, we are all discussing her health. She is fine now but a little weak"

Harrish turned to Kumar and asked, "Kumar, how was your trip to San Francisco?"

Latha smilingly intervened, "I asked that question first"

Kumar retorted jokingly, "You guys are not giving me time to answer that question! It was just great—thanks to Veena. She arranged everything so well."

Latha decided to take charge of the meeting, "Kumar, that is great. Now, focusing on this meeting, Harrish and I were conversing about carnatic music concerts in Chennai in December. I am planning to go and usually Kumar's and Veena's moms attend the music season every year. Harrish and I thought why don't we all get together in USA for a day and celebrate it as a Carnatic-Music-Day. What do you guys think?"

Latha looked at Kumar and Veena. Kumar replied, "Great idea! Let me ask my parents whether we could have it in our house. My mom loves carnatic music and we have a big house"

Veena remarked, "Latha, I love this idea. My mom enjoys singing carnatic music. She and Mrs. Ram have been conversing regularly. The only difficulty I see is that my dad tends to be very busy. Let me call my parents."

Harrish said, " Veena, your dad could come for dinner only."

Veena replied, " Harrish, that might work – especially on Saturday night. He usually travels on Sunday night for a Monday meeting."

Latha observed, " Kumar, Veena, why don't we call our parents and get their inputs regarding time, place and the program and then meet tomorrow."

They all left quickly as they were extremely busy but met again next day.

Kumar started the discussion, "My parents loved the idea and would welcome having it in our house. They suggested Saturday evening and Sunday morning – may be around July 4th weekend." Veena said, "My dad could make it on Saturday evening if he is not traveling to Europe. He agreed to give me a few dates tomorrow."

Latha added, "My mom was all for it. Kumar, why don't you work the date and the social function? Harrish the music program – Veena and I plan the dinner etc."

They discussed the actual program for a while and decided to meet in one week.

Next week, they met again.

Kumar started the meeting saying, "July 4 is perfect. Every one could make it including Dr.Ravi".

All said in almost unison "Great".

Harrish remarked rather excitedly, "I have a great news on the music program. Dr.Geetha will be in USA giving a few concerts around July 8. I am trying to contact her to see whether she could rearrange her program such that she could give us one concert on July 4th."

"That would be lovely", said Latha appreciatingly.

Veena said to Harrish, "Harrish, please call her immediately before her program is finalized. We would share the cost."

Harrish agreed.

Kumar intervened, "Harrish, has Geetha got her PhD now?"

Harrish answered, " Yes, Kumar, just recently"

Veena commented, "Latha and I are planning a great dinner".

Latha concluded the meeting saying, "Let us meet next week again to finalize the program."

Latha left the group immediately. Veena chitchatted for a while with Kumar and Harrish about the music program before leaving. Kumar looked at Veena discretely and carefully; he was looking for some encouraging signals, but did not get any. "She is in her own world," he thought.

Next week, Harrish started the conversation,

"I talked to Dr.Geetha a few times; she told me first she is coming to USA only on July 8th. I requested her whether she could come a week earlier on July 1st – she checked with the airlines and her India program. Juggling everything, she is able to come on July 1st and attend our program"

Everyone unanimously shouted "Great". Harrish continued cheerfully,

"But, we have a few logistics issues; we need to plan her stay from July 1st to July 8th. I asked her to come a few days earlier so that she is not too tired on July 4th."

Kumar said, "She could stay in our house and you could keep her company."

Latha remarked, " She is very welcome in our house."

Veena said excitedly," My mom would love to have her company as she is very much into carnatic music."

Harrish said," Great! Now, we have several options. Why don't Dr.Geetha come to Atlanta on July 2nd and stay in Kumar's house till July 5th while we plan her program in consultation with your parents?"

Kumar replied," Harrish, I will call my parents right away and I foresee no problem in her staying in our house as long as she wants to."

Latha offered, "Harrish, I could come on July 3rd to give her company."

Kumar said, "Great" and Harrish exclaimed warmly, "Wonderful".

Veena proposed that she could stay beyond July 5 if needed.

She added,"We have only two weeks to go. Why don't we finalize Dr.Geetha's program by tomorrow? Let us all call our parents and plan. Why don't we meet tomorrow? We all need to get air tickets etc".

They met the next day; Kumar opened the conversation, "My mom would like to have Dr.Geetha stay with her till July 8th. She would like to extend the invitation to all of you and your parents."

Veena said, "My mom and I can stay a few days after July 5th. My mom has called Kumar's and they are discussing the details".

Harrish remarked,"Great! We have a good program emerging. Geetha would come on July 2nd evening. Therefore, Latha, you need to come only on July 3rd as she would be resting on 2nd evening. The concert would be on July 4th. Informal music sessions would be on fifth, sixth and seventh. Kumar and I would meet her on July 2nd."

As Harrish was talking with great enthusiasm, Latha looked at him with interest admiring his energy and his love of music. While observing him, Latha's eyes met Harrish's for an instant. Latha quickly changed her direction but not before Harrish caught her new interest. Latha was herself astonished. Harrish noted her surprise and decided to ignore the incident. Latha was grateful because she needed time to think.

Veena and Kumar were too busy with the music day planning to notice the exchange between Harrish and Latha. They completed their discussion and decided to meet one more time next week.

As Latha was going towards her room, she thought about Harrish. "He is handsome and smart. My dad thinks a world of him. Moreover, Harrish likes me and has a lot of respect for my sensitive feelings." Latha wondered whether she was beginning to like Harrish. She was not too sure and she said to herself "Let time decide that".

Harrish was amazed at the apparent slow change of heart on the part of Latha. Nevertheless, he wanted to be cautious and wait.

Next week they met again. Harrish smiled at Latha and she smiled back at him. Their eyes met briefly. This time Kumar noticed a difference in Latha; she is showing interest in Harrish even though she probably is not too aware of it herself. Kumar looked at Latha and she appeared a little flustered. Therefore, Kumar decided to put up a blank face. However, Latha caught the curiosity in Kumar's eyes. It made her even more embarrassed. Harrish, who was watching Latha intently, quickly started the discussion on the music day. Latha felt relieved and Kumar too.

Harrish remarked,"Geetha is coming on second evening as planned".

Latha said,"I would be there third evening".

Kumar mentioned, "My mom in consultation with Veena's and Latha's moms is planning the social activities".

Veena affirmed her mom and she would stay on until July 7th evening.

They quickly discussed the logistics and then dispersed.

Kumar walked back with Latha and said to her, " Latha, I was not planning to cause you any embarrassment".

Latha replied, "I understand, Kumar. The problem is that I am not too sure of myself".

Kumar answered, "Latha, take it easy and take your time. I am available for hearing you anytime."

Latha said, "Kumar, I am quite a bit confused. I like Harrish. But I am an ABI and he is an Indian".

Kumar observed," Latha, you are right. You watched on TV "Sesame Street" and he did not. He is Indian but you are an American. The differences are there. The question is how much do you like each other to overcome the differences."

Latha answered, " Kumar, I am not sure that I know the answer to that question now."

"Latha, please wait until that answer is crystal clear."

"Thanks, Kumar" and they said goodbye to each other.

Veena and Harrish were chitchatting in the cafeteria.

Veena asked,"Harrish, you know Geetha well. What kind of a person is she?"

Harrish answered,"She is very one pointed. Her only love now is music. Have you seen an arrow discharged from a bow traveling towards its target? Geetha is focused like that arrow. She is quite beautiful also. She is not that talkative but articulate when necessary. Veena, I think you would like her."

Veena probed deeper; "Harrish, what makes you think I would like her?"

Harrish thought for a moment and said smilingly; "Veena, you are deep and thoughtful—so is she"

Veena smilingly retorted, "Thanks Harrish, if that is a complement. But, do you think compatible people would like each other?"

"Veena, my guess is that at least, there would be less friction."

Veena did not leave Harrish alone. She pushed further;

"Harrish, how about people who are not compatible?"

"Veena, they need deeper understanding of each other."

"Is that possible, given their incompatibility?"

"That is indeed a tough question. It might take more time and more effort. Of course, it might not happen also."

Soon, they departed.

Veena's questions puzzled Harrish, "Why is she asking these probing questions?"

Chapter - 6

Harrish arrived at the Atlanta airport around noon and Kumar met him near the security gate. They shook hands and greeted each other very warmly. Together they went to a restaurant for a quick sandwich at the airport. They were going to receive Dr. Geetha at 2 PM.

Kumar said to Harrish in the restaurant,

"Harrish, I saw Latha take more interest in you"

Harrish replied, "Yes, Kumar. She seems to but there is a reluctance too. Poignant love is not there yet."

Kumar observed, "Yes, Harrish. I talked to her last week. She is concerned about her being ABI and you, Indian.

"I did too, Kumar. But, I changed."

"Harrish, what made you change?"

"Well, Kumar, the more I knew her, the more she captivated me. Her looks, classy style, elegance, innate smartness all charmed me. The differences were made to look trivial."

Kumar remarked, "She is not there yet."

Harrish remarked, "I agree, Kumar and I am willing to wait patiently."

Then, they moved on to talk about the next day events.

After sometime, Harrish and Kumar were standing outside the international arrival area where Dr.Geetha's plane landed. Passengers started coming out of the arrival area. Large were the numbers of travelers coming through. Harrish and Kumar were waiting patiently— no sign of Geetha yet. Harrish was getting a little nervous and Kumar was wondering too.

At that time, a young woman clad in a colorful red and yellow salwar appeared with her bags in a carriage. She walked elegantly and was stunningly beautiful. Kumar could not take his eyes off her. Harrish recognized her and waved his hands saying " Geetha". Geetha waved back and said softly "Harrish". Kumar was still looking at Dr.Geetha admiringly and caught Dr.Geetha's eyes. Harrish turned around and Kumar's adoration of Dr.Geetha struck him. Kumar quickly collected himself and Harrish introduced Kumar to Dr.Geetha.

"Geetha, this is Kumar, my friend. He is doing his PhD in computer science at MIT. We would be staying in his house."

A Tender Melody

Kumar with folded hands said," Namasthe" and she returned it. Kumar observed her closely and she was pretty. He intuitively felt an attraction towards her. However, he checked himself saying, "I don't know her character or her likes and dislikes. Let me talk to Harrish."

Kumar requested Harrish and Geetha to wait while he went out and brought the car. He opened the door in the back seat for Dr.Geetha; Harrish loaded her bags in the trunk.

Harrish asked, "Geetha, how was your trip?"

Geetha answered, " Tiring, Harrish. I left Chennai almost twenty four hours ago. But I am happy to be here and I am looking forward to the concert."

Kumar said, "So are we, Dr.Geetha. We are lucky to have you at such a short notice – thanks to Harrish and you."

Geetha replied, "It was providential that I had concerts planned in USA just a few days later; moreover, I kept a few days free for rest and practice."

"Dr.Geetha, I hope we did not spoil your rest." said Kumar.

"No – In a way, it is better that I came a few days early so that I could get rid of jet lag before the big concerts."

Kumar added, "Well then, Dr.Geetha, next time you come to US, we would plan a similar function".

Geetha laughed and said "Thanks" She liked Kumar's outgoing personality and sense of humor.

Laughingly Kumar said, "I really mean it. You have a band of fans here guided by Harrish"

Geetha said jokingly, "I hope Harrish has not oversold me."

Kumar replied, " Well Dr.Geetha, you know Harrish – very cautious and conservative – he is not the type to exaggerate."

Geetha remarked smilingly, "well – you are putting me on the spot. I have to say, "Harrish exaggerates or I am very good".

Kumar retorted smilingly, "Oh! No! I have a simple solution"

Geetha asked wonderingly, "What?"

Kumar answered, "Let the truth stand wherever it may."

Geetha smilingly said, "Oh! I cannot dispute such a profound statement."

Kumar laughed heartily and Harrish too. Harrish enjoyed this conversation and was surprised at the ease with which they conversed.

Harrish, as they were travelling, showed Geetha the downtown, Georgia tech etc and told her about the civil war between North and South.

Kumar added, "During the civil war, the North's commander General Sherman burnt the city in 1864 to cripple the South's ability to transport freight and troops. He did that because Atlanta was becoming a railroad and transportation hub. The whole city was rebuilt after the civil war. However, the city is still a major transportation hub for bus, train and planes. The city is continually growing."

While talking thus, they soon reached Kumar's house. Dr.Geetha saw a beautiful garden and a grand sprawling home. It was a spacious ranch built in red bricks with a touch of elegant Spanish architecture.

The lovely house and the Garden impressed Harrish and Geetha. As soon as the car entered the portico, Kumar's mom, Mrs. Radha Ram came out to the sit out area in front of the house.

Kumar opened the door for Dr. Geetha and Harrish got the bags.

Mrs.Ram said to Harrish;

"Hey Harrish, it is nice to see you in person."

Harrish said, "Namaskar, Mrs Ram. I am so glad to meet you. Mrs Ram, this is Geetha"

Mrs. Ram warmly took Dr Geetha's hand in hers and greeted her saying, "Geetha, we are so happy to have you on such a short notice."

Geetha greeted Mrs. Ram and then replied," Mrs.Ram, I am very delighted that I could make it. I am looking forward to the concert."

"Geetha, we are excited about the concert. You must be tired. Let me take you to your room."

Mrs.Ram took Geetha to her room with Harrish following with her bags. Kumar took Harrish's carry-on bag out of the car and parked the car. Harrish came down from upstairs after leaving Dr Geetha in her room.

While Kumar and Harrish were in the front, they were both astonished to see a taxi pull into the portico. Out of the taxi alighted Latha. Both Harrish and Kumar screamed in unison" Latha". Kumar hugged her and Harrish held her hands for a minute and said, "I am so happy to see you, Latha."

A Tender Melody

Latha remarked," Hey, you guys, I just could not wait in Boston. I decided to take a flight today. Kumar, I did not call you because I knew that you would be at the airport and taking Dr.Geetha home. So I took a taxi and came."

Hearing the commotion in the front, Mrs. Ram came out and seeing Latha remarked excitedly, " You must be Latha; your mom, Chitra and I exchanged family photographs and I have seen your picture. I am so glad you could come early. You could give Dr.Geetha company. I am quite busy. Let me take you to the room that Veena and you are going to share."

Latha thanked her and followed her while Kumar carried her bag.

Harrish was admiring the beautiful garden until Kumar came.

Kumar said, "Harrish let us go. You are going to be in my room."

After half hour, Latha came down to the living room and Mrs. Ram asked her whether she would like to have a cup of tea.

Latha said, "Let me wait for Dr.Geetha."

At that time, Dr.Geetha came to the living room and Latha went to her and said, "I am Latha".

Mrs. Ram quickly added," Geetha, Latha is doing her PhD in MIT and she is a very good friend of Kumar. Harrish, Kumar, Latha and Veena, who is coming here tomorrow, are all good friends at MIT."

At this time, Harrish and Kumar joined them.

Mrs. Ram said, "Why don't you all come to dining room? We will have some tea and snacks"

Kumar seated everyone and Harrish was between Geetha and Latha.

Harrish turned to Geetha and remarked, "Geetha, Latha's parents live in Syracuse and her mom loves carnatic music. Similarly, Mrs Ram and Mrs.Ravi are experts in music and they go to Chennai every December to participate in the music festival. Mrs.Ravi would be here day after tomorrow."

Kumar added, "Outstanding is Harrish too in music"

Geetha said smilingly; "Harrish and I have known each other since our childhood. Harrish has loved music ever since I have known him. To him, music is divine. He could have had a career in music. As you might know, Harrish's father and my mom are brother and sister. Our grandmother, Kamalam was extremely talented in music. She is a great violinist. Our music love comes from her."

Mrs.Ram added," Geetha, I have heard your grandmother's violin, when I was young. Music seems to flow from generation to generation. My mom, named Gomathy, was a great Veena player. She knows well your grandmother."

"Yes, Mrs. Ram, I have heard her Veena too." said Geetha.

Kumar was watching Dr. Geetha all the time and she charmed him. Latha noticed it.

Mrs. Ram said, "Unfortunately, she passed away a few years ago. We have come to your grandmother's house many times."

While chitchatting thus, they finished tea and snacks.

Latha said to Kumar and Harrish, "I want to chat with Geetha if it is ok with you guys."

Kumar took Harrish to the garden.

While they were alone, Kumar said to Harrish, "I have something serious to talk to you."

Harrish guessed the topic. But said softly to Kumar, "Ok – I am ready "

Kumar remarked, "Well, Harrish – I am attracted to Dr Geetha. Is she engaged?"

Harrish replied,"Not to my knowledge. She is rather busy with music. Kumar, did you think carefully? She loves carnatic music and is dedicated to it. She travels a lot giving concerts. You are doing your PhD in computer science and you want to start a company. Think deep about it."

Kumar replied, "You have a point. Harrish, I have not had much time to think about it. If we really like each other, we can work things out."

Harrish asked, "How about Veena? I thought there was a good potential match there. You are both in computer science. She could help you in your company."

Kumar answered, "Veena is pretty and smart. I admire her and respect her. However, I do not know why Geetha appears so charming to me. I hope it is not a passing fancy. I am a little confused and I need time."

Harrish added, "Kumar, please take your time and think seriously."

Kumar said, "Harrish, could you tell me more about Geetha?"

A Tender Melody

Harrish started telling him about Geetha.

While Harrish and Kumar were thus seriously discussing Geetha, Geetha and Latha sat in the front porch chairs and started chitchatting. Latha asked, "Geetha, are you too tired?"

Geetha replied, "No Latha, I slept on the flight and hence I am ok now."

Latha enquired, "Have you any brother or sister?"

Geetha answered, "I have one brother who is younger to me. He has completed his legal schooling now. Latha, by the way, how did you meet Harrish?"

Latha replied, "Well, Kumar and I have known each other for a while because we have taken some math courses together. Evidently, Kumar and Harrish have been good friends. Through Kumar, I met him."

"Harrish writes to me long letters and always mentions you three guys and I long to meet Veena."

Latha asked jokingly, "Whom does he write about most?"

Geetha answered, "Kumar, of course." But added teasingly, "I know Harrish – the person he says least about is the one close to his heart" and looked at Latha with a mischievous smile.

Latha was a little embarrassed and sorry that she asked the question but she could not do or say more at that time as it would embarrass her more. Geetha noticed her predicament and quickly changed the topic.

Geetha asked, "When is Veena coming?"

Latha made a firm determination to get to know Geetha better and decided to open up to her. Therefore, she ignored this question and said softly, " Well, Geetha, your guess is not too far off the mark. It seems Harrish likes me but I am taking my own time. I have grown up in the U.S.A and he in India. Moreover, I am busy with my studies right now. That is where the issue stands."

Geetha replied quietly," Latha, I have known Harrish all my life. If you have any questions about him, please do not hesitate to ask me."

Latha requested, "Please tell me about his early life."

Geetha answered, " His father got his PhD at Stanford and went back to India. He is a senior department head at IIT and may become its director soon. He took his sabbatical every five years in the USA and hence is quite well acquainted with USA. He has come to America many times and stayed for a whole year each time. Thus, you do not need to worry too much, about his being Indian and you being American. He is a good tennis player and very methodical and thoughtful in what he does. He is not impulsive. If he continues to like you, please remember he has given a lot of thought to this issue."

Latha said, "Thanks Geetha for your input. If I have other questions, I will ask you later."

Latha turned the table on Geetha, "So, Harrish wrote a lot about Kumar but when you met Kumar, did he match your imaginations?"

Geetha was somewhat taken aback by this question. She protested saying, "I did not have any imaginations of Kumar".

Latha persisted, "At least, how did you find him when you saw him?"

Geetha felt that Latha had noticed Kumar's interest in her and so she could not evade her easily. Therefore, she answered, " I came only a few hours ago and have not even spent a day. Whatever I have seen of Kumar, it is positive. Moreover, Kumar may be just having a passing fancy. I am committed to a career in carnatic music. He is in the USA pursuing a high tech career. So there are a lot of issues."

Latha said firmly and quietly, "If anyone can work these issues out, that's Kumar"

Geetha replied, "You think very highly of Kumar."

Latha said, "Yes, I do. Nevertheless, Kumar could be impulsive. Therefore, you need to wait until his liking is steady. So my advice to you is to wait."

While Geetha and Latha were discussing these issues, Harrish was talking to Kumar about Geetha's background.

"When Geetha was eight years old, her father got cancer. He was a famous lawyer in Chennai and she loved him dearly. However, he died when she was ten. She was heartbroken, forlorn and depressed. Her mother, Geetha and her brother stayed with us for five years when her mother finished her PhD in mathematics. During those tough years, Geetha used to listen to music and it gave her immense solace. Soon, she was enchanted with carnatic music; it has now become her soul mate. Eventually, she chose that as her career. It was a tough decision as Geetha is brilliant in mathematics. Her mother is a professor of Mathematics."

Kumar listened with rapt attention and the story touched him. His heart went out to Geetha. He intuitively marveled her decision to pursue music as a career.

At this time, Mrs.Ram came to Latha and Geetha and said, "Please be ready for dinner. Dress well as we plan to have a couple of guests. Latha, could you please tell Kumar and Harrish also? All of you please come to the living room at 6.00p.m."

Chapter - 7

Latha walked through the enchanting garden to tell Kumar and Harrish to get ready for dinner. At that time, she heard a car engine sound and she turned around to see a cab come into the portico. She ran to the car. Kumar and Harrish ran also. Out of the cab, alighted Veena, and was amazed to see Latha. Latha said "Veena" and Veena said "Latha", and they hugged each other. Harrish and Kumar joined them and Mrs.Ram came too.

Veena said, "I just could not stay away and wanted to surprise you guys."

Kumar looked at her; she was well dressed and charming. Kumar had forgotten how captivating she could be. Quite confused was Kumar; stunned was he. Utmost puzzled was he. He even forgot to greet Veena. With a nudge from Harrish, he said "Hi" and took her bags in.

Latha asked, "What made you change your mind, Veena?"

Veena remarked, "The cheerful party spirit, I guess. I just had to be here. How about you Latha?"

Latha added "Same here – I came in the afternoon. Please dress well for dinner. We are supposed to be in the living room at 6.00 pm".

She conveyed the same message to Harrish and Kumar.

At 6.00pm, Harrish and Kumar came down formally dressed in suite and tie. Dr.Ram was there in the living room and Kumar introduced Harrish to him.

Harrish asked, "Dr.Ram, how far is Emory medical school from here?"

"Half hour, by car".

Harrish added, " Atlanta is much warmer and humid than Boston".

"It is warm and nicer in winter," observed Dr.Ram.

While they were thus discussing general topics, Dr.Geetha was coming down the stairs. She was dressed in a beautiful red silk saree with golden border with a matching red silk blouse. Quite attractive was she! Kumar looked at her again. She was pretty and dashing.

Kumar compared her to Veena; the comparison was confusing, both were attractive and elegant. Geetha looked at Kumar and she saw him a little confused. She wondered why.

At that time, Veena came down and Geetha turned around and saw a very beautiful woman coming down. She guessed it might be Veena and then she suddenly understood Kumar's confusion. She was a little hurt but decided to play it cool. Veena saw Kumar look at Geetha and her alternatively and was annoyed. Nevertheless, Kumar ignored her annoyance and persisted in comparing Geetha and Veena. Veena gave him a stern look but Kumar smiled sweetly. When Kumar looked at Geetha again, she was getting upset. Kumar quickly realized that he is making her angry and turned his gaze on Harrish.

Geetha wondered, "What happened to Kumar? He is changed when Veena came here. I have to be careful and I don't want to be hurt."

Veena thought. "What has changed Kumar? Why this newfound interest in me? He is also charmed by Geetha."

Kumar wondered, "What is wrong with me? I am suddenly charmed by both Geetha and Veena. They are getting a little bit annoyed. I care for them deeply. I need to resolve this quickly."

At this time, Harrish moved near Dr.Geetha and escorted her to where Veena was standing. Veena and Geetha were a little embarrassed and felt awkward. Courteous and polite as they were, they quickly recovered and smiled.

Veena said, "Geetha, I am glad to meet you. I am looking forward to hear your concert."

Geetha replied, "Thanks, Veena. I am glad to meet you. You look beautiful in that blue saree".

"Thanks, your red saree matches you elegantly too."

Right then, the doorbell chimed. Dr.Ram opened the door. Dr. Atchuthan and his sister Mrs.Lakshmi Shankar came in along with Lakshmi's son, Dr.Natchikethas. Dr.Ram introduced Dr.Atchuthan as an orthopedic surgeon at Emory Medical School and a close friend of Dr.Ram. He introduced Mrs. Shankar as the sister of Dr.Atchuthan. She lived in India and now on a visit to USA. She loved carnatic music. Her husband, Natchikethas' father, passed away a couple of years ago.

Kumar went to Dr.Natchikethas, and introduced himself and then Harrish, Veena and Dr.Geetha. They formed a small circle while Dr.Ram, Mrs.Ram, Mrs. Shankar and Dr.Atchuthan were conversing.

Kumar asked Dr.Natchikethas, "What field have you specialized in?"

"I am a cardiac surgeon working in the Apollo Hospital, Chennai. I did my residency in Houston under Dr.Debauchy. Quite fascinating is heart surgery!"

Kumar observed," Dr.Debuchy is world famous in the field of heart transplant. Quite fortunate are you to do residency under him."

At this point, Latha came downstairs and she looked gorgeous. Harrish was fascinated and he smiled at her and she shyly returned the smile. Geetha noticed their rapport and felt they were closer than acknowledged by Latha. She said to herself, " I like Latha; Harrish is close to my heart. I hope this works out." Dr.Natchikethas also watched the closeness between Latha and Harrish.

Kumar introduced Latha to Dr.Natchikethas.

Latha asked, "What made you go back to India?"

Dr.Natchikethas replied, " Mine is a simple case. My dad passed away and my mother was lonely and forlorn. That decided it."

Latha observed, "I am very sorry to hear that. What happened to him?"

Dr.Natchikethas said, "He died of a sudden heart attack. He was quite busy running his company."

Kumar asked, "In what field was his company?"

Dr.Natchiketas replied, "Computer and software"

Veena enquired, "What specific area of computer software does your father's company specialize in ?"

Dr.Natchikethas answered, "I am a surgeon and I have not specialized in software or computers. This company makes high-speed processors and develops software for processors. I own the company now and I have a tough time managing it. Far tough is modern changing technology."

Kumar observed, "It's true. Quite rapid is technological growth."

Dr.Natchikethas asked Kumar, "In what field are you doing your PhD?"

Kumar answered, "High Speed computers".

Dr.Nathcikethas remarked, "Well – you are close to my company than I am" – turning to Veena, he asked her, "How about you?"

Veena answered " More in the field of Artificial intelligence".

Dr.Natchikethas commented, "That is fascinating"

Harrish added, "Even though I am in Economics, I have an interest in setting up a software company in India."

Latha said jokingly, "I am not into computers or software but in mathematics."

Dr.Natchikethas remarked, "Well, Math is one of the foundations of computers. I have an idea – If you all could come to my house tomorrow, may be for lunch, I could give you a lot of written material on our company. I would very much like your inputs."

They all agreed and the conversation drifted to the concert on 4ht of July. Dr.Natchikethas asked,"What time is the concert?"

Kumar answered, "at 5.30pm on 4th of July, we will have dinner at 8.00pm."

Veena asked Geetha, "Have you made your final selections of songs yet?"

Geetha replied, " Almost; during practice I shall make the final list."

Dr.Geetha spoke softly and elegantly. She impressed Dr.Natchiketas. Kumar was intensely comparing Geetha and Veena. It was tough.

Veena asked, "How long do you practice everyday?"

Geetha answered, " Carnatic music is vast and deep. It takes years of practice and learning to master it. Excellence demands the very best effort. I work hard to excel."

Veena said, " I understand. My mom spends hours practicing. She came to USA early in her life and hence could not learn as much. She at times regrets not furthering her career in music."

Geetha remarked, "That is sad. I had a difficult decision to make. One thing that makes things easier now, is that music colleges confer advanced degrees and hence it's easier to get into music as a career."

"My mom goes to Chennai twice a year to learn music and then she practices in the USA. Tough is hiring teachers and learning carnatic music in USA. The atmosphere is not there and very limited good teachers. Excellence requires continuous learning."

Mrs.Ram announced that the dinner was ready and they should proceed to the side porch next to the dining room. Dr.Ram led the group to a beautiful porch surrounded by a well-lit luscious lawn. The dinner was arranged in a buffet style and was typical North Indian cusine with malai koftha, mutter paneer, shahi panner with naan, rice and salad. Rasagulla was the dessert.

Chapter - 8

Dr.Ram invited Mrs. Shankar to go first to the buffet table. Little away from the buffet table, was the big dining table with ten chairs. Mrs. Shankar after taking the food items that she liked sat at one end of the dining table. Soon Geetha joined Mrs.Shankar and took a seat near her. Dr.Athcuthan sat at the other end of the table.

The food was delicious and everyone complimented Mrs.Ram. Mrs.Ram and Kumar were busy arranging everything.

Veena was seated between Dr.Atchuthan and Dr. Natchikethas.

She turned to Dr.Natchikethas and asked, "Have you thought of medical electronics for your company?"

Dr.Nathciketas replied, "Yes! However, medical electronics is a vast and deep field."

"Each area, brain, heart, eye, ear etc involves enormous research. For example, brain is a huge and deep field. You know, you are in the artificial intelligence. Our focus in medicine is to cure patients. Whatever helps in that endeavor is great- electronics may help- sometimes it is pharmaceutical discoveries – or gene therapy or complicated surgery. In basic medicine, we also need to understand the basic process of a disease like AIDS."

"In medicinal electronics, what people seem to do is to pick up a technology such as laser and look for applications in medicine. Wherever it fits, they work hard to make it cost effective. Laser is a classic example; from atomic physics to laser to surgery is a great story of research."

As they were just discussing medical electronics, Mrs.Ram came and joined them and the conversation drifted to delicious dinner. Veena remarked to Mrs.Ram, "I love North Indian cuisine. This is great".

Mrs.Ram replied, " Thanks. I learnt it from a North Indian friend of mine."

Dr.Natchikethas added, "Outstanding is malai kofta".

Dr. Athcuthan said, "I love mutter panner"

Harrish who was seated opposite Veena remarked, " I usually love South Indian food but today this north Indian cuisine is very tasty."

Mrs.Ram observed, "I gave it a little touch of South Indian cuisine style. That may be why you like it."

At the other end of the table were, Mrs. Shankar, Geetha and Latha. Laskhmi started the conversation by asking Geetha, "Where do you live in Chennai?"

"We live in Nungambakkam. My mother teaches math at Loyola college. Where do you live?"

"We also reside in Nungambakkam. We shifted to be close to Natchikethas' hospital, the Apollo hospital. We are in Haddows road."

Geetha exclaimed, "What a coincidence! Our house is also on that street!"

Lakshmi invited Geetha and her mother to visit her and they exchanged addresses and phone numbers.

Latha asked Lakshmi, "Do you have other children?"

Lakshmi replied, "Yes. I have a daughter named Vimala. She is probably a couple of years younger than you."

Geetha posed, "What does she do?"

"She wants to understand the origin of languages. She is fascinated by linguistics. She is learning Sanskrit, Latin & Russian. She believes language is the key to life. She had enormous curiosity about languages. Language provides a medium to express oneself –nay – we even think in a language. Knowledge of language is so fundamental."

Latha added, "Linguistics play a key role in modern computer software language research."

Geetha observed, "I am glad she is good in Sanskrit. Dhikshithar songs are in Sanskrit and I can come and discuss their meaning with her."

Lakshmi said, "You are most welcome and I am sure Vimala would love to talk to you."

Latha commented, "My brother is also interested in linguistics, more from a software point of view. He is planning to do his PhD at Harvard in linguistics."

Kumar joined the group. His eyes drifted slyly towards Geetha and her subdued beauty fascinated him. Far impressed was he. He tried quickly to take his eyes off her and but Geetha caught his eyes. Far annoyed was she. Kumar pleaded with his eyes for mercy. She softened a little but was still serious. Kumar averted her and turned his glance to Latha. Kumar quickly picked up the conversation and was in the middle of a linguistics conversation. Kumar commented, "I am impressed by Vimala's ambitious goal. It is a tough subject. Actually, one of my friends at MIT, is doing his PhD in this field."

Dr.Ram said, "Studies have shown that language plays an important role in the growth of the brain."

Geetha observed Kumar. He was energetic and active. He was good looking. Kumar noticed Geetha evaluating him and he gave her a mischievous smile indicating, "you are doing what you blamed me for." Geetha gave back a sportive smile acknowledging his legitimate complaint.

The dinner ended in half hour and the guests assembled in the living room. Mango ice cream with hot apple pie was served with coffee. Everyone was relaxed and great cheer was in the room. Dr.Atchuthan, Mrs. Lakshmi Shankar and Dr.Natchikethas were taking leave; Lakshmi said to Radha, "Let them come to our house tomorrow for lunch and dinner. Dr.Ram, you are also invited. That will help you focus on the concert day."

Radha agreed and thanked her for the fine gesture.

Lakshmi and party departed. Geetha, Latha and Veena helped Mrs.Ram while Kumar and Harrish were with Dr.Ram rearranging furniture. Geetha retired early, as she was tired from the long flight. She went up to her room and got ready to go to bed. While in bed, she started thinking a little about the events of the day. "Harrish" she thought "is in love but Latha is not there yet. However, Latha liked Harrish. Harrish deserves someone like Latha; he is a super guy." Her mind slowly drifted to Kumar. "Kumar is lively, jovial and fun to be with. Well, Veena is pretty and smart. Kumar knows her well but he is not sure yet. Well, let us wait and see. Tomorrow, I need to practice and prepare for concert." Thinking thus, she dozed off.

Veena was sitting alone in the porch and thought, " Why the sudden interest by Kumar in me? I like Kumar but Geetha also attracts Kumar. Dr.Natchikethas is serious, introspective and a very likable gentleman. I will talk to Latha tomorrow. Overall it was a wonderful day." so thinking, she went upstairs.

Kumar caught a glimpse of Veena going upstairs and she looked beautiful. He said to himself ," I need to resolve this quickly – maybe, I will discuss with Harrish today."

Latha was sitting in the side porch, where they served dinner and was quietly watching the full moon when she heard soft footsteps. She turned around and saw Harrish coming towards her. He was tall and handsome. He was in a serious mood. He came and sat near Latha and started talking, "Latha, I have something to talk to you about."

Latha knew that Harrish had something serious in his mind, "Harrish, what is it?"

"I noticed today that Kumar is attracted to Geetha. Geetha is into carnatic music and she stays in Chennai, India. On the otherhand, he will be in MIT, USA finishing his PhD in computer science. He seems to have some liking for Veena – what do you think?"

"Harrish, I am not worried about very different careers or the distance. Kumar is quite capable to handle those issues. However, critical factor is their liking and respect for each other. I wonder how deep is their attachment. Time will tell. Veena's case bewilders me. I do not know about Kumar's interest in Veena. Veena, Kumar is a great possibility but I am not sure about it."

Harrish said, " Well, I understand your point, Latha. If liking and respect are deep, then one can overcome other issues. Nevertheless, if liking and respect are fragile, then everything else becomes paramount."

Now, Kumar who had been looking for Harrish spotted Latha and Harrish in the side porch and joined them. "Hey you guys! What are you discussing? Me?"

Latha and Harrish laughingly exclaimed in unison, "Yes! How did you guess?"

Kumar remarked, "Very easy, you were discussing some secret so quietly. Knowing Harrish, I could guess that he is worried about me. He is probably talking about my interest in Geetha and may be Veena."

Latha jokingly said, " I am impressed by your guessing ability."

"Thanks" remarked Kumar smilingly.

"Well, Kumar, can you bring us up-to-date on your current thinking? Maybe we could help," told Latha.

Kumar replied, " It all started at the airport. Geetha looked gorgeous and I was mesmerized. Moreover, we had a great conversation in the car. However, a funny thing happened when Veena came. She stunned me with her beauty. I had only looked at her as a colleague in MIT. So, I am confused now."

Latha commented, " Kumar, you need lots of time to sort this out; it's a very tough choice."

Harrish added, "Latha said a minute ago, liking and respect are the key. You need to figure that out and how they feel about you."

They chitchatted about these issues before retiring to bed.

A Tender Melody

Mrs. Lakshmi Shankar, Dr.Atchuthan and Dr.Natchikethas reached home and Dr.Natchikethas said he was quite tired and retired to bed.

Lakshmi and Dr. Athcuthan sat in the living room and talked.

Lakshmi asked Dr.Atchutahn, "What do you think of Veena?"

"She is beautiful, smart and also rich .Her father is a tycoon in computers. She is also polite and courteous. I can't say enough in praise of her."

"Good. I like Veena too; she is a very fine young lady. I like Geetha too; she is cultural, she lives almost next door in Chennai. Well, I am worried about Natchikethas' marriage. His father died suddenly and hence his marriage got little attention. Now I want to focus on it."

Dr.Athcuthan asked, "Have you talked to Natchikethas? What is he looking for?"

"Yes. He has an open mind. He wants someone very calm, introspective and with character and with common interests"

"Well that's easily said than done. How does one find such a person?"

"Good question; I don't know the answer," said Lakshmi.

"What is his plan?" enquired Dr.Atchuthan.

"He wants to take time and not hurry the process".

"I hope he gets what he seeks. Well, who are coming for lunch tomorrow?"

"All the youngsters except Geetha who will be practicing her music."

"What are you planning for lunch?"

"Idly, sambhar and ice-cream".

" That looks good. Why should not Geetha just come for lunch with Kumar or Harrish? Someone could drop her back right away. That way she would not be lonely."

"Good idea, we will plan accordingly" said Lakshmi.

Dr.Athcuthan asked, " What time is dinner?"

Lakshmi said, "8.00pm". Then they retired.

Dr.& Mrs.Ram were chitchatting about the evening dinner and the guests.

Mrs.Ram asked, "Ram, what do you think of Latha and Geetha? You were discussing with them".

Dr.Ram replied, "Far beautiful and talented are they. I am very impressed. Why are you asking about them, Radha?"

Radha answered, "Well, Ram, I am worried about Kumar. He is not getting any younger. He needs to settle down."

"Radha, its too early to worry. Kumar is still young".

"I always like to see four steps ahead. I like to worry before it is time to worry".

"Well Radha, it is your privilege to worry. Nevertheless, I am not going to. Please remember Kumar is born and brought up in the USA and he is going to choose on his own. Have you talked to him?"

"Yes. I tried twice. But he is vague."

"May be, he is not sure, Radha"

"But, I feel he likes Geetha- may be, Veena. I am not quite sure"

"Interesting – How do you know? "

"Ram, I watch, I observe and I am intuitive. I am not in the clouds like you."

"Ok, ok. What is your prediction?"

"I think he likes Geeetha. However, he thinks that Veena may be a better match."

"Radha, what do you think?"

"Ram, I agree with him – Veena is a better match."

"Radha, you said he likes Geetha better"

"Ram, realism has to prevail. Geetha is in India and into classical music – He is in MIT and doing computer science. There is so much disparity."

"But Radha, he has to like Veena."

"Ram, Veena is beautiful, lovely – so smart and in computer science – American born Indian. So why can't he like her?"

"Radha, chemistry between people is indefinable."

"Well Ram, that is more poetic than realistic."

"But Radha, life is not just realism. Sometimes, it is reaching for the moon."

"Ram, even the moon has been reached by realistic planning."

"But, marriage is different."

"No, Ram, marriage also requires careful planning. So many marriages fail due to lack of planning. Realism is critical for the survival of marriage."

"True, but marriages also fail due to lack of love."

"Agreed Ram; but, Veena is very lovable".

"True, Radha, but that only Kumar can decide. Moreover, the other person has to decide also."

"Well- all we can do now is wait and see – may be, I will talk to Kumar tomorrow."

With that, they retired to bed.

Chapter - 9

Next morning, around 11.30 a.m., Kumar, Harrish, Veena, Latha and Geetha left for Mrs.Shankar's house in a station wagon. They were in a cheerful spirit and Dr.Natchikethas met them at the entrance. Mrs.Shankar also came and greeted them. The lunch was ready and they ate lightly while chitchatting.

Veena, Kumar and Harrish were in one corner talking in a jovial manner about their life in MIT. They were cheerful and laughing. Geetha noticed that Kumar and Veena were in a lively spirit and she became a little jealous. She was annoyed and decided to forget about Kumar and instead to focus on her career. She wanted to concentrate on her concert the next day and was ready to go back. Latha said she was a bit tired and needed rest. She offered to take back Geetha and soon Geetha and Latha left.

Veena, Kumar and Harrish sat with Dr.Natchikethas to talk about the company. Dr.Natchikethas started the conversation, "Thanks for coming and taking the time to learn about the company. I thought the best way for you to learn is to go through this annual report. I have three copies here. After you have read this, let us discuss it. Then, I also have a latest technology report. May be, you guys want to read that also."

So saying, he gave each a copy of the annual report and then left. Harrish, Kumar and Veena pored over the annual report the next two hours. They agreed to meet and each would tell the others about what they read.

After two hours, they took a short break and got something to drink from the kitchen.

Harrish opened, "The company has enormous potential; it is small but growing vigorously at an good growth rate (35%).

It earns foreign exchange for India and almost all its revenue comes from outside India. It employs around 500 people, mostly top-level technical personnel, and experts in digital signal processor software.

Its annual revenue is around Rs.130 crores ($26 million) and its profit after taxes is around Rs.40 crores ($8 million). The profit is good (around 30%) and the cash flow is comfortable.

The total assets are Rs. 100 crores ($20 million) and cash flow is Rs.50 crores ($10 million). This is a quick summary and we can cover the details later."

Next, Veena discussed her section, "I will cover the technical aspect of the company. It develops "digital signal processors" for the telecom industry. It gets silicon VLSI signal processors from the USA and develops the software in India for them. It specializes in audio and video bandwidth reduction algorithms. This will enable telecom service providers to utilize their transmission media optimally. This is a broad outline."

Kumar said, "In the third section, there is considerable information about the key officers and the directors of the company. Since we don't know the persons, it is best if Dr.Natchikethas could join us now and elaborate on this section".

Veena and Harrish agreed and soon Dr.Natchikethas joined them.

Kumar said, "Dr. Natchiketas, please tell us more about the President, Mr.Sundaram. He seems to be managing the company well. Why are you worried?"

Dr.Natchikethas said, "He is excellent. The problem is that he is getting old and his health is not good. We need a new President."

Kumar asked, "What are your plans for succession?"

Dr.Natchikethas replied, "We have two internal candidates – Dr.Sriram and Dr.Karthik."

Kumar interjected, " I see in this report that Dr.Sriram is Vice President in charge of Research and Development whereas Dr.Karthik is Vice President responsible for Production & Delivery."

Dr.Natchikethas agreed, "They are excellent managers, absolutely top-notch, but they lack marketing and sales experience; in the next phase of the company, we need vigorous sales growth especially in the USA. Hence, I am searching for a candidate with excellent sales background in the USA. Both Dr.Sriram and Dr.Karthik agree with me on that strategy."

At this time, Latha came and joined the group. Veena gave her the annual report to glance while Dr.Natchikethas and Kumar were talking. After hearing some of the discussions between Kumar and Dr.Natchikethas about building up a sales force in the USA, Latha mentioned, "Tomorrow, Dr.Ravi will be here. Why don't we discuss these issues with him?" They all agreed and decided to break the meeting for the day.

Mrs Lakshmi Shankar invited them for tea. Kumar said that he had some errands for his mother in preparation for tomorrow's function. Lakshmi packed a few Vadais (a South Indian dish) for him and Kumar left.

Kumar, after completing his assignments came home. He saw Geetha in the porch practicing for the concert. She was in a serious mood. Her face was away from the entrance and she did not even notice Kumar. Kumar went inside to see his mother. His mother had tea ready. Kumar took a tray with "Vadai" and tea and approached Geetha softly. After hearing his footsteps, she turned around. Quite surprised was she. Then she remembered her resolve of the morning and was quite polite but not enthusiastic. Kumar noticed her reticence but decided to ignore it and talked relaxedly.

After a short conversation during tea, Geetha soon returned to practice and Kumar left for Dr.Natchikethas' house.

While Kumar was away, Latha, Veena, Harrish and Dr.Nathcikethas sat around the dining room table for tea and vadai. Lakshmi joined them also.

Veena started the conversation with a question for Dr.Nathcikethas, "How do you manage your time between the hospital and your company?"

Dr.Natchikethas replied, "It's tough. During weekdays, I spend only one hour on the company, primarily on the phone. On Sundays, I devote about six hours with the President and some key executives going over the details. I look at the progress report and ask questions. It does not leave time for personal things. But the President is excellent and hence, I am able to get away with spending only twelve hours per week".

Veena remarked, "I can see that balancing two different careers is not fun."

Dr.Natchikethas answered, "True"

Veena continued, " You need to either unload the company or reduce your time as a cardiac surgeon."

Dr.Natchikethas said, "That would be tough right now".

As he said that, an idea flashed in his mind. "If I marry someone like Veena, may be she could manage the business." With this thought, he looked at her. She was beautiful and her beauty and intelligence charmed him. He decided that he would like to know more about Veena and Dr.Ravi. Then, he thought he would talk to Harrish.

The conversation drifted to other topics and Kumar arrived. They were ready to go back and at that time, Dr.Natchikethas took Harrish aside and said, " Harrish, could you stay back please? I want to talk to you. I can drop you."

Harrish complied and the rest of them left. Dr.Natchikethas led Harrish to a small private room upstairs and closed the door. He sat next to Harrish and said, " I have a serious question. Please treat this conversation as very very confidential".

Harrish nodded and Dr.Natchikethas proceeded, " I want to discuss Veena. Today, I had an opportunity to observe Veena very closely and talk to her. She is smart and beautiful. She specializes in software area. I am quite attracted to her. Could you tell me if she is engaged to anyone?"

Harrish replied, " I am not sure whether she is engaged or not. Kumar and Veena are close friends. But, I don't know whether this has evolved beyond that."

Dr.Natchikethas added, "They don't look that involved."

Harrish commented, "Kumar likes Veena and Veena likes Kumar. They are compatible in many ways". They soon changed the topic to the company and after sometime, Harrish left for Kumar's house.

When Harrish came back to Kumar's house, Kumar asked Latha," Your parents will be arriving at the airport in an hour. Do you want to come with me to the airport?"

Latha replied, "No- I want to help your mother in preparing for tomorrow's concert. Let Harrish go with you. He knows my parents well." Therefore, Harrish and Kumar set out for the airport.

While driving, Kumar asked Harrish, "Do you know why Geetha might be upset with me?"

Harrish answered, "I am not aware that she is cross with you."

"When I took the tray of tea, she did not even smile at me - so reserved and remote – such a contrast to her warmth the day before – I know she is upset."

Harrish said, "I see your point. May be, she is busy with the concert."

"No, she could still at least smile. It does not take time."

Harrish answered, "I see – may be, she is upset."

Kumar asked " Why ?"

"I don't know – well let us analyze – what could you have done in the last day or so to annoy her?"

Kumar suddenly recalled, " When Veena came down last evening for the party, I was charmed by her. Geetha noticed it – may be she is jealous."

"Well, may be she is jealous or may be she doesn't want to get hurt."

At this remark, Kumar became rather pensive. They arrived at the airport shortly. They rushed to the gate where Gangadharan's were supposed to arrive.

In the meantime, Dr.Gangadharan's flight came a few minutes earlier and when they alighted from the plane, they could not locate Kumar or Harrish. Suddenly, Kumar and Harrish frantically arrived.

Harrish greeted Dr. and Mrs.Gangadharan very warmly. Dr.Gangadharan hugged Harrrish and Mrs.Gangadharan was very affectionate. Kumar was surprised to see how close Harrish was to the Gangadhrans. Kumar thought, "Latha is not this affectionate to Harrish. She is holding back."

Harrish introduced Kumar to Dr.Gangadharan while Mrs. Gangadharan greeted Kumar warmly. Since Kumar is a close friend of Latha, Dr & Mrs. Gangadhran felt affectionate warmth towards him. They all went to pick up the baggage.

When they were in the baggage claim area, Harrish and Kumar heard a voice calling them "Harrish,Kumar" They turned around and saw Dr.Ravi and Mrs.Ravi standing near them. They ran towards them and shook Dr.Ravi's hands.

Dr.Ravi said, "My work was over a little sooner. Therefore, we took an earlier flight."

Harrish and Kumar introduced them to the Gangadharans. As Latha and Veena are bosom friends, they were ebullient and cheerful to meet each other. The Gangadharans and Ravis had a lot to talk about especially regarding Latha and Veena. While thus exchanging pleasantries, the baggage arrived. They picked it up and went to the station wagon. Luckily, the car was atypical; it was big enough to accommodate everyone and the luggage.

Kumar, while driving, mentioned that dinner was at 8.00pm at Dr.Atchuthan's house and explained Dr.Atchuthan's profession. He also described Dr.Natchikethas' company briefly. "Dr.Ravi, he is interested in talking to you tomorrow."

Dr. Ravi requested Kumar to arrange the meeting.

Mrs.Chitra Gangadharan asked Kumar, "Does your mother go to Chennai during the December concert season ?"

"Yes, every year."

Mrs.Aruna Ravi chipped in, "I too go every year."

Chitra said, "This year Latha is planning to go too".

Aruna asked, "Chitra, why don't you come this year ? we can be all together –last year I did not know that Kumar's mother, Mrs.Radha Ram, goes to India every year."

Chitra replied, "Let me think, Aruna."

Aruna continued, "I am asking my husband, Dr.Ravi, to come also. Maybe, you and Dr.Gangadharan can join us and also Radha and Dr.Ram."

Dr.Gangadhran replied, " I like that idea. I could do research for my book. Harrish could join us: also, Radha and Dr.Ram."

Chitra said, "Well, Aruna, that settles that. Kumar why don't you come?"

Kumar said, "I will – with Harrish and Latha there and also all of you guys there – it would be fun".

While talking thus about the India trip, they reached Kumar's house and the car was parked in the front portico. Out came, Latha and Veena. Veena was stunned to see her parents; she ran and hugged them and also Mrs.Chitra Gangadharan whom she had met before in M.I.T. Latha hugged her parents and also Veena's as she felt very close to them. Radha came out and was delighted to see Aruna and Chitra. Dr.Ram greeted warmly Dr.Gangadharan and Dr.Ravi. Everyone was in a cheerful mood and the holiday spirit premeated the room; everyone was talking to everyone.

On hearing the commotion, Geetha slowly proceeded to the front portico. She was wearing a deep blue and white salwar. She was rather pensive. On seeing Geetha,. Latha came to her and introduced her to Ravis and her parents. Both Chitra and Aruna almost said in unison, "We are looking forward to your concert tomorrow". Kumar was watching Geetha; Geetha noticed that Kumar was rather serious and pensive. She was puzzled. "Kumar used to be so jovial and flippant. He is now serious." She looked at him again and he was still serious. She felt better because she thought he would not hurt her flippantly anymore. It relaxed her. She became more jovial and smiled at Kumar. Kumar was relieved that the crisis was obviously over. He smiled back. No one, except Veena, watched this exchange. Veena wondered, "What was this all about?" All of them went inside to get ready for dinner.

Chapter - 10

One by one, everyone assembled in the living room of Kumar's house. They were dressed in casual or sportive attire. Dr.Ram, Radha, Aruna, Chitra and their husbands went in a station wagon while Kumar drove the others in his car. Dr.Atchuthan, Lakshmi and Dr.Natchikethas greeted them. Radha introduced Aruna, Chitra, Dr.Ravi and Dr.Gangadharan.

The buffet was ready with a south Indian menu of sambhar, potato curry, rasam, avial, and curdrice. As everyone was beginning to enjoy the meal, Lakshmi was keen on knowing Aruna and Chitra. She formed a small group with Radha, Aruna and Chitra and they started to discuss music season in Chennai. She invited them to stay in her house in Chennai during the music season, as she had a reasonably big house. After some persuasion, they all agreed. Lakshmi felt good because she would have many opportunities to interact with them.

In the meantime, Dr.Natchikethas sought out Dr.Ravi and briefed him a little about the company. He wanted to meet him next day to discuss some issues. Dr.Ravi and Dr.Natchikethas decided to meet for brunch next day around 9.30 am.

Geetha was in a more cheerful spirit. Kumar stayed away from Geetha and Veena. He was chitchatting with Latha while Harrish, Veena and Geetha were conversing.

Geetha asked Veena, "Are you coming to Chennai in December?".

Veena replied, "I am thinking of it because my parents have decided to go."

"Why don't you stay with me?"

"Utmost thanks. Let me think about it".

Harrish added, "It will be close to where your parents are staying."

Veena asked Harrish, "Is Kumar coming?"

Geetha tried not to listen, however, she heard Harrish say, "Yes! He will be staying with me."

Just then, Dr.Natchikethas joined them. He had heard a little bit of the conversation. He wanted to know Veena better. He asked her, "When did you visit India last time?"

"Three years ago, along with my mother, who goes every year to Chennai during the music season."

"What did you see in Chennai?"

"I went to the music concerts primarily."

"Which concert did you like?"

"The concert by K.V.Narayanswamy was divine. It was outstanding."

"I love his music too. I enjoyed his thodi raga very much."

While Veena and Dr.Natchikethas were busy discussing carnatic music in Chennai, Kumar and Latha joined Geetha and Harrish. They all cheerfully talked about the concert the next day. Veena and Dr.Natchikethas also participated in this merry spirit. Soon, the whole group including parents mingled with the youngsters. All the guests left in a good happy mood to Kumar's house.

When they reached home, everyone went to bed; but Latha could not sleep. She sat in the balcony outside her bedroom and watched the moon and the garden. Something troubled her; it seemed to her that everyone was tacitly assuming that Harrish and she were going to get married. "My parents love Harrish and so do Kumar and Veena. Now, Geetha also adores Harrish. They are all expecting me to agree to marry him because Harrish likes me. I like Harrish too; he is handsome and brilliant with a good character. Nevertheless, I am not sure that I want to marry him. I need to think deeply and come to a decision quickly."

Latha decided to devote sometime to this pertinent issue and started to ponder intensely. As she thought deeply, it became clear to her that compatibility was the key to successful marriages. "Universally, Russians marry Russians, Catholics with Catholics, Indians with Indians and so on. Marriage is a close personal involvement and divisions make that closeness difficult to achieve. At physical, mental and spiritual levels, this closeness has to be nurtured".

"Harrish is born and raised in India and me in USA. The differences are quite deep and though, externally we both are Indian like. To bridge this division, an overwhelming attraction has to be there. However, I do not feel that. I like him but that is not enough to bridge the gulf. I thought time might develop that love but I do not see that happening. I cannot take that chance any more. It is not fair to Harrish or to me. Moreover, people alluding to a romance that really does not exist, deeply embarrasses me. I have to tell this to Harrish after the concert."

She thought about Harrish's feelings. She felt his pangs. Tears came rolling down her cheeks.

Life is an inscrutable drama!

Chapter - 11

Dr.Natchikethas had invited Kumar, Harrish and Veena to join him in his meeting with Dr.Ravi during brunch. The next day, they all assembled at 9.30am.

They took a cup of coffee or juice and sat around the table. Dr.Natchikethas started the meeting with a brief intoduction and brought Ravi up-to-date on all the issues. Now, Mrs.Ram came and said that the brunch dish "vennpongal" with "chutney" was ready. They all went and filled up their plate with venpongal and put chutney on the side.

Dr.Ravi was a blunt person and he started to speak,

"Dr.Natchikethas, thanks for your precise and brief summary. Certain things are very evident to me."

"First, you have a bigger problem than you actually think you have. I think it is extremely serious. Flourishing, profitable companies could collapse in year or two. Your father has built up this company over the years extremely well. The present CEO is running it quite well. However, his health is not good and may retire in two years."

"Moreover, you have no one trained to take over the company now and you think you have to go outside. You are a very busy cardiac surgeon; you are only giving part time attention. That will not do unless you already have a young top notch CEO. It is not that easy to recruit from outside. It is still a young company and not well known."

"Therefore, my sincere recommendation is for you to sell the company quickly while it is growing. One cannot be sentimental about running companies. You cannot do it part time to please your mother. You have to go full time but you are neither trained nor interested."

"You can sell it to a bigger company – that would be less of a headache or look at alternatives. You have to keep it a top secret and work hard on it."

Everyone around the table was stunned. Truth is often unpalatable. Dr.Natchikethas was also stunned and pained. The company had sentimental value for him. Nevertheless, he saw that the company had to survive in the harsh competitive market place. That required experience and hard work.

Dr.Ravi said in a softer tone, " Actually, you have opened my eyes to the succession issue in my company. Like your father, I have not given much time to it". He firmly said, "Today onwards, I am going to work on it."

Dr.Nathcikethan asked, "Dr.Ravi, do you have any interest in buying the company?"

Dr.Ravi replied, "I need to think but I am not looking to buy any company now. I am extremely busy."

They all chatted a little longer and then disbanded.

Veena was wandering in the garden pondering over dad's talk. She thought, "Dad is carrying a big burden. My elder brother is not interested and may be I should get more involved. I have the right technical background and I need to train under dad to run the company. Let me talk to dad about it."

Dr.Natchikethas was driving back and was thanking Dr.Ravi for his words of wisdom. He felt as if a great burden was lifted off his shoulders. He decided to talk to his mom about it.

Kumar was also affected by this discussion. He should think deeply about starting a company. A lot of sacrifice would be needed to run it well.

The meeting influenced Harrish also. Running a company would obviously demand the best of him. He realized how tough the task of developing a company was. He also thought of Latha. He had not seen her the whole morning.

Latha got up early in the morning and after coffee, went for a long walk. She thought through her decision alone once more and finally concluded that it was the right one. She came back to the balcony and reflected on her talk with Harrish. It is going to be emotionally tough and painful. Therefore, she mentally practiced it. After rehearsing it a few times, she felt a little better and went downstairs for a late brunch.

Chapter - 12

The evening was serene and the pointedly cool breeze was soothing to the nerves. Everyone was getting ready for the concert and dressed well for the occasion. Latha wore a beautiful blue saree; Veena chose emerald color salwar with gold and light green chupatha. Both Harrish and Kumar were in suites with colorful ties.

The lawn was sprawling and shining in the evening sun. A dais was erected for the music artists. One by one, the guests started coming; Dr.Ram and Mrs.Ram greeted them. About fifty guests arrived; Dr.Ram introduced them to Dr and Mrs.Ravi, and Dr.and Mrs.Gangadharan. The guests had coffee, tea or soft drinks.

Latha and Veena were busy catering to the guests. Harrish and Kumar were also active in taking care of the guests.

Dr.Geetha was busy preparing for the concert. She was dressed in a colorful grand silk golden color saree with red border. The accompanying artists, the violinist and the south Indian drum (miridangam) player, had arrived. Geetha was working with them fine tuning all the instruments— the violin, miridangam and the sruthi box (tuner). Soon, the artists were ready to perform. Geetha looked gorgeous in her new saree and she was clearing her throat. Dr.Ram introduced Dr.Geetha to the audience and the concert began.

She started "Viribhoni"varnam in "bhairavi ragam". She sang it with swiftness and bhavam (melody). While singing, she noticed Dr.Natchikethas was sitting in the front row and putting thalam (beat) correctly for the song. She was surprised to see his interest and knowledge. She soon closed her eyes and focused on her music.

Latha and Veena dropped their chores to listen to the music and so did Kumar and Harrish.

After a couple of short ragas, Geetha started raga alapanam of "thodi raagam". She was going deep into the ragam and she saw Dr.Natchikethas was fully absorbed and appreciative of the finer nuances. He was totally in tune with her. Outstanding was the raga alapana and the audience loved it. Latha and Veena were thoroughly enjoying it and so were Harrish and Kumar. Geetha chose the famous "koluvai maragatha" song of Saint Thyagaraja. It was outstanding. Dr.Natchikethas was thrilled with her rendition. The swaram she chose was complex but Dr.Natchikethas kept up with the thalam though it was tough. She was very surprised. He gave her a warm applause at the end of the swaram and she smiled acknowledging his genuine appreciation.

She sang two small songs before she took up "karaharapriya ragam" and sang melodiously "sakni raja" song. Everyone loved that song. She ended the nearly two-hour concert with two Meera bhajans. The audience gave her a standing ovation.

The audience rushed to the podium to congratulate her. Joyous were the guests. Latha expressed her special thanks and so did Veena. Kumar came later and congratulated her.

Veena, Harrish, Latha and Kumar were thoroughly enjoying the delicious food.

Geetha was busy talking to the guests and she noticed that Dr.Natchikethas had not yet come and talked to her.

After quite sometime, she went for dinner. As she was looking for a seat, she heard a soft voice, "Geetha, may I join you?"

She turned and saw Dr.Natchikethas. She smiled and said, "Yes, please."

They chatted while they were enjoying the tasty delicacies.

"That was a lovely concert, Geetha", said Dr.Natchikethas.

"Thanks Dr.Natchikethas, I was surprised at your knowledge of carnatic music." replied Geetha.

"In fact, I learnt carnatic music for ten years until I was sixteen. I loved it but I chose medicine as my career. As you know, medicine is a tough field and I could not keep up with music. Geetha, how did you choose carnatic music as your career?"

"In a way, Dr.Natchikethas, it was a natural process. It gave me solace when my father passed away. I began to love it. Then, I learnt it and it came naturally to me. I started to excel. I dedicate every concert to my father. Outstanding was my father's love for music."

"That's sad; I am so sorry to hear about your father. You know, Geetha, after today's concert my interest in carnatic music is rekindled. I am going to devote more time to it. Nothing in the world soothes the soul as well as music. Where and when is your next concert?"

"In Houston, on July 8th."

"Great! I might be there. I did my residency in Houston. I might visit my hospital before going back to Chennai. If not, I will come to your concerts in Chennai, if I don't have surgery on that day".

With that, they departed. Neither thought much about this conversation for a while. It was simply their love for music!

Chapter - 13

Latha went to her room after the concert and she felt relaxed. Excellent was the concert. She thought about the events of the day. One thing bothered her. Her mother was assuming that Harrish and she were going to be married. Her mother did not say it in so many words but was implying it in her covert actions. For example, she was always giving special attention to Harrish. Her mother embarrassed her because she would look wide-eyed whenever Harrish and she

A Tender Melody

were together. It was obvious. She could understand her mothers's anxiety but still it was rather pointedly annoying. Sometimes, even Kumar and Veena were thinking and acting along similar lines. Therefore, she decided to talk to Harrish the next day.

Latha got up early, had her coffee and went for a walk. Then, she looked for Harrish. Kumar and Harrish were chatting and when they saw her, they asked her to join them. She did. The conversation was about the concert and they all liked it. Soon, Kumar had to leave to attend some errands and Latha used this opportunity to ask Harrish whether he had some time to discuss an important issue quietly. Harrish felt that Latha was serious and he suggested they could either walk in the garden or sit way in the back of the garden. Latha preferred the second alternative.

Latha started the conversation, "Harrish, I want to bring to your attention an important issue. Please try to understand my predicament. You had indicated that you like me and I told you that I needed time to think. I have thought about the issue. There are many differences, chief among them, is that you were raised in India and I in the USA. This gulf could be overcome, if there is mutual love. However, I do not feel that. I like you very much as a friend but not romantically."

As Latha was pouring out her heart, Harrish watched her intensely. She was calm but emotionally pained. Harrish slowly began to comprehend her and the more he understood her, the more it hurt. He was shattered; his dreams crumbled. He was slowly realizing that she was making a final statement. However, a lingering hope pushed him to make a vain valliant attempt;

"Latha, why not give it more time?"

Latha saw his pained face and became more emotional and said in a low sad voice,

"Harrish, I see another significant problem, if we prolong this. Sometimes, I do feel embarrassed because my mother, at times, and even Kumar and Veena, assume that we are romantically involved. This embarrassment is not going get better unless we stop this uncertainty."

Harrish was startled to hear this and wondered what else he could say. Then, after a few moments, he offered an alternative, "Latha, I understand your predicament. I have an idea. I am completing my PhD in three months and I might go to California. The physical separation would reduce these rumors."

Latha became thoughtful, "Harrish is trying to prolong this and I am trying to end this."

She was frustrated and said with feeling, "Harrish, it may. However, I am not keen on marriage right now and I am not seriously thinking along those lines now. The physical separation is not going to help us. Moreover, you may find someone in California".

Harrish was hurt and he protested, "Latha, all I want you to have is an open mind."

Latha realized that Harrish was having a tough time in accepting her statements and said quietly, "Harrish, I am willing to have an open mind but you too should, so that you don't close out other opportunities."

To Harrish, it was obvious now that Latha was far far away from thinking of him romantically because romance is pointedly possessive.

He was quite sad; Latha noticed it and said, "Harrish, I am sorry to cause you pain."

Dejectedly Harrish replied, "Latha you had warned me earlier, but I was too hopeful. I was not realistic but was dreaming——today, you have put an end to that dream."

Latha said feelingly, "Harrish, I am so sorry that I ended your dream."

Harrish replied in a tone of resignation, "Latha, life is too fluid and changing to be worried about disappointments. May be, time is the best healer. May be, the physical separation and my work would make me get over this in time".

Harrish was down in spirits and noticing this, Latha had tears in her eyes. However, there was a real gulf between them, which neither knew then, how to cross.

Chapter - 14

Latha quickly departed and Harrish sat there utterly devastated. He pondered over the painful conversation. It was clear that Latha had no romantic feelings for him. Moreover, she was positively embarrassed by any suggestion that she and he were romantically involved. He wondered what went wrong. He realized that he had not taken her warning signals and comments in Syracuse earnestly. He naively thought she would come around in time but never gave any careful consideration that she might not. Harrish chastised himself for not talking her reservations very very seriously.

As Harrish sat there blaming himself and feeling very dejected, Kumar came looking for him. Harrish was too depressed to greet him. Kumar understood that something was wrong. He sat quietly next to Harrish and held his hand. Harrish said quietly, "Latha just told me to forget her and not to think of her romantically."

Kumar replied, "Harrish, I am so sorry to hear that. Did she give any reason?"

"Well; she does not have any romantic feelings for me. In addition, she is quite irritated by people around her especially her mother, assuming that she might marry me. She wants to end the speculation now. I cannot blame her because she warned me in Syracuse but I did not take her seriously".

Kumar observed kindly, "Harrish, don't blame yourself too much. These things happen in life. One has to move on,"

Harrish added ruefully, "Yes, I am planning to go to San Francisco soon."

After some quiet subdued conversation on this topic, Kumar, who was sad for his friend, had to leave to attend some chores. Harrish felt a little better after this discussion.

Latha went to her room and was rather sad and down. As she sat down to think about what happened, there was a gentle tap on the door. Veena walked in.

Seeing Latha dispirited, Veena probed,

"Latha, what is wrong? You look unhappy—the concert went extremely well."

"Veena, this has nothing to do with the concert. You know, people like my mom, and may be you and Kumar, are assuming that Harrish and I are almost engaged. I was embarrassed. Therefore, I told Harrish firmly that I don't have any romantic feelings for him. Of course, it hurt Harrish. I feel sorry for him."

Veena was utterly taken aback by this turn of events. She had thought from the beginning, that Latha was not a good match for Harrish. She even mentioned that to Harrish; he was not listening. She was a little mad at Harrish for getting himself in this painful situation.

Veena, after a pause, said, "Latha, you did the right thing. This could not go on forever."

Latha was astounded with the strong reaction from Veena, " Veena, did you know about this?"

"Latha, it was so obvious. Harrish was not hiding anything and you told me too. I even mentioned to Harrish indirectly whether two people not so compatible could be attracted. He did not pick up the cues."

"Veena, really! I am so glad to hear this, because, I am not alone."

"Latha, you both are indeed different. Harrish did not think carefully though he is smart."

Latha felt so much better and she hugged Veena.

Veena, now, felt sorry for Harrish. She had a soft corner for him. She felt his hurt. After hearing all the details from Latha, she thought about the issue. She decided to see Harrish in the garden.

Harrish was surprised to see Veena. She was calm and collected but was quite serious. Evidently, she knew. She opened the conversation saying, "Harrish, Latha just told me everything. She is miserable and in tears for causing you this pain. You could appreciate her predicament. She is very sensitive and warm. You are also going through hell and I could guess that from your sad face. I came here to talk to you because sharing eases pain."

Harrish looked at Veena. Her sincere concern touched him.

He said, "Veena, thanks for coming. Latha should not blame herself because she warned me in Syracuse. It is my fault entirely for not heeding to her cautious statements. You also mentioned compatibility as an issue. I was not listening."

Veena interjected, "Harrish, don't be too harsh on yourself. You were just optimistic."

Harrish added, "Veena, too unrealistically optimistic!"

Veena commented, "Well, Harrish; you are obviously down and negative. That is understandable now. It may take sometime for this ordeal to heal. By the way, I heard that you are planning to go to San Francisco. I have an idea. We have an outhouse in the back of our house; a one bedroom apartment type which my brother used for studies. He has gone to college and you can use it if you like. You will not be lonely there and there is a kitchen in it for your independent living. Moreover, you would be consulting my dad often and this would enable you to see him frequently."

This fine gesture surprised Harrish, who said, "Thanks, Veena. That is a great offer especially at this time of my life. Let me give it some thought."

Venna added, "Harrish, there is no need to think. This is only a temporary arrangement until you settle down in San Francisco. I am going with my parents today and let me make all the arrangements. I will be there for a month. You just let me know when you are coming."

Veena was quite firm when she said that. Harrish could not help a flicker of a smile at her insistence and Veena, immediately said, "Well, Harrish, I take that as a yes. Ok, will see you soon." She left in a hurry.

Her warm invitation touched Harrish and somehow, it made him feel a little better. He pondered over his future. The more he thought, the more it made sense to him to go to San Francisco immediately. He decided to call his friend in San Francisco and go back to MIT next day to pack. Only a few more chapters were left in his PhD thesis and he could easily finish it in a couple of months in San Francisco. He could also complete the research for Dr.Gangadharan from San Francisco. This decision gave him a future direction and eased his pain a little.

Then, he thought about Latha and Veena's remark saddened him. Therefore, he decided to go and see her. He knocked on her door and Latha was surprised to see Harrish.

Harrish said in a low voice but seriously, "Latha, Veena told me that you are miserable about causing me grief. I thought about it. It is entirely my fault. You had told me that you do not feel any romance and not interested in marriage. I did not heed it. Therefore, I take full responsibility for my grief. I am going to San Francisco soon and I plan to reconstruct my life. I want you to look ahead and forget the past."

Latha came close to him, took his hand in hers, and said with feelings, "Harrish, I sincerely wish you all the best in your life".

Harrish said warmly, "Latha, I wish you all the very best happiness in your life. Let us part as friends and keep in touch".

They shook hands with a tear or two in their eyes and they parted.

Life indeed is an inscrutable drama!

Chapter - 15

Dr.Natchikethas woke up early in the morning and went for a walk. During the walk, he thought about the concert; it charmed him. It rekindled his interest in carnatic music. His mind drifted to Geetha; he was impressed by her dedication to music at such an young age. He loved the intensity and care with which she sang. He decided to go to her concert in Houston and made up his mind to visit her in the morning to get the address etc.

He came home and left for Dr.Ram's house around eleven in the morning. In the side portico, under a canopy, were assembled Dr.Ravi and his wife, Dr. & Mrs.Gangadharan and also Dr. & Mrs.Ram. Veena and Latha just joined them. Dr.Ravi and the party were departing for the airport shortly and a brunch was set up. Dr.Natchiketas went to the buffet table filled his plate and sat with them. Kumar and Harrish came at the end.

Geetha arrived last and everyone instinctively got up and gave her a spontaneous applause appreciating the performance of the previous night. Geetha was touched and thanked them. The brunch and the get-together made everyone cheerful. Even Harrish forgot his pain and the joyful spirit was catchy. Dr.Ravi and others soon departed for the airport; Dr.and Mrs.Ram went to the airport to see them off as they had become quite close in the last couple of days. Kumar drove one car with Harrish. Dr.Ram drove the other. Geetha wanted to rest and stayed back.

Dr.Natchikethas and Geetha waved them goodbye. Dr.Nathcikethas turned to Geetha and said, "Geetha, that was an wonderful concert last night. I would love to attend your Houston concert if possible. Could you please give me the address and phone number and also the time of the concert?"

Geetha was a little surprised but did not show it. She went up and got the address etc. for him. Dr.Natchikethas left and Geetha went up to take rest.

While coming back from the airport, Kumar told Harrish,

"Harrish, please stay here a few more days. Geetha will be here. My mom and Mrs.Ravi plan to have long music sessions with Geetha. You really love music and you cannot get another opportunity like this. Moreover, Latha has left. You would be lonely at MIT."

Harrish thought about it—the idea of spending quality time on music with Geetha appealed to him. It would be lively and cheerful here in Atlanta. Therefore, he decided to stay.

That afternoon, around 3pm, they had their first music session. They focused on theoretical discussion on raga alapanam and swaram. Mrs. Aruna Ravi was very knowledgeable and so was Mrs.Radha Ram. The three, Aruna, Radha and Geetha went deep into music theory. It was so lively that Harrish forgot his pain. Later, he also participated actively. Veena was happy to see Harrish's enthusiasm.

In the evening, Kumar was strolling in the garden. Veena joined him. Veena remarked,

"Kumar, it is great, you persuaded Harrish to stay. He was relaxed in the music session."

"Veena, I am glad it is working out. Veena, do you understand how all of this happened?"

"Kumar, I told you in San Francisco that Harrish was not paying attention to warning signals from Latha. If he had understood Latha's lack of interest, he would not be suffering now."

"Veena, you are too harsh on Harrish."

"Okay, Kumar, what is your opinion?"

"Veena, I feel Latha also shares the blame. She is too sensitive. If Latha did not get embarrassed so quickly, this would have moved smoothly. Harrish would have sensed, in time, Latha's lack of interest. He is quite smart."

"Kumar, I do like Harrish. I am not just picking on him."

"Veena, Harrish is outstanding in many areas."

Veena was touched by Kumar's high regard and affection for Harrish.

Next day, Dr.Natchikethas came to see Geetha briefly. He told her that he had to return to Chennai immediately to take care of a patient. He regretted his inability to attend her concert in Houston.

The next two days of intense music-sessions, had a wonderful therapeutic effect on Harrish. On the last day, before Geetha's departure, Kumar and Harrish sat in the side portico after dinner.

Harrish asked Kumar, "Kumar, what have you decided about the summer project? Are you coming to San Francisco?"

"Well, Harrish, after hearing Dr.Ravi's stern message to Dr.Natchikethas, I realized how tough running a company was. I have decided to focus on PhD first and then worry about starting a company. Therefore, I am staying put in MIT."

"Kumar, it might have been fun with you in San Francisco, but I understand your reason. Thanks a lot for asking me to stay back. It helped me a lot to cope."

"Harrish, wish you all the best in San Francisco. We will be in touch"

Chapter - 16

Harrish was in the one bedroom apartment–type outhouse in San Francisco arranging his things brought from MIT, Cambridge. It had a small living room combined with dining, a bedroom and a kitchen. The weather was lovely and the view from the living room window was magnificent.

There was a knock on the door and Harrish opened the door. Veena stood there with a smile. Harrish greeted her warmly and said, "Veena! This is a lovely place and quite cheerful."

Veena replied," Harrish, I am so glad you like it. Do you play golf?"

"Yes, I am reasonably good at it but not great."

"Good; my brother, Chandran, is coming tomorrow and he is a good golf player and so is my dad. I am an ok golfer. Let four of us go and play some golf. I will let you know tomorrow when and where."

The golf course, green and sprawling, was basking in the morning sun and the foursome, Veena, Dr.Ravi, Harrish and Veena's brother, Chandran started the game early in the morning. Veena teamed with Chandran and Dr.Ravi and Harrish formed the other team. They played foursome; Dr.Ravi, and Chandran being better players started with teeing off. Both Veena and Harrish followed them with the next stroke. All of them chitchatted in an amicable spirit, as they walked from the teeing ground to the putting green. They were enjoying the beautiful weather.

During the chitchat, Chandran, a medical student said he would be going to Atlanta Emory University to do a one-month sub internship in neurology under Dr.Ram. Dr.Ravi was happy and said they had a wonderful time in Atlanta. Veena added that the concert by Dr.Geetha was simply divine.

She turned to Harrish and asked, "Harrish where is Geetha now ?"

Harrish replied, "She is in Detroit now and coming to Los Angeles next week."

"Harrish, my mom was wondering whether Geetha could come to San Francisco. Is it possible for you to call her today and see whether she could come to San Francisco and stay in our house for a few days?"

"Veena, I would love to. I want to see her also."

"Do you have her number?"

"Yes, I have her contact person's number in Detroit. I will call tonight."

"Great! I hope she can come. Then, we will have a grand time," said Veena with feeling.

Harrish approvingly smiled.

After some golf and general chit chat, Dr. Ravi asked Harrish, "Harrish what do you think of Dr.Natchikethas' company?"

"Dr.Ravi, it is a small but fast growing high tech company. It is solid, very profitable and well run. The only issues are succession of the President two years from now and the fact that Dr.Natchikethas does not have time."

Dr.Ravi asked Veena, "Veena, how do you assess the technical strength of the company?"

Veena answered, " I like their innovative spirit. They have an outstanding digital-signal –processor-software-technology. Overall, I rate their technical skills highly. Dad, why are you asking these questions?"

"Well, I am thinking of buying that company. Dr.Natchikethas does not have time and I do not want that company to go down."

Harrish interjected, "Dr.Ravi, there may be one problem. Dr.Natchikethas' mother is emotionally attached to her late husband's company. She may not want to sell."

Dr.Ravi became pensive.

Harrish added, "Maybe, she might sell a portion of her share. She knows her son is a surgeon and very busy. She has met you and Veena. She might be willing."

Dr.Ravi's face brightened and he said, "Harrish, I have an idea. You want to start a company. You know, I first worked in a company to learn the ropes. You could work with me to acquire this company and help me run it."

Harrish observed, "Dr.Ravi, that is a thoughtful proposal. Let me talk to my friend, Aravind."

Dr.Ravi continued, " Harrish, could you please arrange a meeting with Dr.Natchikethas in Chennai in the early part of August? I am going to be in Europe, I could fly from there, and you could be there ahead of us."

Harrish agreed to call Dr.Natchikethas that evening and try to arrange a meeting in Chennai.

After some more golf, Veena said, "Dad, I might come to San Francisco. My professor has suggested that I come to Stanford to work under a great Artificial Intelligence expert in Stanford for a period of nine months. I am seeing that professor in Stanford next week."

Dr.Ravi was delighted and said "I hope it works out."

They obviously had a relaxed and lovely golf before returning home late in the evening.

Chapter - 17

When Dr.Geetha came out of the security area in the San Francisco airport, Veena greeted her with a big hug and Mrs.Chirtra Ravi held Geetha's hands warmly. Veena drove the car and they conversed about the Atlanta experience and about Geetha's recent concert tour. It was now evening and after a light dinner, Veena asked Geetha whether she was tired. Geetha said "No". Veena said, "Can we talk?" Geetha agreed readily.

They went to Veena's room which was spacious and well furnished. They sat in a conner where a love seat and a chair were placed.

Veena asked Geetha, "Do you know about Harrish and Latha?"

Geetha answered, "Not really – I knew that Harrish liked Latha and Latha was indecisive."

"Well, Latha made up her mind. She felt that Harrish is not her choice and told Harrish about her decision. Harrish, of course, is disappointed."

"Did Latha cite any reasons?"

Veena told her in detail that basically Latha did not have any romantic feelings for Harrish and she was embarrassed by her parents and other alluding to one. Geetha, as a woman, understood Latha's feelings, but she was sad for Harrish. It hurt her because she loved Harrish deeply.

Veena held Geetha's hands and said with feeling, "I do not want to hurt you. However, Harrish is hurting more and someone needs to talk to him. This is a delicate topic and I cannot discuss this with him and he may not confide in me. But you are here and you are close to him and you can make him share his feelings."

Geetha was touched by Veena's concern and assured her that she would talk to Harrish. After some light conversation, Geetha retired to bed.

Geetha got up early in the morning and knocked on Harrish's apartment. Harrish opened the door and was surprised to see Geetha but he was happy. He made her coffee and they started a conversation.

Geetha asked, "Harrish, please tell me all about Latha in your own words. Veena gave me an outline yesterday."

Harrish started with a sigh, "Let me tell you from the beginning. When I first met Latha at MIT, she impressed me as intelligent, music loving and beautiful. She was also courteous and classy. Therefore, I was attracted to her. I met her mom and we clicked. Her father liked my work extremely well. But Latha expressed some reservations at Syracuse."

Harrish was pained as he recalled Latha's reservations; he slowly walked to the window and looked out. After a pause, he continued in a sad tone, "I promised her then that I will be professional. I was that way in Syracuse. That relaxed her and made her cheerful. She seemed even encouraging at MIT. In Atlanta, I was in good spirits and so was she; however, her mother assumed that we were involved romantically. This bothered Latha because she was not that attracted to me. She told me that and wanted me to accept it."

Harrish thoughtfully returned to his seat and was in low spirits. Geetha was touched by his sad tale and was emotional for a few minutes. Then she asked, "Harrish, how did you feel at that time?".

Harrish replied with anguish, "Well, Geetha, I was devastated. I had built castles in the air and it all came tumbling down. Utmost heartbroken was I. While in MIT, old memories haunted me. The trip to San Francisco was a savior."

Geetha perceived a silver line and enquired, "How do you feel now?"

"I am busy completing my PhD thesis and also I am on Dr.Ravi's project to acquire Dr.Natchikethas' company. We are coming to India in a few weeks. Only time could heal this wound. Both my busy schedule and the support of Veena and her family are keeping this pain from explosion."

Geetha probed gently, "Harrish, do you feel any regrets or remorse?"

Harrish answered feelingly, "Yes, Geetha; often, I feel that I should have been more careful. I am paying for my lack of vigilant thoughtfulness. I should have thought seriously about Latha's reservations. I was heedlessly optimistic. This is my regret."

"Harrish, you are down on yourself a little too much. In the first love, a touch of optimism is quite human."

"Geetha, tell me frankly. What do you think went wrong?"

Geetha answered, "Harrish, I feel lack of communication is the problem. You did not ask her earlier what she thought about the issue. You did not probe her deeply. You let too much time pass before it exploded. Two people think differently. Unless they communicate frequently, how could they know each other's mind? This is true in business, true in family and true in every endeavor where two or more persons are involved."

Harrish, after some deep reflection, saw Geetha's point and thanked her for it. They had some general chitchat and Geetha returned to her room.

After Geetha left, Harrish sat quietly and was absorbed in contemplation. The villain became very evident to him—thanks to Geetha——the lack of communication had indeed created the havoc. He analyzed the sequence of events. The more he thought about it, the better he felt. A mystery was resolved. His tension reduced and he was more relaxed.

In that calmer mood, he thought of Latha and the sadness this had caused her. He wanted to ease her pain. Therefore, he wrote her a warm, soothing letter, sharing his newly acquired intuition and wisdom.

When wisdom dawns, peace ensues!!

Chapter - 18

Geetha spent two days of music sessions with Mrs.Ravi and Veena. Harrish joined them whenever he could and was in better spirits. Geetha and Veena forged a closer relationship because music created a friendly, cheerful spirit. Veena also thanked Geetha for talking to Harrish.

When Geetha returned to Chennai, she had an important marriage to attend in two weeks; the marriage of her cousin sister, (*i.e.* her mother's sister's daughter) Vanaja. Geetha and Vanaja had been close playmates in the early years and have kept in touch. They were quite intimate friends. Vanaja had graduated in astrophysics, a fascinating subject. Geetha was looking forward to attending the wedding; weddings are a grand affair in India with all the relatives mingling with good food and a catchy cheerful atmosphere.

On the day before marriage, in the evening, Geetha was dressed in a beautiful blue saree with a matching blouse, a pearl necklace and an elegant earring and was involved in talking to the bride, Vanaja, on the marriage dais, waiting for the marriage function to start. It's called "Nitchyarthartham", where both parties solemnly agree to the marriage next day. The bride and the groom are given new dresses and after they wear new clothes, they exchange garlands. The function was going to start in five minutes, when Geetha heard a man's voice calling her "Geetha".

Geetha turned around and she saw Dr.Natchikethas in total surprise but was smiling broadly. She could not help smiling but was in utter shock.

"What a surprise!" said Geetha.

"Well! I am cousin to the groom. How about you?" asked Dr.Natchikethas.

"Oh! I am cousin to the bride!" answered Geetha.

"Geetha! We are going to be close family members."

"I guess so!" said Geetha laughingly.

"Geetha, you look dashing," said Dr. Natchikethan said admiringly.

Geetha smiled shyly.

At that time, Vimala, Dr.Natchikethas' sister, came up to the dais. Dr.Natchikethas called her and said "Vimala, this is Dr.Geetha whom I told you about. She is bride Vanaja's cousin sister. We are going to be family relatives."

Vimala took Geetha's hands warmly and Geetha said, "Hi Vimala – I heard a lot about you from your mom. I will contact you later about Sanskrit Dikshithar songs."

Now, the ceremony started between the two parents and the elders on both sides. Soon, the bride and the groom left to get dressed in new clothes and there was a lull in the ceremony.

Geetha spotted Mrs.Laskhmi Shankar, Dr. Nathcikethas' mother. She took her mother along to meet Mrs.Shankar. Geetha addressed her,"Mrs Shankar, namaskarams"

Mrs.Lakshmi Shankar was astounded, "What! Geetha!"

"Aunty, I am the bride's cousin sister; I saw Dr.Natchikethas – we are going to be family relatives".

"Oh! I see" .

"Aunty, this is my mother, Parvathi."

Lakshmi was so overwhelmed that she hugged Parvathi and said, " I have been wanting to meet you and tell you that Geetha gave a splendid music performance in Atlanta. We were so thrilled."

Parvathi was pleased and said, "Lakshmi, we are going to be related. I am the bride's aunty and you are the groom's. So, we will meet often."

On the dais, Dr.Natchikethas was being introduced to a number of the bride's relatives. Someone said, "This is Pavitran, Geetha's brother."

Dr.Natchikethas was delighted to meet Pavithran.

"Hi! I am Dr. Natchikethas."

"Oh! I heard so much about you from Geetha."

"I hope its good," said Dr.Natchikethas.

"Of course, excellent"

Then, they exchanged further information. Dr.Natchikethas found that Pavithran was a lawyer specializing in corporate law. He had both law and MBA degrees.

The bride and the groom just arrived on the dais wonderfully dressed and there was silence in the hall. It was a solemn, auspicious and lovely moment and they exchanged garlands committing themselves for a joyful partnership in life. It is the custom for Nadaswaram (a long winded instrument) and drum to play carnatic music to symbolize gaiety and jubilation. To impart solemnity and sacredness, ancient Sanskrit Vedic mantras were chanted by Vedic scholars.

The ceremony was over in half hour. The invited guests were led to a large dining room for dinner. Lakshmi, Parvathi, Geetha, Dr.Natchikethas, Vimala, and Pavitran were busy with the guests. The inner family on both sides remained at the end and they went for dinner. Dr.Natchikethas was with the groom, Krishnan and Geetha was with the bride, Vanaja. They sat together and enjoyed the delicious meal.

Dr.Krishnan was an associate professor in Physics at Emory University, Atlanta. He knew Dr.Ram and Dr.Atchuthan in Atlanta and he missed Geetha's concert as he was away attending a conference.

"Dr.Geetha- I am sorry I missed your concert. Natchikethas told me that it was outstanding."

"Thanks" said Geetha.

"Well, next time you come to Atlanta, please stay with us."

"I will, Dr.Krishnan. Actually, to stay in Vanaja's and your house, I don't need an invitation."

"Dr.Geetha, tomorrow evening, I will get a chance to hear your concert" said Krishnan.

Dr.Natchikethas teasingly said, "Krishnan, you will be too busy looking at Vanaja that you will hardly hear the concert."

Everyone laughed.

Krishnan added, "That may be true but I will try my best."

Thus, merrily, they talked and enjoyed the muticourse finely prepared dinner.

Chapter - 19

Geetha got up early in the morning around 4.00 am and dressed elegantly for the marriage function that is to start at 5.30 am. The early morning matched best for auspicious timing. She arrived at 5.20 am and Dr.Natchikethas came a little later.

He spotted Geetha and asked her, "Geetha, you are dressed gorgeously – where can I get a cup of coffee?"

"Upstairs" said Geeetha with a smile.

"Do you want one?"

"I am very busy"

"I will get you a cup, Geetha".

"Thanks."

Dr.Natchikethas brought Geetha a cup of coffee but she was running around with so many chores to attend to while sipping coffee.

The first major function that is fun is called "oonjal" where the bride and groom sit on a swing and while they go back and forth, ladies take turn to sing songs and certain ceremonies are performed. That function started right away and Vanaja and Krishnan were on the swing outside on a beautiful lawn. Geetha started the music with three melodious songs which were so touching.

Early in the morning, as the sun was radiating its golden colorful rays, Dr. Natchikethas closed his eyes and was totally immersed in the lovely songs. They were soothing to his nerves in the enchanting serene early dawn. Geetha saw his utter absorption in the music and that was inspiring to pour her soul into the divine songs.

When the last song was about to be over, Dr.Natchikethas opened his eyes and saw Geetha beautifully dressed and singing like a nightingale. He sensed a special warmth towards her and expressed it in a smile. She felt the fond admiration and was touched by it.

The function shifted indoors and the ancient Vedic mantras were chanted before the sacred fire. The guests started to arrive and fill up the hall. Soon, the big hall was full. The most important ceremony, rather the pinnacle of the marriage ceremony was just about to start. The groom is supposed to tie a thread with auspicious and sacred golden imprints called "Thirumangalyam" around the neck of the bride. That consummates the formal marriage ceremony.

Vanaja was seated on her father's lap and Krishna had the "Thirumangalyam" ready. Both the families were on either side. The nadaswaram started playing music. The Vedic mantras were chanted loudly. Krishnan tied the knot – nadaswaram and drum were really loud to announce the union of the couple. Vimala tied the second knot, as Krishnan's sister could not come from Australia. The close family members were emotional; Lakshmi hugged Parvathi, Geetha hugged Vimala and Dr.Natchikethas shook hands with Pavithran.

The parents of the bride and groom embraced each other. The marriage is as much a union of the two families as it is a union of the bride and groom.

After an hour, almost all the guests had the special breakfast. Dr. Natchikethas was planning to go for breakfast and was looking for his sister, Vimala. However, he saw Geetha busy but tired. He went up to her and asked, "Geetha, did you have breakfast?"

"No. Not yet – kind of busy".

With concern, Dr.Natchikethas asked, "Geetha, aren't you giving a concert today evening?"

"Yes"

"Won't you be too tired? What about your voice, Geetha?."

Geetha saw his point. A larger audience would be there in the evening. She could not disappoint them. They looked for Vimala and Pavitran and all the four went for breakfast. Dr.Natchikethas suggested that he take Geetha and Vimala home and Pavitran bring both the moms later. Therefore, the first party left so that Geetha could rest and practice for the concert.

Dr.Natchikethas arrived at six in the evening at the marriage hall. The bride and the groom were in the final adjustments of their splendid attire; the hall was glittering. The reception would start soon and the guests would soon be arriving.

The concert would start at six thirty. Dr.Natchikethas told Vimala that he planned to listen to the music and could mom and she greet the guests. She agreed. Bride and groom would be at one end of the hall greeting guests and the concert would be at the other end.

The concert started exactly at six thirty with Geetha dressed in a golden saree with red border. Lovely she looked. Dr. Natchikethas was seated in the front and gave her a warm smile. She returned it while thanking him in her mind for ensuring her rest in the morning. She was well rested and started the music in a fast and vigorous tempo with the majestic Thodi ragam varnam "Yennara pai". The music began with a cheerful gusto and Dr.Natchikethas was enthusiastically putting the thalam. Geetha moved next to a fast paced song "Nenna runjira", it set the tone of the concert and awoke everyone to the marvel of the music. "Marubahalga" was sung with hearty zest and vigor.

Geetha moved to a major ragam "shankarabaranam"; Dr.Natchikethas had a beaming smile, as he loved the ragam which in his opinion was really outstanding and captivating. His infectious, enthusiastic smile propelled her deep into the very soul of the ragam. Her poignant melodious rendering of the ragam moved him profoundly. Thus, they were intensely in their own world of music oblivious of the outside world.

During the next two hours, it seemed that they were in unison with their souls deeply in the splendor and glory of music.

Chapter - 20

Veena knocked on Harrish's apartment in the morning about four weeks after his arrival in San Francisco.

Harrish opened the door and said, "Hi! Veena"

"Harrish, I came to discuss our trip to Chennai to investigate Dr.Natchikethas' company and reserve the tickets."

"Okay, Veena. Would you like a cup of coffee?"

"Thanks, Harrish."

With coffee in their hand, they sat near the table.

"Harrish, what is your plan?"

"Well, Veena, first, I just completed my PhD thesis and my professor has corrected it through the email. Now, I have to go to MIT and take care of some formalities."

"Harrish, that is very fast."

"Yes, Veena, I have been working very hard at it so that I could devote time to the Natchikethas' company from now on."

Veena marveled his energy and dedication.

"Harrish, how is the acquisition of Dr.Natchikethas' company coming?"

"Veena, Dr.Ravi wanted at least fifty one percent and more. After long deliberation, Dr.Natchikethas' mom agreed to sixty percent. This is subject to Dr.Ravi inspecting the company next week in person. Therefore, next week is critical to the final agreement."

"Dad asked me to look deeply at the technical aspects of the company along with Kumar." said Veena.

"He asked me to study the financial aspects," remarked Harrish.

"Harrish, I want to ask you an important question that is bothering me."

"Veena, what is it?"

Veena replied, "Well, you see what is happening to Dr.Natchikethas' company. His father worked hard to build the company and none of his heirs are interested in running it. My father is not getting younger. Should I complete my PhD or help him in the company?"

Harrish got up, walked to the window and looked out. He was thoughtful. He looked handsome to Veena. He turned around and said, "Veena, learning from a top CEO like your dad, is worth, in my opinion, ten PhDs. That is why, I jumped at the opportunity to work with Dr.Ravi, when he asked me to help him acquire Dr.Natchikethas' company."

Veena asked, "Should I do an MBA?"

"No! The most poined need is to learn from him first. Then, you can augment it by taking executive training programs in selective areas for three months at a time. Excellent programs are available at Stanford, at Harvard and at Sloan school."

"Harrish, I have another question. Why didn't dad ask me to help him?"

"Well, Veena. He probably wants to see real burning interest form you. One cannot run a growing, outstanding company with half-hearted interest. Otherwise, he might sell the company to a bigger company as he advised Dr.Natchikethas. A

A Tender Melody

top company could go down quickly if not run well as the market is very competitive."

"I see."said Veena." The ball is in my court now. I will think hard and make a decision. Now, what is your plan?"

Harrish answered," Today is Monday. I would like to leave for MIT tomorrow morning and then depart for Chennai with Kumar on Thursday evening."

"How about your return?"

"I could return with Dr.Ravi and you."

"Harrish, my plan is to join dad at Frankfurt, Germany on Thursday. We are leaving Friday and will reach Chennai Friday late at night. We will return next Friday."

"Veena, you probably know that Dr.Natchikethas has requested Dr.Ravi and you to stay with him"

"Yes; Geetha's house will be close. She has requested that I stay with her for a couple of days."

"That's great. I would like Dr.Ravi and you come and meet my parents."

"Of course, we would love to meet them."

With that, Veena left.

In the evening, around 4pm, Ashok, Veena's younger brother, knocked on Harrish's apartment. Harrish opened the door and saw Ashok.

Harrish cheerfully asked, "Hi ! Ashok, what is up?"

Ashok replied, " Harrish, Veena told me that you are a good Tennis player. My partner could not make it today. Could you please play with me?"

" Okay,Ashok. However, you are a great player and I am a bit rusty. Is that okay?"

"Harrish, it is fine. I need practice today."

Soon, they set out for the court nearby. They started to play and Harrish was slowly getting better and better. At that time, a car pulled up. Ashok stopped to watch and it was his brother's car, a Porsche. Out came, Veena and Chandran dressed for Tennis.

Veena asked,"Ashok, could we play doubles?"

Ashok replied, "No, Veena, I need practice. Harrish is hitting well now and I am getting excellent practice. Why don't Chandran and you play singles?"

Chandran retorted,"Ashok, I am a bit off today. I cannot play singles."

Reluctantly, Ashok agreed. Veena and Ashok formed one team, Harrish and Chandran the other. They had a great time playing together and even Ashok enjoyed the doubles game.

Next day, at the Logan airport in Boston, Kumar met Harrish and Kumar noticed right away that Harrish was more cheerful. When enquired, Harrish said, " I had a long talk with Geetha and she pointed out that lack of communication as the central issue. The more I thought of it, the more it became abundantly clear to me that good communication would have cleared the misunderstanding much earlier. Moreover, Veena and her family are very supportive; therefore, I am in better spirits."

Kumar was happy to hear that. They went to a good Indian Restaurant and while enjoying the food talked about their trip to Chennai and Dr.Natchikethas' company.

Chapter - 21

Two weeks later, Veena was dressed splendidly for the dinner hosted by Dr.Natchikethas for the guests from USA who had been working hard on the company for four days. He had invited Geetha and her family, to join them for dinner. When Veena came down to the dining room, Lakshmi was impressed by her beauty. She wondered if Dr.Natchikethas married Veena, then the company would still be in the family. That thought attracted her to Veena; of course, Veena was also beautiful, smart and very cultured.

Dr.Natchikethas came down and saw Veena well dressed. He commented,

"Veena, you look radiant"

Veena said, "Thanks"

Lakshmi saw this exchange and she thought they liked each other. Dr.Natchikethas saw his mother's looks and it hit him that she wanted them married.

He wondered "why". Soon it dawned on him, if that were to happen, the company would be in the family. On thinking more, he could not fault his mom because he himself thought about marrying Veena and let her run the company. He even talked to Harrish about Veena in Atlanta.

The doorbell rang and Dr.Natchikethas opened the door. Geetha, her mom and her brother were at the door and Dr.Natchikethas greeted Geetha with a warm,

A Tender Melody

cheerful smile and she returned it. Lakshmi noticed the warmth between Geetha and Natchikethas. She dismissed it as mutual love for music. Veena came running and hugged Geetha.

Geetha said to Veena, "Veena, you have been very busy. You could not come to our house nor call"

"Geetha, I am very sorry. The company issues have been very demanding and this is a short trip. I have been thinking of you and I will come tomorrow."

The doorbell rang again. In came Kumar and Harrish.

Geetha hurried towards Harrish and Harrish hugged her. Geetha complained, "Harrish, you have been too busy even to call."

Harrish replied, "Yes, Geetha. I apologize. We have been extremely busy. We came Friday late at night. Starting Saturday afternoon, around 2.00p.m, we had long meetings with Dr.Natchikethas and his top officials. On Saturday evening, two senior Vice Presidents from Dr.Ravi's company flew in from USA and we had further meetings all day Sunday. We split the team into three groups and each team had been very busy Monday, Tuesday and Wednesday mornings. This afternoon, all of us assembled for a final discussion."

Geetha asked, "How is it coming along?"

Harrish answered, "Great- the final decision is up to Dr.Ravi and Dr.Natchikethas."

Dr.Natchikethas came over and smilingly said, "Harrish, no company talk now – all of you just relax and enjoy."

Harrish smilingly agreed and of course, Geetha voted for it with all her heart.

Dr.Ravi just joined the dinner party and he saw Geetha and went up to her and said, "Geetha, your music in Atlanta is still ringing in my ears. Unfortunately, I was too busy in San Francisco when you came to our house. Could you please sing a few songs informally today?"

Veena joined him in the request and so did Harrish. Geetha agreed. Fortunately, she was preparing for a concert and she decided to rehearse a few key songs here.

The doorbell chimed. Harrish's parents arrived. Harrish's father Dr. Sridhar and Dr.Ravi hit it off being in computer technology. Dr.Ravi agreed to visit IIT and give an address next time he visits India. Harrish, Geetha, Parvathi, Harrish's mom, Lakshmi, Vimala, Pavithran and Dr. Natchikethas talked about Vanaja and Krishnan's marriage and their new family connection.

Lakshmi prepared a grand gourmet dinner for everyone to enjoy and relax. Everyone sat around a big around table and was served by trained professionals.

Kumar was seated next to Veena and Kumar asked Veena, "Veena, when are you flying back?"

"Kumar, I was planning to go with dad but he has to leave early morning tomorrow to Singapore. Harrish will take care of completing the report here. I decided to stay back to be with Geetha and see Mahabalipuram."

Kumar added, " Great! I did not want to go back early. I am glad that Harrish is returning late. Harrish and I were so busy that we didn't get a chance to talk about our return plans. May I come with you to Mahabalipuram?"

"Kumar, of course. Harrish, you and I will go. May be Vimala would join us"

Lakshmi observed the closeness between Kumar and Veena. They seem to have known each other for a long time. "Are they closer than she thought?" Then, she got a little upset with Dr.Natchikethas; "Why is he not taking care of himself?"

She looked for Natchikethas. He was seated next to Dr.Ravi, who was leaving next day morning. The other side of Dr.Ravi was Geetha. The three of them were having a jolly, cheerful conversation. Lakshmi did not know what to make of it. Dr.Natchikethas caught his mother's look but he did not know what to make of it either. Then, he saw Kumar and Veena chitchatting amicably and he understood his mother's concern. He remembered what Harrish told him in Atlanta about Kumar and Veena. He decided to let it go then as he was having a grand time with Dr.Ravi and Geetha.

After dinner, they all sat around on the floor in the spacious living room – dining room combined rooms. Geetha started the informal music with "kapi"ragam song "yentha sowkhyama". She sang it melodiously. The group forgot about the company issues and were immersed in the music. Geetha next sang "Kalyani ragam" and the song "Nithijala sukhama". The audience was enthralled. Dr.Natchikethas was totally involved in the music and was in a different world. Geetha next sang "bhairavi" ragam and the song "kamakshi". It was so touching; she sang it so well that the group only thought of music. Geetha completed the informal music session with two lighter melodies.

Kumar, when he returned home after dinner, could not sleep right away due to jet lag. The party, especially the music, totally relaxed him. He found out that Mrs.Shankar was very interested in the radiant Veena and was following her always. He understood why. Geetha, of course, shined with her subdued beauty. Kumar could not, yet, choose between them. He simply decided to wait.

Chapter - 22

Kumar and Harrish came the next day morning to Dr.Natchikethas' house; Pavitran and Vimala decided to go with them to Mahabalipuram. All the five, Veena, Kumar, Harrish, Vimala and Pavitran cheerfully started off for their trip.

Lakshmi and Parvathi shared in the preparation of the lunch. They packed for them pullianchatham (tamarind based preparation), coconut rice, potato curry, appalam (fritters), Yogurt rice. The ride was about an hour and a half. They rented a cottage and ate lunch while chitchatting lively about the history of Mahabalipuram.

Mahabalipuram was built by an Indian king to commemorate the Great king "Mahabali". It has beautiful, breathtaking sculptures of panchapandavas of mahabharatham, an epic drama of India. They set out to see the sculptures; Kumar, Pavitran, and Vimala went in the front and Veena and Harrish were following them.

Veena started the conversation with Harrish, "Harrish, I talked to dad about my joining the company. He was thrilled with my interest."

"Great – that is wonderful, Veena. When are you starting?"

"Next Monday."

"So soon, Veena!."

"Actually, Harrish, dad has already given me an assignment to be completed in ten days."

"Veena, that is surprising."

"Dad has been looking at a young high tech startup company for possible acquisition. He wants me to analyze the company, visit the company and make an assessment whether he should buy that company. Actually, Harrish, I would appreciate it if you could help me with this assignment. I need your help in analyzing the financial aspects of the company."

"Veena, I would be glad to. Please give the relevant documents when I reach San Francisco."

"Harrish, I have all the papers here with me. We don't have much time."

"Veena, that is fast – please give me a copy."

"I have already made a copy for you. It is in the car."

"That is, indeed, super fast! Please tell me a little about the company."

"Harrish, the company develops high speed computer boards. It was started four years ago and it is profitable. It is located in Los Angeles. The President is a technical expert and the Chairman is a lawyer. If you read the financial report, you may get deeper information."

"Okay Veena, I will go through it tonight and I will come and see you tomorrow."

"Harrish, tomorrow, I will be staying with Geetha"

"Okay, Veena, I will come around 11am to my aunt's house and we can discuss this company in detail."

Now, Kumar, Pavithran and Vimala joined them.

Kumar commented, "Harrish, Veena; you guys are immersed in deep discussion."

Harrish answered, "Well, Kumar, Veena has made a major decision. She is joining her dad's company next week."

Kumar commented, "That is a great and a tough decision. She will learn enormously."

Pavithran said, "I am so impressed with Dr.Ravi, I agree with Kumar."

Veena felt better about her difficult decision after hearing these comments.

The group went to a breathtaking, uniquely sculptured temple on the seashore. In the twilight of the evening, it was such a divine sight with waves caressing the outer walls of the temple. They all sat on a few rocks and watched the ocean. It was so peaceful and serene. Veena and others felt relaxed and they all decided to stay there until dusk. When night fell, they returned to Chennai.

Next day morning, Harrish arrived at Geetha's house around 11 am. Geetha greeted him and soon Veena joined them. Geetha requested Harrish to stay for lunch and Harrish agreed.

Veena and Harrish started their discussion on the new company.

Veena asked, "Harrish, did you read the financial reports? What is your opinion?"

Harrish answered, " Veena, I read through it several times. First time, I saw the financials, I felt very good about the company – excellent product., great profit and it seemed to be a very well run company."

"That is great, Harrish"

"However, Veena, on the second perusal, I wondered how the profit was generated. I was surprised that most of the profit resulted from "other income". I dug deeper as it was not clear where and how the "other income" came from. Finally, I saw a footnote that said that the "other income" resulted from the profits of the subsidiaries. All this report gives in another section are the names of the subsidiaries."

Veena asked with concern, " Harrish, are there no details about what the subsidiaries' businesses are, their income statements, etc?"

"Veena, that is what bothers me. The major profit is coming from subsidiaries and there is precious little information about them."

With worry, Veena said,

"Harrish, that is strange. How can we judge this company without detailed information about the subsidiaries? I will call dad today in Hong Kong when he arrives there later in the evening and inform him about this issue. May be, he could get for us more detailed information about the subsidiaries."

Harrish said, "Veena, may be, we should investigate quietly, without the company knowing. Otherwise, we may get false documents."

Veena was surprised to hear that. With anxiety she asked, "Harrish, do you think something fraudulent is going on here?"

"Veena- I don't know – may be! .It is better to be very cautious from now on. Basic facts are not given. Something seems wrong. Has dad invested any money already?"

"Yes, dad has invested five million dollars already."

With concern, Harrish commented:

"Veena, let us proceed very carefully and cautiously. Let us hope everything is ok."

Geetha came and said that lunch was ready. Harrish and Veena terminated their discussion. Veena requested Harrish to stay until she called her dad. She wanted Harrish to talk to dad also. Harrish consented. As they arrived at the lunch table, Geetha saw their faces grim. She said, " "Hey, you guys – relax – please leave the company issues behind. Let us enjoy the lunch."

Harrish and Veena smiled and they changed the topic to music. That relaxed them quite a bit.

At 2.00pm, Veena called her dad, "Dad, Harrish and I have gone through the papers of the company. Harrish has a very important concern. Most of the profit of the company comes from "other income" i.e. subsidiaries. But there is no information or income statements of the subsidiaries. Here is Harrish, please talk to him."

Harrish said, "Dr.Ravi, it is rather strange that they have not furnished you, an investor now – and possibly a major investor in the future – enough information. Do you have further information on the subsidiaries?"

"Harrish, no! I gave all the information to Veena. You are right- they should have given us all the information. I am surprised that my VP-Finance did not pick this point up."

"Dr.Ravi, we need to proceed cautiously. The company should not know that we are doubting them. We should investigate quietly."

"Yes Harrish, I will call my company lawyer and discuss the case with him. Please let me talk to Veena."

"Veena, please. Harrish and you proceed immediately to San Francisco – I will meet you both at home. I will call you if I have further information."

"Ok, dad"

Veena and Harrish agreed to leave the next day. Veena changed the flight plans and they were to leave for San Francisco via Singapore next day morning.

Chapter - 23

Dr.Natchikethas came to Geetha's house that night and rang the doorbell. Veena opened the door and gave Dr.Natchikethas a big smile. Dr.Natchikethas returned it and said, "Veena, Harrish called me at the hospital to inform me that both you and Harrish would be leaving for San Francisco tomorrow morning. I came here to say goodbye in person and also to discuss a few company issues."

Veena replied, " Dr.Natchikethas, please come in and be seated."

After sitting down, Dr.Natchikethas continued, " Most of the company issues have been resolved. There are a few items that Harrish is working on. He and I will be in constant touch through email. He might come back in three weeks. I think we can wrap up the merger in two months."

Veena remarked, "It looks that way. Dad is happy with all the information that he collected here. He plans to discuss with his Vice Presidents next week and then call you. "

Dr.Natchikethas asked with concern," Would Harrish be very involved with the new company in Los Angeles? "

Veena continued, " No – he is just helping me. Dad has couple of Vice Presidents working on it. But, there are some basic issues that I am looking at and Harrish is a good asset in that investigation. He might be busy next week but then others would take over."

"Veena, I feel better. Harrish is very much needed to complete this merger. He is excellent. I am glad that he would continue to work on this merger."

At this time, Geetha came downstairs and saw Veena and Dr.Natchikethas engaged in some deep, intimate conversation. That triggered a little jealousy in her. She saw in the previous day dinner, Lakshmi, Dr.Natchikethas' mother dote on Veena. "She probably wants them married. Veena is beautiful, smart and rich. Their company merger would bring them closer." Then she wondered, "Why should I be so concerned about Dr.Natchikethas?" She looked at him and he was handsome. She remembered the rapt attention with which he would hear her music. Dr.Natchikethas turned and met Geetha's eyes and smiled. She smiled back and then forgot her annoyance.

Veena saw Geetha and told her, " Geetha, we have just completed discussion on the company. Please join us and we could talk about music. Both Dr.Natchikethas and you love music."

Dr.Natchikethas and Geetha looked at each other and could not help smiling. Three of them had a lively chitchat about Geetha's next concert's line up of songs. Dr.Natchikethas left for home after some time and then went to his room after dinner. There, he sat on the sofa and started thinking about Veena and Geetha. He just had an opportunity to see both of them together and he decided to collect his thoughts and see where it leads.

Veena struck him as a very beautiful, smart, cultured and above all a woman with class. She had decided to join Dr.Ravi's company and hence would be working on the merger. If he were to marry her, the company would be in the family. His mother adored Veena. His mother loved his dad deeply and the company was his dad's legacy. Hence, his mother would very much favor Veena.

Then he thought of Geetha. Geetha was beautiful, intelligent and very devoted to music. He remembered the concerts in Atlanta and Chennai. The ragams were ringing in his ears. Ever since he heard Geetha's songs, his interest in music had soared. Geetha made him spend more time in music which he enjoyed deeply.

Dr.Natchikethas wondered what Geetha thought of him. He felt he should talk to her soon and find out her views. He decided to go there some morning when Pavithran and her mother would be at work and she would be practicing music.

Couple of days later, on a morning when he did not have surgery, he came to Geetha's house and rang the doorbell. When Geetha opened the door, she was stunned to see Dr.Natchikethas. She became nervous and annoyed. "Why didn't he call first?"

She was almost speechless for a moment. Then, she forced a smile and requested him to be seated. She politely asked whether he would want a cup of coffee. Seeing her nervous face, he felt that making coffee might give her time to collect herself and said, "Thanks – that would be great."

When Geetha came in five minutes with a cup of coffee, Dr.Natchikethas assured her that he would only take ten minutes. That made her feel better.

Dr.Natchikethas started, " Geetha, I want to discuss an important issue with you. Please relax. There is no immediate urgency. As you know, I love music. In the last few months, you have created deeper love of music in me. I have some pressure from my mother to get married. Then I thought of you."

When Dr.Natchikethas said that, Geetha's face became red and she was very nervous and very annoyed. She blurted out with an undertone of irritation, " "Dr.Natchikethas, I am not interested in marriage now. I am very busy with my music career. Marriage is the last thing on my mind now. Moreover, the medical profession is very hectic with untimely hours. For example, you could not come to Houston concert. I am not sure that I would want to marry a doctor."

Dr.Natchikethas was pained with her answer; because he expected a more conciliatory reply. Her irritation convinced him that he should leave right away and let her think alone. Therefore, he abruptly got up and thanked her for the frank answer and left.

After Dr.Natchikethas left, Geetha was so high strung that she paced up and down the living room. She was so furious with Dr.Natchikethas to bring up this issue of marriage. Her own mother was putting a lot of pressure about marriage and she had been resisting it. Now, Dr.Natchikethas opened an old wound. Both her mother and Dr.Natchikethas did not know what it took to shine in music. It required total dedication. She needed to devote her full time for the next few years. Moreover, the medical career was a very demanding profession. One might get emergency calls anytime. Call nights would be extremely exacting. The music career and the medical career would not match well.

Chapter - 24

After Dr.Natchikethas left, Geetha was fretting and fuming; a little later, her mom and her brother Pavithran arrived. That took her mind off Dr.Natchikethas. She had lunch with them. After lunch, the doorbell rang and after opening the door, she saw Vimala. Geetha had totally forgotten that she had an appointment with Vimala to discuss Dikshithar kritis (songs composed by Dikshithar). She forced a smile and asked Vimala to be seated.

They exchanged views on Dikshithar kritis and examined deeply the meanings of the songs. During the discussion, Geetha looked at Vimala; she had a lot of resemblance to Dr.Natchikethas. Her mannerisms were similar; moreover, she was very polite, courteous and cultured like Dr.Natchikethas. There more she talked to Vimala, the more she was reminded of Dr.Natchikethas' fine gentlemanly character. Therefore, when Vimala left, she began to wonder whether she was too rude to Dr.Natchikethas.

The more she thought of it, the more she became convinced that she was indeed very irritable. She wondered "why?". She discovered the idea of marriage created that irritation in her. But she could have controlled it and could have been more polite. She became rather contrite. She felt she should do something to correct it. She remembered what she told Harrish – communication is very important. She did not communicate well. She thought she should apologize. There was no need to to change her views but seek apology for her impoliteness. She would also thank him for thinking of her so positively. She would also acknowledge their common interest in music. But, marriage was a different issue.

She became convinced that she should talk to him. But she did not want to go to his house because his mother would be there. The idea struck her – why not the hospital?

Couple of days later, one morning, she called the hospital and she was told that he would be out of the Operation Theater around, 2.00pm. She reached the hospital at 1.30pm and the Operation Theater around 1.45 pm. She waited in the waiting room. Dr.Natchikethas came out sometime later and went straight to the patient's relatives. She moved close to the exit door so that he could not miss her when leaving the room. When he came out near the exit door after talking to the relatives, he could not believe that he was seeing Geetha. He was so astounded. Geetha, without losing time, said, "Dr.Natchikethas, could I talk to you quietly for ten minutes?"

Dr.Natchikethas was speechless in the beginning and then quickly recovered, "Geetha, of course- let me get a quiet room. Please give me five minutes."

She waited while Dr.Natchikethas was arranging a room. Dr.Natchikethas came back shortly and escorted her to a quiet room. After they were seated, he asked her with concern," Geetha, what's up?"

Geetha was a little nervous and was not sure where to begin. She started slowly,

"Dr.Natchikethas, you came to my house couple of days ago and talked to me. First, I want to apologize; I was very irritable on that day."

She paused, as she could not proceed. She was filled with emotion. Dr.Natchikethas came near and said with feeling, " Geetha, I should be the one to apologize. I came barging into your house without any forewarning and I opened a topic that is very annoying to you. I was very thoughtless; somehow, I assumed that you might agree. That was rather poor judgment on my part."

At that point, Geetha interrupted,

"Dr.Natchikethas, it was not poor judgment. We both have deep love for music. In my annoyance about marriage, I overlooked that point that day. I have been fighting with my mom about marriage; my music demands enormous time. Marriage would consume time. That is my big problem."

Dr.Natchikethas said, "I agree. Carnatic music is a tough field in which to shine. That night, I felt miserable that I did not see that point earlier. I can understand that you need to think about it a lot."

Now, there was a loudspeaker announcement calling for Dr.Natchikethas to report to the Operation Theater immediately. He left abruptly telling Geetha that he would call her later.

Geetha felt relieved that the conversation ended quickly and went home in a more relaxed mood than was her mood when she came in. She had accomplished what she had set out to do in the first place; she had apologized. An unexpected event was——he apologized too—he seemed to understand her plight——she felt good about it.

Chapter - 25

Veena and Harrish had agreed to meet at the check in counter of the Airlines at Chennai International Airport. Whoever arrived early would wait for the other person. Harrish arrived at the counter at 5 am and Veena a few minutes later. They both checked in, went through the security and waited in the lounge. Then Harrish commented,

"Veena, last night, I was going through this new company's documents again. I am surprised to find that two of the subsidiaries are in Singapore. Look!"

Veena saw the document and she was flabbergasted; two companies' addresses were in Singapore.

Veena remarked in amazement, "Yes, Harrish, They are both in Singapore. Should we not change our plan and investigate these in Singapore?"

Harrish replied, "Veena, I agree. We need to investigate right away. Please call Dr.Ravi and inform him. He may have other ideas."

Veena called her dad and she was able to reach him. She briefed him about the two companies in Singapore and he agreed that they should explore immediately. He told her that he would call his office in Singapore and the office would make all the arrangements for their stay. Some one would come to the airport to meet them.

Veena and Harrish, shortly, boarded the plane and they discussed further during breakfast on the flight.

Veena started, "Harrish I can't believe this. They have an international operation."

Harrish agreed, "Veena, it seems they are sophisticated. I will go and look up the companies. If you come, your last name will raise suspicion. Moreover, I could go to these companies seeking employment. You proceed to your office. I will go directly from the airport and I will meet you at the office. I will take your office phone from the staff and keep you informed."

Veena agreed and they followed the plan at the Singapore airport. When they came out of the customs, two persons from their office met them. A fine looking Chinese woman and a man smilingly escorted them. Harrish got the telephone number and general instructions about Singapore and distances to these locations. He left immediately and Veena went with them to the office.

He located the first company; it was a good-looking industrial complex. When he went in to ask for a job, he was told that it was a small company buying components like integrated circuits from Far East for their parent company in the U.S.A. They didn't do anything else here and they were not hiring. To Harrish, it looked like a bonafide company but it was too small and nothing exotic to generate large profit.

Harrish proceeded next to locate the next company. It was a long drive and the locality was poor. At the location of the company, was an old dilapidated building. Harrish went up and knocked the door. An old Chinese guard opened the door and said in broken English that no one worked there. It was just a storage place. Old furniture and paintings were stored and no high tech equipment nor products were there.

Harrish left quickly and told Veena from the car, that he would explain everything in person; he would meet her in half an hour.

They were both hungry. They went to a choice restaurant, sat in a corner and talked in a low tone. After ordering the food, Veena asked with anxiety, " Harrish, what happened?"

Harrish answered in a soft, sad voice," Veena, not good news- I am afraid. The first company has only ten people and they buy components from a Far East Company for the parent company."

"Then, it can't generate so much profit" said Veena

"Exactly!. It can't be the source of the other income. The other company is worse; it is located in a poor locality in an old building. No one except an old guard works there. It is simply a storage place for old furniture and some very old paintings."

"Harrish, that can't be the source of other income either." interjected Veena.

"Absolutely true, Veena. Unless we discover something good in Los Angeles, we are in deep trouble." said Harrish

"Yes, we will lose five million dollars." remarked Veena.

"Veena, it doesn't end there, we may also be in a lot of legal issues. " said Harrish.

"What legal issues?"

"If something fraudulent is going on, we will have to report to the Government authorities. If we do that, the company executives would be mad at us and would not give us a penny back. If we do not report, we would be part of a conspiracy. If it ever became public, we would also be held responsible."

"Boy! That puts us in an unique and tough situation. But, we have to do what is right."

"Veena, we need a lot of discussion with our lawyer to find out what our legal obligations are. We cannot ignore 5 million dollars either."

"Harrish, it is 7.00pm here and it is too early to call San Francisco. When we return to the hotel, we can call dad and get further instructions."

Thus, they were engrossed in this issue as they finished the dinner and then returned to the hotel.

At 10.00pm, they called Dr.Ravi and briefed him about what they had found. He was shocked but was prepared for it. He requested Harrish to fly directly to Los Angeles and someone from his office would meet him at the airport. After the call, Veena changed the flights. Harrish asked Veena, "What time are our flights?"

"I set it up a little later so that we could get some sleep. Yours is at 1.00 pm and mine is at 2.00pm"

"Great,Veena. Let us meet for a late breakfast at 9.00am. Please get some sleep"

"Same to you, Harrish, good night".

Harrish left and went to his room. He was exhausted and slept immediately. Veena, was thinking about the events of the day. She was quite impressed with Harrish's excellent business acumen and his insight into company financials. She then decided to put on a carnatic music CD in order to get some sleep.

Chapter - 26

At 9.00 am, Harrish knocked on Veena's door and Veena came out smilingly.

"Hi, Harrish - Did you have a good sleep?"

"Great, Veena – I am totally rested – How about you?"

"Me too"

They selected a spacious lounge and sat in a quiet corner. They ordered breakfast; both of them decided not to talk business. Veena was dressed casually and was pretty looking. Harrish was in a colorful sports shirt and jeans – he looked relaxed and handsome.

Veena said, " Harrish, last night I heard M.S.Subhalakshmi's song "Oranga Sai". It was totally relaxing."

Harrish commented, "Good, Veena. Have you heard Semmangudi's rendition of "Oranga Sai? "

"No, I haven't."

"Well, Veena; I have a tape in San Francisco and I will give it to you. You would love that."

"I generally find Semmangudi fast paced and deep."

"Yes, that is true, Veena, but some of his songs are simply superb. "Oranga Sai" is one of them."

"Ok, Harrish, I will listen to it."said Veena, "By the way, Harrish, have you heard from Latha lately?"

Once she asked that question, she bit her lip, suddenly realizing that bringing up Latha might hurt Harrish.

Harrish saw worry and anxiety on Veena's face and reassuringly held her hand for a minute and smiled.

"Veena, I am quite relaxed about Latha now. Thanks to you. You sent Geetha to talk to me. After hearing my story, she said the basic problem was that we did not communicate directly and deeply. The more I thought about it, the more the mystery got resolved for me. Really, Latha and I never sat together face to face and discussed the issue till the very end. If we had done so earlier, we would have discovered that there was less compatibility. You alluded to that too. At least, I would have been less hurt. I wrote Latha a long letter explaining all this and she wrote back immediately. We are on good terms as friends. I just got another letter from her before I left for India. As I see it now, it was one of those fancies pursued in a childish way." said Harrish; he paused, "But, I am over it now, Veena" smilingly he reassured her.

Veena was relieved. She commented,

"Harrish, I am glad you are relaxed and are in good terms with Latha."

Veena looked up the watch and commented that they should leave shortly for the airport. Soon, they departed for the airport. Harrish boarded his plane first and Veena, half-hour later.

In his plane, Harrish planned his investigation in Los Angeles. He had gotten hold of a Los Angeles' map at the airport and used it to map his strategy. He wrote all the addresses down from the financial report and planned his moves. Once he completed this task, he thought about the conversation with Veena.

He wondered whether Veena really believed him; but she seemed to. He thought of the service Geetha had done; he was too busy in Chennai to talk to her deeply. Therefore, he decided to write her a letter which he completed on the flight. He took a short nap and then changed his clothes to be ready for work in Los Angeles.

Veena boarded the flight on time; first, she thought about the conversation with Harrish. She could not believe that Harrish could be so relaxed about Latha. She decided to call Latha and get her view point. Then, she plunged into the work that her dad had already given her.

At the Los Angeles airport, Harrish met the Gigabit company executive who Dr.Ravi had asked to meet him. The executive had already arranged for Harrish a car with a driver. As Harrish had his plan ready, he set out to see the first company. It turned out to be a reasonably big company with about hundred employees making precision high tech components for the parent company. It seemed like a well-run company but could not be generating a lot of profit. The other two companies were located in different parts of the town; they turned out to be just one-man shows.

By now, it was late in the evening. With all the travel, Harrish was exhausted and retired to the hotel. Next day, early in the morning, he started the investigation; all the other three companies turned out to be small with less than ten persons. It was around noon time and he called Veena with all the information. She suggested that he go quickly to the airport and catch the next available flight to San Francisco. Dr.Ravi, would be at the San Francisco airport to catch a flight to Paris around 5.00pm. They could possibly meet him before he left. Harrish loved the idea and agreed to rush to the airport. Veena said she would book the ticket and call him.

Harrish arrived at the San Francisco airport around 4.00pm and Dr.Ravi and Veena met him at the baggage claim. They went to a restaurant for just juice and talked.

Dr.Ravi started, "Harrish, I want to thank you for finding the "other income" item. My people at the office are still reeling as how they missed it. How did you find it?"

Harrish replied, "Dr.Ravi, I usually write down by hand the top four items of income, expense, assets, and liabilities. I look for "80/20" rule. 80% of income comes from 20% of products; 80% of expenses are caused by 20% of the expense items. When one writes down, they become crystal clear. It takes only one hour but one gains enormous information. Usually, it is straightforward. In this case, "other income" was the second biggest income item but no detailed information was forthcoming. That is why I became worried."

Dr.Ravi commented, " Good, methodical procedure, Harrish. I am going to insist on following this procedure at the office. Harrish, I am seriously thinking of not investing any further in this company unless you get believable information from the company. Veena and you talk to my lawyer tomorrow; if you wish, all of you could visit the company. The company has very good high-tech product and the President is a fine technical guy. I do not know who is behind this "other income" scenario – may be, the Chairman – but, I have not met the Chairman."

Veena and Harrish agreed to further investigate the company.

Dr.Ravi continued, "Harrish, Veena; please follow the advice of the lawyer on the issue of informing other authorities."

Dr.Ravi left for his flight and Veena and Harrish saw him off.

Chapter - 27

Veena and Harrish entered the Gigabit senior counsel's office on the twenty fifth floor in a sky rise building in downtown San Francisco. They saw a breathtaking magnificent view of the San Francisco bay area ocean.

Veena said, "It is just beautiful, Mr.Viterbi"

John Viterbi, the chief counsel said, " Well, Veena —I love this view and so I took this floor. Veena just call me John. Let us go through this company. Why don't we start with what Harrish had observed in Singapore and Los Angeles. "

He led them to a corner sofa / love seat arrangement.

Harrish briefly recounted his experiences.

Veena asked, "John, what are the chances that we could get more information from this company?"

John answered, "Not much, I am afraid."

"Why not, John?"

"Because they have excellent backing from the top accounting company. It is the biggest in the world. It has good reputation. The high tech company has a good product line which your father thinks is great. They are getting investors right now. Therefore, why should they change? I called their lawyer and this is exactly his line of reasoning."

Harrish enquired, "Could we not report them to authorities?"

John answered, "What could we report? There are ten subsidiaries whose income are lumped into "other income". They would say again, a top accounting company created the report. We don't have further concrete evidence. Moreover, they could file a defamation suit against us and try to collect millions of dollars from us."

Harrish was stunned, "Defamation suit, why?."

The lawyer put a counter question,"Why not, Harrish ?"

Harrish replied, "What motivation would we have?"

Lawyer continued, "Easy, you want to reduce the stock price so that you could take over at a low price, or buy it after it goes bankrupt. Remember Dr. Ravi loves the product!"

Harrish exclaimed, "That is a bit far fetched."

"Not so fast, Harrish. In the business world so much happens — so many companies are taken over in similar situations."

Harrish replied, "That is hard to prove, John."

"Harrish, even if they do not prove it finally, they have dragged "Gigabit" to court and given it bad publicity. Moreover, this could go on for years."

Veena asked with anxiety, "John, could we pull out our money, five million dollars?"

"Not easily, Veena. They came up with a tough contract. I warned Dr Ravi. He was very impressed with their technology — so we went ahead. We cannot pull our money out for five years unless they let us go. What motivation would they have? Gigabit is a well-respected company. Our investment gives them credibility with the investors."

Veena enquired "John, if we are respected and since we are a billion dollar company, won't we have leverage?"

John replied, "Even if we have, they would not acknowledge it, but could negotiate hard. Moreover, they have grown bigger now and could be independent of us."

Veena asked in frustration, "John, what is our next step then?"

John answered, "I am trying to arrange a meeting with the Chairman. He has the power to give us more information. I would hold the 20 million dollar investment as a carrot. Let's see what happens."

Veena commented, "John, you don't sound that hopeful."

"Well, Veena, something fishy might be going on. If that be the case, he would not give us any information. He would stall, delay and buy time."

Veena asked incredulously, "What is their objective?"

"Easy, Veena. They have a great product, their profit is okay but not that great. Therefore, they enhance their profit with "other income". Most people miss it. We missed it too until Harrish caught it. Hence, they look excellent with a great product and a good profit."

Veena questioned, "John, where do they find money for their "other income"."

"Veena, that is not difficult — they have lot of cash from investment."

"But, John won't the accounting company catch it."

"Not easily, Veena, if they fudged the financials of the ten companies. It is a lot of work for the accounting company to investigate ten companies. Moreover, this is a small company and not yet publicly listed. Therefore, they have no motivation to be very thorough."

Veena and Harrish drove back in frustration.

Harrish commented, "Veena, the business world is complex."

"Harrish, I can not believe what I have learnt in two weeks; you do not learn this in school."

"I don't believe the extent to which people go in creating wrong documents."

"It is all motivated by quick money. They do not want to work hard. They want it all fast."

Talking thus, they reached the office. Harrish and Veena had their office next to each other so that they could work together. They could not stomach the discussion they had with the chief counsel, John Viterbi; they met in Veena's office to discuss their next strategy.

Veena asked, "What do you think we should do?"

Harrish answered, "First we should go to Los Angeles and investigate further. We need to understand the personalities of the vice-president-finance, President and the Chairman."

"Why?"

"Only then, we could find out who is behind this operation. We could try to isolate that person."

"Harrish, what if we get zero information ?"

"Then we have to go up, we should contact the directors and investors."

"What if they don't believe us?"

"Dr. Ravi has the reputation and credibility. If he were to call, they would believe him, Veena"

"The company could sue us with defamation charges."

Harrish got up and paced up and down thinking. Veena was also quietly thinking. Suddenly Veena said,

"Harrish I have an idea— maybe, we should contact a top criminal lawyer. My dad once had to use an expert lawyer. Let me ask him if such a lawyer could give us guidance. If there is a fraud, they might not be able to sue us. If there is no fraud, maybe we would invest more and there is no suit."

Harrish commented,

"But our case is not yet strong; on their side, they have a powerful accounting company to justify their actions."

Veena said, "Let us ask that lawyer by pointing out to him our suspicions. There might be a fraud— we have invested $ 5 million and our reputation might be on the line. What are our rights as an investor? What would it take to get more information? Could we get back our $ 5 million ?"

Harrish agreed, "This is definitely worth a try. "

Harrish looked at his watch it was eight thirty in the night. He enquired with concern,

"Veena, did you call home? Do they know you are coming late?"

Veena answered, "Thanks for your concern. I work late nowadays and hence, mom would not worry."

Veena continued,

"Harrish let us summarize our immediate action plan. First, let us meticulously plan our trip to "Saturn". Let us write down all the questions we would like to ask the Chairman, the President and the chief financial officer. Second, let me call dad and John Viterbi about the criminal lawyer; anything else, Harrish."

Harrish commented, "That looks good. Let me think further."

They returned home rather late in the night.

Chapter - 28

Kumar was just seated in the MIT cafeteria, to start his Monday lunch, when he heard a familiar voice "Kumar!". He looked up and there was Latha, beautiful as ever. He was stunned to see Latha and exclaimed, "Latha, when did you come?"

" I just came this morning," said Latha

"Latha, you took a long vacation"

"Kumar, it was totally relaxing"

Kumar looked at Latha. She was cheerful and well rested.

"Well, the vacation has done good for you. You are indeed totally relaxed.".

"How was your trip to India?" asked Latha.

Kumar was extremely surprised.

"How did you know that I visited India?"

"Easy, Veena told me".

"Do you talk to Veena often?"

"Yes, once in three days, either she calls me or I call her".

"Latha, do you know that Veena has joined her father's company?"

"Yes. We talked at length about it before she made the decision. I encouraged her because time is of the essence. Her father is past middle-age. She could always come back to academics later on if she wanted that".

"How is she doing?"

"She is doing ok so far. She finds it very demanding. But Harrish is helping her a lot. He seems to have business savvy. "

"Well, I too noticed it in India. Harrish spends a lot of time with Veena. The arrangement is working out for both of them because I saw Harrish quite relaxed and happy." said Kumar.

Then he stopped, thinking that he might be touching on a sensitive subject.

Latha looked at Kumar and then smiled.

"Don't worry. Harrish and I are on great terms".

"How is that?"

"Well, it's a long story but let me be brief now. Maybe, Kumar, someday, we will explore that in detail. Essentially, both Harrish and I were rather sad leaving Atlanta. Veena became intensely aware of Harrish's sadness and arranged for Geetha to talk to him. Geetha told Harrish, after hearing the episode, that he and I never really sat down and discussed the issue at length. This lack of communication led to the explosion in Atlanta. Harrish wrote me a long letter and it made sense to me. We have been corresponding regularly and it has eased considerably the pain in both of us."

Kumar was so relieved to hear this. He said emotionally, "Latha, I am so glad to hear this. Harrish is a very close friend of mine and you too. This has pained me so much that I could not even talk to Harrish in detail about this. I am really grateful to Veena and Geetha for what they have done. Harrish briefly mentioned it. You can't believe how happy I am hear this from you".

Latha also said emotionally, "Thanks so much for your concern, Kumar."

For a moment, they were in touch emotionally. After an one-minute pause, Kumar said softly, "Latha, Harrish is coming here tomorrow."

"Tomorrow! Veena didnt tell me two days ago."

"It was a last minute decision. Harrish called me last night."

"Oh, I see."

"He is coming here to defend his thesis which is on Monday. He will stay here, study, and prepare."

"Great! Kumar, I will get a chance to meet him and talk to him. That is wonderful." said Latha cheerfully.

Kumar was happy to see her cheer and he left to meet his advisor.

When Harrish came out of the terminal gate in the Boston Logan Airport, he could not believe what he saw. Latha was standing there smiling. He was stunned to see her; but was very happy. He went near her and held her hands and said with feeling,

"Latha, I am so glad to see you."

"Harrish, I came to MIT yesterday and Kumar told me that you were coming. He had to attend a seminar. So, I have come. He will join us a little later."

Harrish commented, "I am so pleased that you could come. Actually, we could use the time alone to complete our ongoing dialog in person."

They drove to a nice restaurant after picking up all the baggage. As it was early, the restaurant was not crowded. They could get a quiet corner and they continued their conversation.

Harrish commented, "Latha, you look relaxed and cheerful."

"Yes, Harrish, there are two reasons for it – one is the long vacation at home-second your letter – that soothed my spirits. Thanks Harrish for that letter."

"Really, Latha, you should thank Geetha and Veena. Geetha hit it on the nail. She said we should have sat together early on, face to face and should have discussed deeply the pertinent issues."

Latha interjected,

"You know Harrish, when I read that letter, that point made so much sense to me"

Harrish continued, "Latha, right in Syracuse we should have discussed in detail your reservations."

"But, Harrish, they were vague then."

"Yes, Latha, but they did not change in the end. If I had asked you penetrating questions, you would have thought deeply and come up with some answers – maybe a litter later – maybe a few weeks later."

"I agree Harrish. If you had posed deep questions, it would have forced me to think. As you said, the feelings did not change that much but it got worse being wrapped up in other person's opinions and wishes."

"Latha, this is what I learnt from these events. It is better to know the full truth early on. It may be painful but will avoid a disaster. Untruth may be soothing in the beginning but painful in the end".

"Very well put, Harrish – very well put, indeed." said Latha.

They moved on to discuss Harrish's present job when Kumar joined them. Kumar was delighted to see Harrish and Latha relaxed and chitchatting cheerfully.

On Monday, by noon, Harrish had defended his thesis successfully. Kumar met him and congratulated him. Kumar told Harrish that Latha and he planned to take him to dinner at 6.00pm. They were going to a top restaurant and requested Harrish to dress formally.

Kumar came to take Harrish to the restaurant. Harrish was in a new suit and a colorful tie; he was relaxed and good-looking. Kumar said, "Harrish, you look dashing."

Harrish commented, "Thanks Kumar. Where is Latha?"

Kumar replied, "Latha has an errand to do. She will come directly to the restaurant. Let us go."

Harrish and Kumar waited for a few minutes in the spacious well-decorated lobby of the restaurant. Harrish saw Latha come tastefully dressed and charming. In a minute, as he advanced towards Latha to greet her, he thought he saw another person. In a few seconds, he was amazed. It was Veena, gorgeously dressed and smashingly pretty.

Harrish exclaimed with emotion, "Veena!"

Veena said smilingly,"Harrish, it was Latha's idea. I had some errands at MIT. Latha told me "why not come and give a dashing party to Harrish?" It was a splendid idea and so I came."

Harrish held Latha's hands for a minute and thanked her for the great suggestion; He also thanked Veena for coming. Kumar suggested that they go and sit down.

After being seated, Harrish asked Veena.

"When did you come?"

"Yesterday, Harrish"

Harrish exclaimed, " I did not see you, Veena".

Latha laughingly said, "Harrish, we hid her from you."

They all laughed. Harrish really appreciated Veena coming all the way from San Francisco and was very happy to see her.

Veena asked Harrish jokingly,

"Should we call you Dr.Harrish, hereafter?"

Latha intervened, "Of course, Veena – he has earned it."

Kumar smilingly said, " No – I am just going to call him Harrish"

Latha turned to Harrish and asked, " How does it feel to complete your PhD?"

Harrish replied, " I love it; it ends an important chapter of my life. I am thrilled. But, since I started working, the euphoria is a little subdued. The real life is so complex"

"So, you are happy but this is not the end of the world – isn't that so, Harrish?"

"Exactly, Latha- you got it."

Veena chipped in,

"The business world is so complex. I have learnt so much in the last few weeks about the real world"

Kumar observed, "That is why I postponed the idea of starting a business. I want to watch you guys operate in the real world".

Latha asked, "Kumar, you did not tell me yet how your trip to India was".

"Well, Latha – it was all business in the beginning – the high point was our trip to Mahabalipuram."

Veena added, " Another highpoint was informal, impromptu music recital by Geetha.- it was simply divine."

The food that they had ordered arrived and they started to enjoy it.

Kumar asked, " Are all of you coming to Chennai in December for the music season?"

Latha assured, "Kumar, I am definitely coming. I have not been to Chennai for several years"

Veena said " I am too" and Harrish also voted for it.

Harrish, Latha, Veena and Kumar were in a jolly mood and thoroughly enjoyed the dinner. Veena saw that Latha and Harrish were close, relaxed, happy and were on great terms with each other. They were joking and teasing – they were great friends. Veena was so happy to see this and she felt that her trip was worth just to watch this.

Latha and Harrish felt that their face-to-face meeting and this dinner did a lot to heal the remnant of their aching pain and to start a new level of friendship.

Chapter - 29

After dinner, on the way out of the restaurant, Veena asked Harrish,

"Harrish, could we get together tomorrow morning?"

Harrish replied, "If it is urgent, we could meet today."

"No, Harrish. You had a busy day. Please take rest. Tomorrow morning will do."

Next morning, at 8 am, Harrish and Veena met in the cafeteria over a cup of coffee.

Veena started, "Harrish, yesterday's dinner was totally relaxing for me especially after hectic weeks."

Harrish commented, "Veena, thanks again for coming. It was just a wonderful party – it was so good to meet and talk with friends. What is going on with Saturn?"

"Well, John said that the schedules of the Chairman and the President are so tight that it was difficult to coordinate. Finally, he got a date for a full day at "Saturn" a month from now. We will meet both the President and the Chairman."

"That meeting is very important. We simply have to wait. Then, we could focus on Dr. Natchikethas' company, V-Digitronics. There are many issues to resolve. May be, I should go to Chennai from here."

"Harrish, I thought of the same idea. Therefore, I brought all the reports from the various Vice Presidents – research, development, production and sales – their ideas of implementation of the merger. You could go through it and discuss with the corresponding Vice Presidents in V-Digitronics."

"Let me read the reports. Why don't we discuss it at 3 Pm before I leave?"

"OK"

At 3 pm, Veena and Harrish discussed at length all the issues and before Harrish's departure, Veena said,

"Please give my regards to Geetha and Dr.Nachikethas and also to their moms. I will probably be there in ten days and as per Geetha's request, stay with her."

Veena next called Latha to find out whether she could walk with her. Soon, Latha and Veena were walking along the beautiful Charles River in the serene evening.

Veena said, "Latha, I really enjoyed the dinner last night. What a wonderful surprise it was that Harrish and you were cheerful and were back as close friends. Harrish told me about it in Singapore and I did not quite believe him, but it was great seeing it to be so true yesterday."

Latha added, "Veena, it is indeed amazing. But, you should know that you contributed to that by getting Geetha to talk to Harish."

Veena replied, "But Latha, what surprises me is how one conversation could make that much impact ?"

Latha became thoughtful and then answered after a pause,

"To answer this question properly, one needs to know who Harrish is. You, probably know him a little now. He has a strong mind, a good character and an ability to grasp things quickly. He had been pondering over the issue when Geetha talked to him. He is not the type to push things on me that I don't like. He saw clearly once he talked to Geetha, that he could have seen my wishes if he had probed deeply in the beginning. That would have ended the matter. Because of his strong mind, he stopped fretting and fuming after he realized that. That is my guess."

Veena added, "Knowing Harrish a little now, I probably would agree with your guess. Let me ask one more question. Is there any negative about Harrish that turned you off?"

Latha, rather quickly, responded, "No, No, No! It is not Harrish. It is me. I was just not ready; I am still not ready for marriage. But, my parents assumed that Harrish and I were romantically involved. So did you and Kumar. That embarrassed me. Moreover, Harrish was going full blast. He would have been totally devastated if I had just went along, but changed my mind a year from now. So, I had to act fast to stop it. That is the full story, Veena."

Veena was rather pensive and so was Latha. They walked in silence for a while.

Latha turned to Veena and held her hands and said with emotion, "Veena, you work closely with Harrish now. In case, you like him and he likes you, please don't hold this against him."

Veena looked into her eyes and said with feelings, "Latha, I am not into marriage at all now. But if it were to happen, I would just think that he had a wonderful taste but somehow things did not work out."

Latha was touched by her comments and simply hugged her.

So the friends walked, talking deeply thus.

The telephone rang and Geetha picked it up and said, "Hello, this is Geetha."

The voice at the other end said, "This is Harrish, Geetha."

A Tender Melody

"Harrish, what a surprise! Where are you – Planet Mars?"

"Geetha, I wish I were! But I am here on earth, here in Chennai."

"Harrish, what a surprise that you could find time to call me! You are a busy, busy businessman. Last time, you did not even talk to me."

"Forgive me, Geetha! Profuse apologies! That's why I am calling you now."

Next day evening, they met and after dinner, sat down for conversation.

After some light chit chat, Geetha said, "Harrish, I have a serious topic for you."

"Geetha, I am listening."

"After you and Veena left, a few days later, Dr. Natchikethas came unannounced. I was very surprised. He came just to talk to me. He said that he was under pressure from his mom about marriage. Because of our common love of music, he thought about me."

"How did you feel and how did you respond, Geetha?"

"Harrish, as you know, I am also under pressure from my mom about marriage. But, because of my music career, I am dodging her. Any talk of marriage now, creates an annoyance in me. So, I was irritated and said rather cryptically and with an undertone of vexation, that I was not interested in marriage now due to my music career. He left abruptly."

"Geetha, did anything happen after that?"

"Yes; after I calmed down, I felt I was too irritated and my tone showed it. So, I saw him in the hospital and apologized to him. He also apologized for just barging in and throwing an unpleasant surprise. He called a few days later and said that there would no pressure from him and I could take as much time as I needed to think. This is where we are. What is your opinion?"

Harrish started to walk up and down, as it was his habit when a serious topic hit him. Geetha, who was knew him well, just waited.

Harrish started with a question, "Suppose you did not have a music career, would you consider marrying Dr. Natchikethas?"

Geetha thought for a minute and said, "That is an unfair question, Harrish. I do have a music career."

"Agreed. But could you please answer my question?"

"Dr. Natchikethas and I do have an outstanding common interest. He loves music and so do I. Moreover, he has a deep knowledge of music like me. He is also a perfect gentleman and has a pleasing personality. So, I would seriously consider marrying him. But, I do have a serious career issue."

Harrish continued, "Yes, Geetha. But, let us again set aside career for a while. Looking at long term, do you like to remain single or like to be married and have a family?"

Geetha was taken aback by this question; but, quickly saw its relevance. So, she thought for a while and answered, "I am enjoying a family life now. But Pavitran may get married and move away. Mom is not getting younger. I could live a single, lonely life. I am not a loner. I like people. So, I would have to say, long term, I would like to marry and have a family."

Harrish replied, "Well, now that you have decided on marriage long term, we have to explore whether to postpone it or consider it now."

Geetha said, "I am for postponing. I can build my career and then consider marriage."

Harrish responded, "Geetha, you can always postpone at any time. But the tough thing is to evaluate the opportunity in front of you. If it is deemed mediocre, you could postpone. On the other hand, if it is outstanding, won't you owe it to yourself to consider it. If you reject it without thinking through, won't you regret it the rest of your life?"

Geetha became rather pensive. She could not refute this logic. Both were silent for a while. Geetha then, asked softly,"Harrish, how do I investigate?"

Harrish said, "Geetha, write down on paper how much time you need for music. Include your practice time, concert preparation time, travels etc., then, talk to Dr. Natchikethas about what is possible after marriage. Discuss Dr.Natchikethas' schedules and his time management issues. You both have demanding careers. Think through them and then talk again."

Geetha said "Thanks, Harrish for your time. Let me mull over these ideas."

Harrish left shortly after enjoying his favorite Mango sundae that Geetha had prepared.

Chapter - 30

Latha was having her lunch at the MIT cafeteria when Kumar joined her.
Latha said "Hi! Kumar."

Kumar greeted her back, "Hi! Latha, how are things?"

"Kumar, something interesting is happening in my home. My father's book will be coming out soon and it has taken five long years. He is very excited about it. However, we have some work ahead of us. We have to officially release the book."

Kumar observed, "Latha, I am so glad to hear this. But your father has a weak heart and your mother is very busy running the real estate business. May be, my mom and I could help. I will call my mom today."

Latha interjected, "Kumar, I did not tell you this for your help. We could manage."

Kumar replied with a warm smile, "I know, Latha. May be you can manage well. But my mom and I would find this an interesting and challenging project."

Latha saw that Kumar was firm and was enthusiastic about the project. She knew, with her dad's health, she and her mom could use the help.

So she said, "Okay, in that case, you are really welcome. Please when you call your mom, find out her interest."

"I know my mom. She would love this project."

Next weekend, Mrs. Radha Ram and Kumar arrived in Syracuse to discuss the arrangements for the book release. Dr. Ram accompanied them to give support; Latha met them at the airport. Chitra Gangadharan was thrilled by their interest. She could use all the help she could get. Moreover, Radha Ram did an outstanding job arranging the music function in Atlanta. So, she was very happy to see Radha.

They had light lunch; rested a bit and got together after tea around 2:30 pm. Dr. Ram started the discussion, "Dr.Gangadharan, could you give us all, a little bit background, on the book?"

Dr. Gangadharan said, "A few years ago, I began to wonder about the Indo-US trade. It bothered me why it did not take off like FarEast. I started to read a lot about the subject. Soon, I was becoming an expert. So, I decided to put down all my thoughts in a book form."

Dr.Ram added, "Very good topic, indeed. What title have you chosen? When is it coming out?"

"Dr.Ram, I finally chose this title after a lot of discussion – "Gone a golden moment – is it?; Indo-US trade." The book would come out of the printers in a month, I am told by the publishers."

Chitra chipped in, "We are planning to have the function two months from now. In case, the book is delayed, we still have time. Moreover, we need the time to prepare."

Radha asked, "Chitra, where do you plan to have this function?"

Chitra answered, "Radha, New York city because the New York senator Tom Brooks has agreed to release the book. As you know, he was the Ambassador to India. He would be the chief guest."

"Chitra, when is the function?"

"Yesterday we got three possible dates from his office. We need to finalize on one in a couple of days."

"Chitra, what about the speakers?"

"Well, Dr.Gangadharan's classmate, Economics professor at Harvard, Prof. Bill Malcolm, will give the key note speech on the book. He could make it on all the three days. The High court judge, Justice Joseph Gore, can make it on two days. He will preside over the function. We need to book a hall in New York immediately on one of the two days and finalize the date. I have a list of halls from the publishers."

Kumar intervened, "Mrs.Gangadharan, I can go to New York, check out the halls and call you on Monday."

Radha asked, "Chitra, can you go with Kumar?"

Chitra answered, "No, I have a public relations director of the publishers coming here. I have to complete the guest list and be in touch with the senator's office on Monday."

Latha chipped in, "Mom, I could go with Kumar."

It was decided that Latha and Kumar would fly on Monday to New York.

Radha asked, "Chitra, are you planning an invocation or a short music recital?"

"I was wondering about it, Radha."

Kumar interrupted, "How about Geetha?"

Latha exclaimed,"That would be lovely."

They were all smiles about it.

Chitra asked Kumar,"Would she come?"

A Tender Melody

Kumar replied, " I will call Harrish, who is in Chennai."

Chitra said with concern, "We cannot ask her to come all the way for a short recital."

Kumar replied, "I can arrange a concert in Boston."

Latha said, "I have a few friends in New York."

Radha commented, "They would love to have her again in Atlanta."

Chitra, Radha and Kumar were deeply involved in the guest list while Latha took Dr. Ram to the airport and Dr. Gangadharan took some rest.

On Monday morning, both Latha and Kumar, dressed in a conservative business outfit, landed in New York early at 8 am. They took a cab and reached the first hall at the opening hour of 9 am. They looked it over and it was good at a reasonable price. The second hall was lousy and was a waste of time. The third hall was almost the same as the first.

The fourth hall was excellent and the décor was elegant and tastefully done. It seemed particularly suited for a book release. But, it was expensive. It was available only on one of the two days. They had a couple of other potential customers interested. It was around 2 pm.

As Kumar and Latha skipped breakfast, they were quite hungry. They went to an Italian restaurant close by to have lunch. Latha called her mom from the restaurant while eating as time was of essence. Chitra liked the fourth hall but was concerned about the price. She said she would call back in ten minutes. Chitra called, "Latha, this function is very significant for dad. Top dignitaries like the Senator are coming. So the fourth place would be lovely."

The time was 2.30 pm. Kumar called the place right away. They said that the deposit should be given to them by 4 pm for them to reserve the place. There was another party waiting.

Kumar panicked because, the bank Latha was supposed to get a check from, was a little far away. They stopped their lunch midway and caught a cab. They got to the bank at three and received the check by 3.20 pm as there were many formalities. They were in a dilemma. A cab could get stuck in the traffic. They took the subway but the direction was not perfect. They got off one station too early. It was 3.50 pm. They had a few blocks to cover. Kumar told Latha that he would run to the place; Latha could only walk because of her high-heeled shoes.

Kumar rushed to the office one minute before 4 pm. But, he forgot to pick up the check. He quickly came up with an idea. So, he told the lady that he wanted to fill up the form and the check was ready. She gave him the form and he filled it slowly and deliberately to buy time. Fortunately, Latha came in time and they completed all the formalities in one hour.

Kumar and Latha were totally exhausted but were in a cheerful mood. They did not finish their lunch and so were hungry. They decided to have dinner before flying to Boston. They would also avoid the traffic.

At the restaurant, Kumar said with a smile,

"Latha, when I reached the fourth hall office, I realized I forgot the check. I was petrified for a moment. Then the idea of form came to my mind. That saved the day."

Latha laughed and said, "Thank God. You came up with the idea of the form. That was clever. The minute I knew I had the check, I took my shoes off and ran barefoot."

Kumar commented, "That is why you came early – I was wondering."

"Kumar, I did not think of the form. If I had, I would have walked."

"Latha, I am so glad you ran. If not, I would have had a heart attack – I was nervous and sweating."

Latha laughed heartily.

Kumar said, "Latha, I feel so happy for your dad. It is so hard to stop one's career in the prime of one's life. But he has struggled and chosen another career."

"Yes, Kumar. I am so happy and proud of him. That is why mom and I are putting forth enormous effort. I am so thankful to you and your mom."

"Thanks. We are finding this a challenging project."

Thus, chit chatting, they enjoyed the gourmet dinner and left for Boston.

Chapter - 31

Veena and Harrish returned to San Francisco after a hectic two weeks stay in Chennai finalizing all the details of the merger of V-digitronics with Gigabit. They came early to prepare for their meeting with "Saturn Computing." They decided to be very pleasant and conciliatory.

A Tender Melody

Next week, John Viterbi, Harrish and Veena drove to the "Saturn' headquarters from LA airport and were met by the company President in the lobby. Dr. Joe Chang, the President, is a meticulously dressed Chinese American with a perfect American accent. Dr.Chang gave an excellent technology overview of the company which Veena enjoyed very much. She was very impressed by his grasp of the technology – he came across as a knowledgeable and experienced technocrat.

In the afternoon, they met the Vice President – Finance who gave a good overview of the finance of the main company that Dr.Chang runs. He said the subsidiaries directly report to the Chairman who looks after their financial matters.

At 3 pm, they walked into the Chairman Jack Taylor's office. Jack was an absolutely charming gentleman on the outside. He was very well dressed. He welcomed them warmly and tasty tea was served.

Jack asked Veena, " Miss.Ravi, how did your visit go so far?"

"Mr.Taylor, excellent; Dr.Chang gave an outstanding presentation and the VP Finance gave a very good report."

"You see, Miss Ravi, we run an outstanding company. Dr.Ravi was so impressed that he invested $ 5 million in one week, almost a year ago, when we were much smaller."

"Mr.Taylor, I can see that from what I observed so far."

"Well then, we are making very good progress. We would definitely welcome more investment from Gigabit. I guess, there is but one minor hitch. Your lawyer, John Viterbi, wanted more information on the subsidiaries. I checked with our accounting firm. They feel the information given in the annual report is sufficient. But since you are a favoured investor, I dug out this report on one of the subsidiaries to give you an idea on how we run them."

Veena said after receiving the report,

"Thank you very much for your extra effort. We would convey our impressions to Dr.Ravi who would make the final decision."

They shook hands and the visitors left.

John, Harrish and Veena did not talk about the Saturn Computing in the car or the plane, as it was a confidential matter. They waited until they came to John Viterbi's office in San Francisco. It was around 7 pm and they ordered pizza and coke. Then, John asked Veena, "Veena, what do you think of the company?"

Veena answered, "I can see now, John, why dad invested so much money in this company. Dr. Chang gave an excellent overview. It is very well run. However,

Jack Taylor is playing games thinking he is helping the company. He is charming but dangerous. If we get rid of him, the company would be fine."

"Veena, you seemed to have changed your mind. You wanted to flee the company."

"I would, John, if I can't get rid of Jack Taylor. But we have very little information. The only thing we have is a report of a well run subsidiary."

Veena kept quiet, John turned to Harrish, "Harrish you are silent."

Veena intervened, "That means he has an idea." Smilingly, asked Harrish, "What is it, Harrish?"

Harrish smiled back and said, "Well, I read the report a few times on the flight."

Veena asked, "Did you discover something again?"

Harish smiled and said, "No Veena – but Jack gave us an excellent lead."

"How?" asked Veena anxiously.

"Veena, he gave us the name of the company, as Roberts & Co, that prepared the report."

"So what?" said John impatiently.

"It could be everything, John. You see, I have thought of a way to get more solid information about the subsidiaries."

"Harrish, don't be naïve – that company is not going to hand it over to us in a platter – they are being paid by Jack Taylor."

"I know that, John. But Dr. Ravi is very busy. It is our responsibility to get him solid information. We have given him only vague notions. Time has come to collect good, verifiable information. So, we have to use efficiently every lead we have."

Veena asked inquisitively, "So, what do you propose?"

"Veena, I want to go to LA immediately and check this company out. Let us see what we can get. Right now, we have nothing."

Veena said, "I agree. Let us try. We need to protect our investment. Saturn is basically a good company."

John agreed, "It is worth a try."

Therefore, it was agreed that Harrish should go to LA next day.

A Tender Melody

Next day, early morning, Harrish left for Los Angeles. He went to Roberts & Co. He met the receptionist who asked, "Whom do you want to see, Sir?"

"I want to meet Steve Roberts."

"Please talk to his secretary." She called the secretary who came to the lobby to take a look at Harrish. She was impressed with his classy business suit and his courteous demeanor.

"What can I do for you, Sir?" she asked.

Harrish replied, "My name is Harrish Sridhar. I have a PhD in economics from MIT Sloan School. I would like to meet Mr. Roberts."

"For what purpose?" she asked.

"That is private; I will not take more than fifteen minutes of his time."

She felt that he was sincere and so she asked him to call her at 2 pm. Instead, Harrish came to the company at 2 pm. The secretary was pleased as she had set up a short meeting at 2.30 pm.

When Harrish entered Mr.Roberts room, Roberts came to greet him. He was a tall, well-groomed young man of thirty five. He got to the point quickly,

"Mr.Sridhar, how could I help you?"

"Mr.Roberts, I have a PhD from MIT Sloan school in economics and have taken a number of business management courses. I plan to start my own company in a couple of years. In the mean time, I am looking for a part time job – even one day a week will do. I can analyze a company well; but I lack law background. I thought I will pick up some of it from this job. Your company is ideally suited as it is small and has a unique combination of Law and Accounting."

Harrish gave him his PhD certificate and letters of recommendation. Mr.Roberts thought for a minute. He could use Harrish's help especially as a part time worker,

"What salary do you want?"

"$ 100 /Hr."

"That is high – How about $75 /Hr."

"Okay, but you should increase it to $100 in three months."

"Okay – but I am offering this job only for one month. If I am not happy, I will cancel it."

"Okay."

"Well, you come tomorrow at 8.30 am."

"Okay, Mr.Roberts. If you have something for me to read, please give me. I can read today but I will not charge you."

Mr.Roberts liked free bees and he gave him a file to read.

"Please read this file especially the latest letter of the President. I need to reply it tomorrow. I want your thoughts on it."

Harrish left Roberts & Co and was thrilled. He called Veena from his hotel and she was delighted. He started poring over the file, because he wanted to make a good impression on the first day. After he read the file a couple of times, he got the gist of it. "Apollo Computing is a small high tech computer company. A bigger company is suing it on patent infringement. This small company will go bankrupt if they get an injunction from the court against them. They want Roberts & co to fight this case for a small fee."

Harrish called Veena on the technical aspects of the case. She felt that it is a deep technology and the court could not decide it without top expert's help. Kumar also felt that the technology was very high-tech. Harrish thought through the case and wrote out his position on his laptop until late in the night.

Harrish was standing in front of the company ten minutes before eight thirty; the door was locked. Roberts arrived a few minutes later and he apologized, "I have to get you a key, Harrish."

They went in. Roberts said, "Harrish, coffee will be ready in two minutes. Let us take a cup, sit in the lounge as nobody will be here before nine."

As they sat in the lounge, Steve asked, "Harrish, what do you think of the case?"

Harrish briefed him quickly and then said, "Steve, this technology is complicated. We need to convince the Judge that the top officers of this company are talented technical leaders. Then, the judge will hesitate to pass a quick injunction order. Deeper study will take time which will benefit this company."

"But, Harrish, long litigation will cost effort and money. This company cannot afford to pay me. Have you thought of that angle?"

"Steve, I have. You seem to be an entrepreneur. With your talent, you could be in a top law firm, making a lot of money and in an absolutely modern office. Instead, you chose to run this small company in this small office. Similarly, you ask for a generous stock option and may be a seat on the Board. That might satisfy your entrepreneurship spirit in the short term – may be big money long term."

"That is brilliant – you have really understood me. I will see the President today. I have handled patent infringement litigation before. Please prepare a letter to the President on the lines you outlined today. Let me read this file."

Harrish gave him his written report also and Steve was very pleased with that. Steve felt he was getting a bargain in Harrish!!

Chapter - 32

The phone rang and Geetha answered, "Hello, this is Geetha."

"Hi! Geetha, this is Dr.Natchikethas."

"Hi! Dr.Natchikethas."

"Geetha, I noticed that you are giving a concert in Rani Seetha hall this Sunday at 6 pm. If I were to attend, would it embarrass you?"

Geetha was not sure and noticing the silence, Dr.Natchikethas said, "Geetha, please think. I will call in half an hour. Either way is fine with me. The key is that the concert should go well."

Geetha thought, "Dr.Natchikethas always inspires me sitting in front and putting thalam. He is always focused and serious. Would he embarrass me now?" After some reflection, she felt that awkwardness would go away if he came early. Dr.Natchikethas agreed to come early.

On the concert day, unfortunately, Geetha forgot about the curtain and that prevented her from seeing the audience before the start of the function. At the start, nervously she saw Dr.Natchikethas in front smiling; she felt a flicker of embarrassment. Fortunately, the fast pace of the first varnam song erased it quickly. The major ragam she chose was Kambodhi with "Sri Subramanyaya Namasthe" Dhikshithar song. She sang it superbly well and Dr.Natchikethas was absolutely absorbed. His concentration inspired her all the more.

Dr.Natchikethas congratulated her at the end of the concert and she said with a smile that she would focus on his question, as her next concert was two months away. He replied with a smile, "Please take your time" and he left.

As promised, Geetha arranged a meeting at 6pm with her uncle, Dr.Subramanian, a renowned neurologist, to discuss the medical profession. Promptly at 6 pm, Dr.Subramanian met Geetha and stated briskly, "Geetha, you are here for a purpose. Why don't we discuss that first and then if time permits go on to pleasantries."

That suited Geetha fine.

Geetha started, "Uncle, I have a busy career in music – I travel quite a bit. My mom is putting pressure on me to marry – but I am avoiding that issue. Recently, a cardiac surgeon was interested in me. I know medical profession is a very demanding one. I wondered how hectic life would be after marriage?"

Dr.Subramanian was thoughtful for a moment and then said, "That is a tough question – you really have to decide that. All I can say is that medical profession is indeed a serious one. Moreover, cardiac surgeons and neurosurgeons have heavy responsibilities and have to be ready at anytime. But, nowadays, they share to reduce the burden. Moreover, university hospitals abroad have more research. But, as you may know, my son Shankar has an MBA and works for a large firm.He is as busy as a doctor. His wife is an architect. You need to ask them how they manage their married life."

After some more discussion, Geetha left.

When Geetha came home, the whole house was quiet. Geetha got some time to reflect, "It is obvious that Dr.Natchikethas' profession is very demanding. I don't think it will mix well with my music career. Best thing is to postpone the marriage. As Harrish suggested, let me talk to Dr.Natchikethas next week. But, I don't think that would change the facts."

Soon, both mother and Pavithran arrived. Geetha had early dinner and went to bed right away, because she was exhausted with thinking and with the busy schedule last week.

In the middle of the night, around 12 pm, Geetha felt a light touch. She heard a faint voice "Geetha". She woke up slowly and then realized that it was her mother's voice. She knew her mother's voice would not be so faint.

So, with great anxiety, she asked, "What is up, mom?"

Her mom replied almost in a whisper, "Geetha, I am having chest pain for the last half-hour. I thought it would go away. But, it is increasing every minute. I cannot breathe well."

Geetha jumped out of the bed, "chest pain – chest pain – chest pain – heart— the only person I can think of now is Dr.Natchikethas. He is a cardiac surgeon. My dear mom's life is in danger."

Though it was the middle of the night, she decided to call him. She had his emergency number. He had given it to her. She ran to the desk and got that number and called. Every ring was like eternity," Oh, God, let him pick it up."

One ring

Second ring, Third ring—eternity-

"Dr.Natchikethas" came the voice.

"This is Geetha," she said in tears.

With great anxiety, Dr.Natchikethas asked, "Geetha, what's wrong?"

"My mom is having severe chest pain."

"Geetha, I will be there in five minutes. Please call this number and get the ambulance. Don't panic. Ask her to rest and give her three aspirins. Don't worry."

He hung up the phone. Geetha, with tears flowing from her eyes, called the ambulance, woke up Pavithran, gave mom the aspirin and kept softly massaging her.

Dr.Natchikethas arrived in five minutes and was very very serious. He checked Parvathi and. gave her emergency medicine. The ambulance arrived immediately. They gave her oxygen. Dr.Natchiketas sat next to Parvathi in the ambulance and kept checking her. The ambulance left with Geetha in the front seat.

When they reached the hospital, Parvathi was quickly wheeled into the "Cardiac Lab" with Dr.Natchikethas walking fast beside her. He vanished into the lab and Geetha was pacing up and down outside.

Pavithran arrived and Geetha told him everything. Soon, to Geetha's surprise, Vimala came. Geetha hugged her and she could not help crying on her shoulders.

Vimala said with great affection holding Geetha's hands, "Geetha, don't worry. Dr.Natchikethas has handled many tough cases."

Soon, a junior doctor came out with all the forms to be signed and said, "Dr.Natchikethas has wheeled your mom into the Operation Theater. She has several blocks and her valve appears weak. The operation may take several hours. Please go to the Operation Theater waiting room."

They all went to the waiting room. Geetha asked Pavithran and Vimala to go home and get some sleep. Pavithran said, "Geetha, I can doze off here – at home, I will not get a wink of sleep."

Vimala felt the same. They both were soon half asleep.

But, Geetha was wide-awake. It was probably around 2:30 am.

In that dark night, Geetha was all alone thinking of her mom.

"My mom has been my sole supporter after my dad's death – what a tragedy that day of my dad's death – heart wrenching – now my dearest dear mom is fighting for life – Oh God! Please save her." Tears rolled down her cheecks.

"Oh God! I would be extra nice to her from now on. I would listen to her. Please save her."

Then she thought of mom's wishes – they were very few – but one was very, very dear to her – her marriage.

"Now, I know why she worried so much – she could die – she wanted me to be married before that."

That thought was far, far away from Geetha – now, it was not.

Then, her mind drifted to the Operation Theater – There her mother was – her heart was open.

Then, she thought, "Who is operating her? Dr.Natchikethas – without a wink of sleep in the middle of the night, he is meticulously performing the operation. How serious was he when he came ! When he arrived, a big burden was off my shoulders. All the burden of saving her is on him. I am just sitting here. But he is racking his brain in the middle of the night trying to save my dear mother. What a strange twist of fate!! Just early this night, I thought that medical profession and music would not mix. But now he, a medical doctor, is saving a musician's dearest mother – how mysterious is life!"

Thinking thus, she, totally exhausted, closed her eyes and was half asleep.

Geetha felt a tap on the shoulder and heard a voice "Geetha". She woke up startled and Vimala gave her a cup of coffee; she held her hands and said softly.

"Geetha, everything is OK. A nurse came to tell us that the operation is going well. Dr.Natchikethas would be out in half hour."

Geetha got ready and Dr.Natchikethas came towards them in forty minutes. He was surrounded by a few young doctors and three nurses.

Dr.Natchikethas was exhausted but still had a faint smile for Geetha and said, "Geetha, your mom should be OK."

Geetha was so happy to hear that. Tears welled up in her eyes. She said faintly,"Thanks, thanks, Dr.Natchikethas, what happened?"

"She had several blocks and also her valve was weak. We removed all the blocks and repaired the valve."

Geetha with worry asked, "Would she be OK from now on?"

Dr.Natchikethas touched her shoulders softly and said,

"Geetha, don't worry. She should be fine. But, this week is very critical. We have to make sure no complications arise."

Geetha asked with anxiety,"When will you see her again?"

Dr.Natchikethas said, "I will come in the night. Dr.Kamath is an experienced cardiologist. He will be watching her. If anything is wrong, please call me on my emergency number that you have."

Then, he introduced Geetha to Dr.Kamath. Dr.Natchiketas gave instruction to his junior doctors. He then turned to Geetha and said, "Geetha, I have another operation later on. I postponed it by a few hours. I need to go and take some rest and be ready for that operation."

He quickly turned and walked briskly along the corridor. She watched Dr.Natchikethas along the corridor; though tired, he was moving fast. Then, her thought turned to her mother, "Oh, my mom's heart is OK. I lost my dad but my mom is okay. Oh my God! Thanks, Thanks." Her heart leapt with joy.

In that joyful spirit, as she watched Dr.Natchikethas at the end of the corridor, she thanked him again and again in her mind and in that silent moment, without her knowledge, her heart went out with him.

Chapter - 33

Geetha ran to see her mom as soon as Dr.Natchikethas turned the corner. Parvathi was in the Intensive Care Unit. She was hooked up to many gadgets and was unconscious. But, Geetha was so happy to see her; "She is alive." She thought to herself. After couple of hours, Parvathi regained her consciousness; she gave a weak, wane smile to Geetha; Geetha was thrilled. Geetha held her mom's hands softly but soon, Parvathi dozed back to sleep.

The whole day was spent in and out of sleep except when Dr.Natchikethas came in the late evening. Dr.Natchikethas was quite serious but Parvathi had a broad smile for him. She has formed a warm affection towards him.

Geetha was surprised at the gravity with which Dr.Natchikethas examined her mom. Actually, this went on for the next six days. Dr.Natchikethas was always very grave and examined her mom seriously and said very little except for a few pleasantries with her mom. On the seventh day, however, he was quite relaxed. After examining her mom, he gave Geetha a big smile. Geetha was surprised but happy.

Dr.Natchikethas took Geetha aside and said with a smile, "Geetha, post-operative care is as important as surgery. I was very worried that some complications might develop. By God's grace, those symptoms vanished. Therefore, I am relaxed. She should now pull through."

Geetha felt so relieved and she had almost tears in her eyes. Before she could thank him, he continued, "Geetha, I have something else to tell you; please don't say no right away."

Geetha was stunned by these introductory comments. Looking at her surprised face, Dr.Natchikethas said softly, "This has nothing to do with the question I posed before."

Geetha was confused.

Dr.Natchikethas did not want to keep her in suspense too long. He continued,

"Your mom would be discharged in a few days. Your mom and mine are very close. We are relatives now. You and Vimala are good friends. We have a spacious house. If your mom came and lived with us for a few weeks, you will have support from my mom and Vimala. My mom was the one who suggested this first. Moreover, I could see your mom everyday. I think your mom will recover faster talking to my mom every day."

Geetha was in awe at this proposal. She didn't know how to respond. She thought for a minute. The proposal would be great for her mom; but she would be somewhat embarrassed. The benefit to her mom far outweighed her own personal feelings. To Dr.Natchikethas' surprise, Geetha agreed. Dr.Natchikethas was happy and thanked her for the decision.

Geetha replied, "I should be the one to say thanks."

Dr.Natchikethas smiled and then left shortly.

In a few days, Geetha and her mom came to Dr.Natchikethas' house. They were greeted warmly by Lakshmi and Vimala. Parvathi's room was arranged on the ground floor and Geetha's was adjacent and also connected to her mom's on the same floor. After they were settled, a few days later, Dr.Natchikethas examined Parvathi and then asked Geetha, "Geetha, have you seen the room adjacent to yours on the other side?"

Geetha said, "No."

Dr. Natchikethas took her to that room and Geetha saw a beautiful carpet in the middle. On the one side was a "Thambura" and on the other side was a tape recorder. Next to it were cassette tapes. Geetha was startled to see a large collection of great masters' music tapes. She asked, "When did you get these wonderful tapes?"

Dr.Natchikethas replied, "I told you I was very much into music before I went to medicine. I collected all these tapes at that time."

Geetha said, "Wow! You have a large collection of Semmangudi, Ariyakudi, Madurai Mani, M.S., Maharajapuram and D.K. Jayaraman."

"Geetha, please listen to them when you have time."

Geetha thanked Dr.Natchikethas for his thoughtfulness.

A few days later, on a Sunday evening, Geetha was reading a magazine in the living room. Dr. Natchikethas came and asked, "Geetha, may I talk to you for a few minutes?"

Geetha wondered what it was all about.

Dr. Natchikethas said, "Geetha, today is Sunday; I was home all day. I don't think I heard you sing today."

Geetha was startled by this comment, "Why is he making this remark?"

Geetha replied, "Well, ever since my mom's heart operation, I am emotionally high strung. I am not calm. Music needs a calm mind."

Dr.Natchikethas said sympathetically, "Geetha, I understand. After an operation like this, it is quite reasonable to be restless. Last week, Pavithran came and asked me whether he could go back to work. I said he should. It is good for your mother if children get back to their normal work. So, as you know, Pavithran is back to work. I see that music is different."

Geetha got his point and so she asked politely, "Dr. Natchikethas, do you have any idea how I could get back to music?"

Dr.Natchikethas thought for a while and then said, "Let us try this, Geetha. When you get up in the morning, don't see your mom first. That will bring back all your worries. I will request Vimala to bring you coffee at six am and stay with you for company. As soon as you are ready, please start the music right away. You are fresh and energetic in the morning."

Geetha felt that it was a good plan. Next day, she got up at five am, took shower and was ready at six when Vimala came. After coffee, they started music immediately. Geetha first got her throat into shape and Vimala played the thambura for sruthi (tone). Then, Geetha was not sure whether she should sing simple songs or go for the big ones. After a little thought, she decided to go for the tough ones because she wanted to know where she stood. Geetha started with the "Bhairavi" varnam, "Viribhoni" which is a master piece. It was tough going but she struggled valiantly. Finally, it turned to be OK. She decided to perfect it and sang repeatedly until it was almost near perfect. She felt very good.

With that confidence, she made up her mind to try a difficult song, "Sri Subramanyaya Namasthe" in Kambodhi ragam. After a few tries, it came out okay and she was happy.

Next, she went for the best raga, Thodi. She sang the ragam first and then the song "Koluva maragatha." This time, it all flowed naturally and nicely. She was thrilled.

At this time, Vimala said that it is time to go for breakfast.

When Geetha came out in a happy mood, she saw Dr.Natchikethas with her mom. She was surprised. She asked Dr.Natchikethas, "Don't you have hospital this morning?"

Dr.Natchikethas answered, "Geetha, I had been very busy these three weeks. So, I arranged no operation today. I just have to go to hospital in the afternoon. By the way, your "thodi" came out very well."

Geetha smiled and asked, "Do you really think so?"

Dr.Natchikethas answered, "Yes, it is almost there – just needs a little bit more fine tuning."

They all went for breakfast and were in a cheerful spirit. Music has that cheer in it.

Couple of days after, Geetha was singing in the music room in the evening. Dr.Natchikethas came and waited for her to finish her song. Then he asked, "Geetha, could I talk to you?"

Geetha silently assented. Dr.Natchiketas continued,

"I talked to Harrish today. He was probing whether you could come to the Book Release Function in New York five weeks from now. I told him that your mom is recovering very well and should be almost normal in five weeks. I talked to Pavithran who supports your going. I also discussed with Vimala and my mom who want you to go to New York. I am your mom's doctor and will watch her."

Geetha was totally taken aback by this proposal. She was speechless for a minute. Her first reaction to herself was "No way, am I going to leave my mom— —especially after all these heart wrenching problems. I cannot leave her alone. She needs me and so I am staying. Period."

Dr.Natchikethas had come to know Geetha well. Noticing her silence, he said, "Geetha, please talk to your mother and then decide."

He left quickly.

Geetha went to her mom's room to check her out. Her mom said, "Geetha, I heard from Pavithran that they have invited you to New York to sing in the Book Release Function. I think you should go and sing there. They are impressed with your music and you need to build your career. I see that you are happy ever since you started your music this week. My health is good. Dr.Natchikethas is taking excellent care of my health. In five weeks, I would be normal."

Geetha said, "Mom, I cannot think of leaving you emotionally. You may be right technically. But, after so much happened, I cannot think of leaving you. So I have to really think deeply."

"Okay, please talk to Pavithran, Vimala and Lakshmi and also to Dr.Natchikethas and decide."

Geetha sat alone in her room. She was deeply in thought. "What is happening? I thought Dr.Natchikethas' profession will stand in the way of my music career. Now, I am refusing to go to New York. Oh! My mom is just recovering. How can I leave her and go?"

Then, she remembered what she told herself in the hospital. "I promised that I would listen to my mom. Now, mom says that I should go to New York. She feels Dr.Natchikethas and others would take care of her. I am in a fix."

She decided to talk to Pavithran and Vimala. She did not want to talk to Dr.Natchikethas as she already knew that he supported her going. But, Pavithran and Vimala also urged her to give the concert. So, reluctantly, with a heavy heart, she decided to travel to New York and sing the invocation and also give a few concerts in USA.

Chapter - 34

Harrish was worried that after four weeks of working in Roberts & Co, there was still no mention of Saturn Computing. By now, Steve Roberts liked Harrish immensely. But, the main goal was not yet accomplished. Veena, Harrish and John Viterbi got together to consider the next move. Should Harrish continue or should he quit? They decided to try for three more weeks and if not successful, discontinue the operation.

Nothing happened next week. Harrish wondered what else could he do. Shortly, Steve Roberts called him to his room to discuss a tough case. At the end, he tossed a few reports at Harrish and said, "These are not important. Spend the least amount of time on them. The company is not paying much money. Just check the telephone numbers, address and small things and then approve them. I have already checked in detail one of these companies."

Harrish looked at the reports- it said "Saturn Computing" on top! Harrish could not believe his eyes! His heart almost stopped. He was ecstatic. However, he quietly left Steve's office. He hurriedly went to his desk and started reading the reports. One report was on a subsidiary that he knew was only "one-security guard" company. However, the report showed a huge profit for this company; it had large income, expense and profit. Harrish was stunned.

Two other reports were of the same vintage. Harrish made a copy of the reports quickly and ran fast to his hotel room. He hurriedly called Veena.

"Veena, something great happened! I got three subsidiary reports today. I can't believe it. They are indeed fraudulent."

Veena was thrilled. Harrish suggested that Veena go to John Viterbi's office right away and then, three of them can strategize the next move. Veena at once left for John's office. Harrish called John's office an hour later and three of them discussed the immediate step.

John suggested, "Why don't you, Harrish, come back immediately with the copy of the reports?"

Harish replied, "John, I think I have a different idea. Steve Roberts is a good guy and if we could get him on our side, we would be on a strong footing. Jack Taylor had asked Steve to verify the reports. Therefore, if Steve Roberts checked and found the reports to be fraudulent, then our case would be strengthened."

Then, John questioned, "Why would Steve stick his neck out and fight Jack Taylor, a well known lawyer in Los Angeles?"

Harrish answered, "Two reasons, John. First, Steve does not like to be involved in criminal activities. He does not want to get caught in the future. Second, he likes to earn well. If we pay him handsomely, he will give an excellent performance."

Veena probed, "Harrish, what you are saying is, if Steve approves these reports without checking and if someone finds out the truth, then Steve would become a co-conspirator. Steve would not like that. Is that it?"

Harrish replied, "Yes, Veena. Steve likes to stay within the law. He hates to be outside the law."

John intervened, "How much would he want?"

Harrish commented, "Just the going rate for his time and probably a bonus if he does a good job. Plus, a promise of future job from Gigabit would go a long way."

John said, "Harrish, I don't see any problem with it. Do you, Veena?"

Veena commented, "No, John. It would be great to get Steve on our side."

Harrish summarized the next step, "Well then, I will go now to Steve's office and talk to him briefly. Then, we will call you guys from his office. Why don't you both stay there and wait for our call?"

Harrish, then, almost sprinted to Steve's office. He wanted to catch Steve before he left the office as it was almost 6 pm.

Harrish knocked on Steve's door.

Steve said impatiently with a frown, "Harrish, be quick. I got to leave now."

Harrish commented, "Steve, there is an immediate job opportunity from Gigabit, a billion dollar company. They are willing to pay. Their corporate lawyer, John Viterbi, is waiting to talk to you."

Steve's eyes widened; he said with a smile, "Please call him right away – Gigabit – Wow, that is great !"

Harrish, called at once John and said, "Mr. Viterbi, I mentioned to Mr. Roberts that you told me that you have an important and an immediate job opportunity for him. Please explain to Steve Roberts the job."

John started the conversation by saying, "Please call me, John; I will call you Steve. Here with me, Steve, is Ms.Veena Ravi, daughter of our Chairman Dr.Ravi and also an assistant Vice President of Gigabit Inc."

"Hi! Veena" said Steve.

John asked, "Steve, what do you know about Gigabit Inc?"

"John, I know Gigabit as a billion dollar company and very high tech. Dr.Ravi is a well respected high tech business leader."

John continued, "Good, Steve. Let me now explain the project I have for you. Dr.Ravi has invested $ 5 million dollars into "Saturn Computing." We are planning to invest more, but, while investigating, noticed a peculiarity in the annual report. They show a huge income from subsidiaries. But, the report does not give much information about them."

Steve quickly realized why Gigabit was interested in him and he wondered what Harrish was up to.

Guessing Steve's mind, John proceeded, "We checked a couple and they are just one – man operation."

Steve countered, "I checked one and it was okay."

"Steve, that is the good one. Have you carefully checked the others?"

Steve felt that he was on the carpet. He defensively said, "I just received the reports for checking."

"Okay, Steve. Please check these out thoroughly. We will cover the costs."

Steve suddenly remembered that Jack Taylor did not want him to check these carefully. Now, he wondered why. Steve was deeply in thought. Noticing Steve's silence,

John asked, "Steve, do you have any problems?"

"John, Jack Taylor told me specifically not to check these out carefully. Now, I am puzzled."

"Steve, do you realize how serious this is? Our $5 Million investment is at stake. If state or federal authorities question these, all of us would be in trouble."

"I see, John, how serious this is. Especially my company would be found in serious violation of law. John, thanks for calling."

John commented, "Steve, you really need to thank Harrish. He is the one who found this out from the annual report. He checked out two companies in Singapore and two in Los Angeles and he found them to be one - man show."

Steve smilingly said, "So, it is probably, Harrish's idea to come and work for me so that he could get hold of these reports. The moment he got these reports, he had called you."

Veena, John and Harrish laughed.

Steve continued, "Okay, John, Harrish and I will start working on these reports right away."

John remarked, "Steve, time is very critical. Could you please finalize them in a few days. Today is Tuesday. Could we meet on Saturday in San Francisco?"

Steve agreed, "If we don't run into any big hurdles, that would be fine."

John asked worriedly, 'Do you have anyone in Singapore and New York?"

Steve replied emphatically, "Yes, John, I have excellent contacts. We will do a thorough professional job."

John was relieved, "Great, Steve. Please call me on Friday on the status."

"John, we will."

"Good bye, Steve."

Thus ended an important, strategic conversation.

Steve turned to Harrish and said, "Harrish ,let us go and eat. I am starved. We will discuss our next move during dinner.'

Steve and Harrish worked diligently night and day during the next three days and met with Veena and John on Friday itself. Dr.Ravi's meeting was scheduled for Wednesday.

Chapter - 35

It was a Saturday morning. The weather was perfect; sunny, lightly cool and breezy. Veena looked out the window and she loved the weather. So, she decided to go for a long walk. She quickly changed her dress and set out for her walk.

As she walked, she thought a little about her projects and then her thought drifted to "Saturn Computing." "Well, Harrish did an excellent job in getting those important reports through Steve. Now, we have solid evidence. But, given Jack Taylor's contacts and his smartness, the next steps are not going to be easy. Anyhow, on Wednesday, we will discuss it with dad."

Her mind moved to Harrish, "What a guy! So talented in business, so hard working and intelligent. Why didn't Latha like him? Well, Latha wasn't too interested in marriage. She worried about conflict with non NRIs and Harrish also is a little too serious for her. Nevertheless, he has so many strengths. Well, that is where, probably, the chemistry comes in. What is chemistry though?– not so easy to define – is n't it- I wonder whether there is chemistry between Harrish and me – Well, definitely we have in business – We get along famously there. What about outside business?" Veena was puzzled with this question "Why am I asking this? I am not sure – may be , it is time to find out – Harrish said communication is important – I and Harrish have always been working on business issues – why not go out for dinner and not talk about business?" The more she thought about it, the more she liked it.

Veena was the type who implemented her ideas quickly. Therefore, she decided "why not this evening ? What should I tell Harrish? – just let us have dinner and not talk about business." When she mentioned it to Harrish, he was more than willing. Actually, Harrish said that would be wonderful.

So, in the evening, they went to a nice, small restaurant in Palo Alto.

Veena started the conversation,

"Harrish, I thought we have been working very hard – hence, I felt why not go out and just chit chat."

"Thanks, Veena – Excellent idea – Last two months indeed have been hectic."

"Harrish, I chose this restaurant as it is quiet and also have good food."

"Yes, Veena, the décor is good. By the way, Veena I was just talking to Dr.Natchikethas this afternoon. He told me that Geetha's mother, my aunt, had chest pain and he had to operate on her."

"How is she now?"

"Okay, now. She is recovering well."

"I want to call Geetha and I want to give her support." said Veena.

"Me too – I could not get her – she is in the hospital."

"When you do, could you also transfer it to me?"

"Okay."

Then after some light chitchat, Veena said,

"Harrish, I want to ask you a question"

"What?"

"Well, in Singapore you said, that if you had better communication with Latha, things could have been less tense – let me ask you – what would you have asked Latha?"

"Veena, that is a good question. I have thought a lot about it. I would have asked her in Syracuse, whether she was interested in me.'

"How would she have replied?"

"Probably, she would have said —I don't know—"

"Then, what?"

"I would have requested her to think about it and let me know."

"What then?"

"Then, a few weeks later, she would have thought and said —no."

"Are you sure?"

"Yes, from the way things worked out – the chemistry was not there."

"Why do you say that?"

"When I went to Syracuse, she was annoyed rather than be happy about it – At that time, I was too naïve."

"So, what does chemistry mean to you ?"

"Well, I think a mutual liking and interest in each other's company."

"In retrospect, how was the chemistry?"

"I think it was all one sided – the other side was not sure and noncommittal."

"So, what would you do in the future ?"

Harrish responded, "Veena, I really don't know how and when these things happen – All I can say is, I will communicate a lot."

Harrish returned the question, "Veena, why are you asking so many questions?"

"Harrish, the reason is I talked a lot with Latha about it. You are right in Singapore. She is very relaxed after getting your letter."

"Yes, her major concern was I – whether I –was OK with her decision, but her decision was firm and final."

"Yes, she is now happy but how do you feel about it?"

"Fine now – I finally realized what happened. Knowledge has a strange power to quell the restless mind."

Veena smiled at that phrase, "That is a fascinating point, Harrish! Well, I talked at length with Latha and so I wanted to close the loop. I have done that now. We could move on to other topics. By the way, I heard Semmangudi's "Oranga sai" It is indeed superb. Thanks for giving me the tape. Do you have anything else in Kambodi raga?"

"I do; I have "Sri Subramanyaya namasthe" also by Semmangudi."

"Great. Harrish, why don't you periodically give me good tapes."

"Okay"

Then they talked about music in general. Thus, they enjoyed the dinner and Harrish complimented Veena on her selection. They had a pleasant evening.

When Harrish reached home, he could not sleep. He thought about Veena – "Strange, she thought of the dinner idea and asked me so many questions – why? Is she interested in me? May be – I am not going to worry about it now – I have gone through a disaster – let me cool it."

But he could not help thinking of Veena. "She is beautiful and a wonderful person – absolute class act – Is there chemistry between us? Yes, in the office – How about outside?"

Now, he saw why Veena arranged the dinner – she wanted to find out – whether there was mutual liking.

She wanted to find out whether he was pining away for Latha – Harrish smiled, "Hey, this Veena is a smart cookie. She is already trying to implement the "communication" idea. She doesn't want to be hurt like I was. She is being very careful and communicating."

Harrish smiled again. Harrish was impressed with Veena.

Veena came back from dinner and started thinking about it. "Well, did they communicate well? Well, I did indeed asked some tough questions. It is clear, Harrish is fully aware of what went wrong with his interest in Latha; he looks at it as an amateurish, naïve mistake. What else? He again emphasized the need for communication. Do they have have anything in common outside work?" She was not sure. She thought some more. Then, it hit her – "Music" – "Harrish is great at carnatic music. I have begun to love it. My knowledge is less."

She remembered that she was good at singing. Her mom had told her that her voice was excellent. Then it struck her, "Why not learn music? But how?— My mom – she is an expert in carnatic music and sings every day – why not learn from her?"

Again, Veena was quick at carrying out ideas.

She looked for her mom and found her in the living room. Seeing Veena, mom said,

"Veena, you are not in bed yet."

"No Mom, I was thinking – you know I like carnatic music – I was wondering why not learn it?"

"Veena, I always told you that you have a good voice and good listening capacity. Therefore, definitely you can learn."

"Then, mom, would you please teach me? I know I should have, when I was young."

Her mom hugged Veena, "Veena, I will any day. However, do you have time?"

"Morning, everyday lesson. Saturday & Sunday I will practice. This will give me something outside work. I am really excited about it, mom."

But, her mom did not know then, that Veena had another interest. She wanted to explore whether there was chemistry between Harrish and her by creating a common interest.

Chapter - 36

On Monday morning, Veena got up early in the morning around 5.15 am. She took her coffee and shower. She wore a simple saree and went to the pooja (Prayer) room and prayed for ten minutes. Then, exactly at 6 am, she came into the music room. Veena's mother was already there waiting for her.

Veena smilingly said, "Mom, you are up early."

"Yes, Veena – you wanted to learn carnatic music and I am so thrilled. So, I was up early."

"Great."

Mrs. Ravi loved carnatic music dearly. She had dedicated a room for that. It was a spacious room with pictures of Thyagaraja, Dikshithar and Shyama Shastri—the three great composers of carnatic music——adorning the wall. There was a beautiful carving of Saraswathi (Goddess of Learning) with Veena (a stringed musical instrument) it was so captivating. In the cabinet, were cassettes, books—almost a small library.

Veena's mom started with a simple song. She said this would make it interesting and not boring. Amazingly, Veena was able to sing very well. She had a good voice and good listening capacity. The lesson was fun for Veena.

When the lesson ended, Veena got ready to go to office. Dr. Ravi was at the breakfast table. He said, "Veena, you look cheerful!"

Veena replied, "Yes, dad. I took my first music lesson from mom today. Somehow, it is so relaxing and gets your mind in a great mood. The office is always worrisome."

Dr. Ravi commented, "You know what I do, Veena. I just focus deeply on the problem at that time and I also anticipate all the negatives. Next,, I decide on a course and then I forget it. If I worry about everything, I cannot sleep."

Veena said, "That is a good advice, dad. Let me practice that."

After breakfast, she came to the office in the same happy mood. When she passed Harrish's room, as it was her habit, she stopped and said, "Good morning, Harrish."

"Veena, Good morning. You are in a great mood today."

"Yes, Harrish, I started my carnatic music lesson with mom today."

Harrish was stunned, "Really, Veena?"

"Yes, Harrish – I wanted to learn something outside office that would be peaceful."

"True, Veena – carnatic music can be soothing."

"Only thing is, Harrish, I am learning at a late stage in life."

Harrish protested mildly, "No Veena – you are so young. You know Geetha learnt it very well in five years. Only for professional singing, she spent several additional years."

"But, she did it full time."

"No, at that time she had two years of school and then college."

"Really?"

"Yes."

"That is encouraging, Harrish."

Then Veena looked at Harrish and asked, "Harrish, you once told me that you don't sing though you have so much knowledge of carnatic music."

"Actually, Veena – that is true. When Geetha was learning, I was too interested in cricket and did not learn to sing. That is one of my regrets."

Veena was thoughtful for a minute and then said with a smile, "Harrish, I have a great idea. Why don't you learn along with me?"

Harrish did not know how to answer that. He felt it might embarrass Mrs. Ravi and he might not be too comfortable.

"Veena, it may be awkward for your mom to teach me."

"No, Harrish – You don't know my mom. She loves carnatic music so much that all these small things don't matter to her."

Harrish, by now, knew Veena well. "Once an idea like this gets hold of her, she will push it. Let Mrs. Ravi decide that".

He said politely, "Why don't you ask your mom? Please don't push her."

A Tender Melody

Veena smilingly said, "Harrish, I don't need to. She would love it – She gets two students."

Veena called her mom right away and her mom was a little surprised by Veena's request. But, she knew Harrish well and Harrish had deep knowledge of carnatic music. Noticing Veena's enthusiasm, Mrs. Ravi agreed.

Exactly at 6 am, next day Harrish arrived. He came in the traditional South Indian dress with a veshti, shirt and Vibudhi on his forehead. Veena opened the door and said smilingly, "Harrish, you are in Chennai!"

"Yes, Veena."

Mrs. Ravi saw Harrish in the South Indian dress and smiled, "You look traditional, Harrish."

"Well, Mrs. Ravi, I am going to learn carnatic music."

Mrs. Ravi started to teach Harrish the same song so that he could catch up to Veena. Harrish struggled. It did not come that easy. But, because of his knowledge, he pulled it off okay.

Next, Veena sang the same song. It was so melodious. Harrish closed his eyes and listened deeply. Veena had a great voice and a wonderful grasp of carnatic music. It came to her so naturally. Harrish was deeply touched. When she finished, Harrish said, "Veena, carnatic music comes so naturally to you. You also have an wonderful voice."

Veena was so happy to hear that from Harrish, who is so knowledgeable.

Mrs.Ravi said,

"Harrish, I always felt Veena would do well in carnatic music. But she was busy with technology."

"Mrs. Ravi, she is still so young. She can pick it up fast as she is so talented. Geetha learnt it quite well in five years. This will stay with Veena throughout her life."

Mrs. Ravi said, "That is true. Even now, I come here to this room and sing. That gives me so much solace and cheer. Often, Dr.Ravi travels a lot; those days I spent my time here."

Harish commented, "That is why, I am learning it though it may be a little hard for me. I can then sing any time. I think I would enjoy listening it more."

Mrs.Ravi added, "That is true; Once you learn to sing, your appreciation of music will soar."

When Veena was driving her car to the office, she involuntarily hummed the tune of the song. It was just spontaneous. As usual, she stopped on her way at Harrish's office.

"Harrish, how did you find the morning session?"

"Veena, it was great. Your mom is a good teacher. All my reservations were proved incorrect. The biggest surprise was your singing. You have kept it a big secret."

Veena said in a happy mood, "Well, I never really believed my mom. I was too interested in math and computer science."

"But, Veena, you are still young."

"Harish, you too!"

"Veena, I am very happy. Today, I was singing in the car – I used to hum the tune but not correctly – Today, I could really sing and I am so thrilled – Thanks a lot for arranging the session."

Veena felt good and she thought, may be, this music might give them a common bond outside office.

Chapter - 37

As planned, on Wednesday, Steve Roberts, John Viterbi, Veena and Harrish met at 4 PM in Gigabit's conference room. Dr.Ravi would join them at 4.30 PM. They briefly touched base with each other to ensure they were all in unison on the plan. Dr.Ravi joined them promptly.

The session started with Steve Roberts presenting his official report on the subsidiaries of "Saturn Computing".

"Dr.Ravi, since your time is limited, I want to be brief. Did you get a chance to read the reports?"

"Steve, yes. They are all very well written and to the point. It is very clear that five out of the eight subsidiaries do not have proper record and no substantiation of the profit of these companies."

"Dr.Ravi,I tried to bring out the facts in a telling manner, so that if there is a litigation, we are clear and safe."

"Thanks, Steve" Dr.Ravi turned to John and asked, "Where do we go from here, John?"

John replied, "Actually, Steve had asked Harrish to prepare a strategic plan. Veena and I went through it last Friday and I had given you a copy."

"Yes, John. I have read that report. It is very impressive and I feel it is an excellent plan. But, I have a number of questions. First, it says that I should talk to the President, Dr. Chang. How do we know that he is not friendly to Jack Taylor?"

Steve intervened, "Dr.Ravi, we do not know that fully. But, we know this – that Dr.Chang does not run the subsidiaries and has very little knowledge— at least, as he and his VP finance have said so. Even if he were friendly to Jack Taylor, when he sees the extreme seriousness and almost duplicitous nature of these transactions, then he would not side with Jack on this particular matter."

"I see, Steve. What you are saying is, even if Dr.chang knows, he would not publicly support Jack Taylor now. Only Jack could implicate him if he wanted to."

"Yes, Dr.Ravi. We are assuming Dr.Chang does not know. Veena pointed out we should anticipate the worst. What we are saying is that even if Dr.Chang knew, he would find it advantageous to support us now. If he did not support us, he would face dire consequences as we are very determined now."

"But, what if he tips off Jack?"

John intervened, "You mean, what if he played both sides?"

"Exactly."

Veena interrupted, "Dr.Ravi, in your meeting, you have to be very, very stern that if he played any games he would be prosecuted under law. The matter is very serious now."

Dr.Ravi said, "Okay, we are depending on Dr.Chang being rational and reasonable. Let us see how that works out. Now, let me turn to my second worry. When we contact the Board of Directors, the cat is out of the bag. Anyone of them could contact Jack Taylor."

John intervened,"Yes, Dr.Ravi, there is that risk but as you see we are contacting the Board of Directors only one day ahead. So, if things don't go smoothly, we may change our plan totally" Dr.Ravi asked, "Change to what?"

John answered,"We have to go the litigation route, and criminal justice system. We would have no recourse if matters get out of hand."

Dr.Ravi pointed out," That could be a long process, John"

"True, but we have no option at that point because Jack Taylor would move on that front anyhow. However, we have carefully chosen the four Board Directors who may not be friendly to Jack, but there is no hundred percent guarantee."

Dr.Ravi, now, turned to Harrish and said,

"Harrish, you are rather silent."

Veena, smilingly said, "That means he is thinking."

Dr.Ravi asked, "What?"

Harrish answered, "Dr.Ravi, I see your concern. If we talk to Dr. Chang and the Board of Directors, some one might tip Jack Taylor. We chose this path because it was fast. There is another way, probably, much more safer and deliberate. That is, we could go to the investors first. They have a personal, vested interest in the company; probably, they are more worried about their money than Jack Taylor. Obviously, this would take time but safer because Dr.Chang needs money for growth. If half the investors pull out, his company would probably go bankrupt. He has already put too much time and effort for that to happen. The Board of Directors also would not want half the investors withdraw because the company would fold."

There was silence in the room and everyone started to think.

Steve Roberts spoke first,

" I agree with Harrish. When we go to Dr.Chang, we would be in a very strong position. This approach would definitely take more time but is more of a sure bet"

Dr.Ravi asked, "Do we know whether investors would side with us?"

John answered, " Dr.Ravi, we have obtained a list of all the investors and we have studied their background. About fifty percent of them are in San Francisco and they do not know Jack Taylor. They have invested because, we, Gigabit, have invested. So they would listen to us and most probably side with us. Fifty percent would be a blow to Saturn Computing,"

Dr.Ravi said, "Well, then, that would be a better approach, John, even if it takes time. Why don't we contact all the friendly investors and then let us get together:"

Dr.Ravi left shortly and the rest of them sat and planned the next steps.

Veena asked,

"What should we tell the investors?"

Steve Roberts answered,

"First, I would present my report. Next, we point out that this is illegal and Gigabit can't be associated with this illegality. We would be forced to terminate our association with Saturn. We would also be legally obligated to tell the authorities."

Veena asked,

"What if they say—— why not let it run as is. Why rock the boat? Who is going to find out?—"

"The answer is simple, Veena" said John, "We, as a publically traded company, couldn't be involved in this illegality. We have to take action"

Next, they looked at the list of investors. They picked the most friendly investor, named, Robert Kelly. He had invested $ 1 million in Saturn when he heard about Gigabit's investment.

When they met and explained to him the situation, he was enraged at Jack Taylor. He could not believe that he would do some thing so stupid. He totally supported Gigabit.

Next, they met two other friendly investors. They backed Gigabit. The fourth investor, Joe Petrocilli, was very tough to handle. He was extremely worried about his money. He did not want Gigabit to take any action. He threatened to call Jack Taylor immediately, if Gigabit proceeded. He did not care about all the legal ramifications.

John Viterbi borrowed two days time to consider all his objections and promised no further action would be taken in the meantime. Four of them met to discuss his strong opposition. They were in a quandary as to how to handle this case. At that time, Veena said,

"I have an idea. Why not buy this guy out? His major concern is his money."

"May be Veena, all he want is a guarantee that we would protect his investment if something wrong happens"

Dr.Ravi preferred to buy him out because he was worried that other investors would want similar guarantees. Joe Petrocilli was very happy to sell his shares ($ one million) and they agreed to enact an agreement in such a manner that the company or Jack Taylor need not be notified immediately. Joe, now, fully supported Dr.Ravi's moves. Now investors with about $7 million investment were on Dr.Ravi's side. In the meantime, Robert Kelly called his friend, a fellow investor in LosAngeles. That investor became furious with Jack Taylor and agreed to totally support Dr.Ravi. He had invested two million dollars in Saturn computing. Dr.Ravi now had (including Gigabit), $14 million out of a total $20 million, supporting Gigabit.

Chapter - 38

On the next Monday evening at 3pm., Dr.Ravi, Steve Roberts, John Viterbi, Veena and Harrish got together to discuss Saturn Computing.

John Viterbi started the discussion;

"Dr, Ravi, we have contacted the friendly investors and we have on our side $14million out of $20million. Therefore, we have the majority of stake holders fully backing us. We need an action plan next. Time is of the essence and we need to move fast."

Dr.Ravi asked,"John, what plan do you all suggest?"

John Viterbi answered,

"Dr.Ravi, the time has come to contact the Board of Directors. We want you to call John Williams of Nanotech today at 6:30pm Newyork time or 3:30 our time. You know him well and we have set up that telephone call immediately. Tommorow morning you could contact three others. We have prepared a short two page summary for you to use in the phone conversation"

Dr.Ravi said, "Okay, John, please join me in my room at 3:25pm and I would call from there"

They all gathered in Dr.Ravi's room at the appointed time and John Viterbi called John Williams. His seceratry answered and said John Williams would pick up the call in one minute. John Viterbi gave the phone to Dr.Ravi and when John Willams answered, Dr.Ravi said, " John, Hi, this is Dr.Ravi. How are you?"

After exachanging pleasantries, Dr.Ravi said, "John, I have something very very serious about Saturn Computing. Dr.Harrish Sridhar of my staff noticed large income from the subsidiaries that raised his eyebrows."

John interrupted, "Dr, Ravi, we noticed it in our Board meeting too and asked Jack Taylor to get it approved by a top accounting company"

Dr.Ravi continued, "Yes, John. That request for verification came to Roberts and company in LosAngeles and its President, Steve Roberts, is here in this room now. He has found no substantiation of the large income. Steve Roberts has worked on this problem intensely and has prepared a detailed official report of his work. I can either fax it or e-mail it now as you wish."

John answered," Dr.Ravi, Please fax it now so that I will have it as we talk."

A Tender Melody

John Viterbi went to the next room to fax the report while Dr.Ravi continued the conversation. Dr.Ravi said, "John, for the sake of conversation, let us assume that this is true. Then, we need an action plan. I suggest we contact three other Board of Directors who are not friendly to Jack Taylor. By the way, we have contacted key investors with investment of almost $14 million out of $20 million. They are against Jack Taylor."

John Williams answered, "That is great. That would be absolutely convincing to other Board of Directors and would call for immediate action by the Board of Directors. Dr.Ravi, do you know any other Board members?"

Dr.Ravi said, "No, John."

John continued,

"In that case, Dr.Ravi, let me call them. Actually, let me take charge of this problem now; please have your staff support me. Please introduce them to me."

Dr.Ravi answered,

"Well, this is John Viterbi, my chief counsel. He is overall in charge of this operation.

Next, is Steve Roberts, who I told you is the President of Roberts and co. He has done a remarkable job of unearthing this episode; Dr.Harrish Sridhar has just joined Gigabit and has a PhD from MIT Sloan School. He has been very very instrumental in this investigation. Finally, Veena Ravi is my daughter and she has interrupted her PhD in MIT to join me. She has been working very very closely with Harrish in this enquiry."

John greeted, "Hello! John, Steve, Harrish and Veena. I will be in touch with you guys throughout this evening."

Dr.Ravi concluded, "John, let me suggest that your organize an emergency Board meeting on Wednesday at 1pm. I have informed the key investors and they plan to attend. I am planning to come to Los Angeles. I am meeting Dr.Chang at 10am.on Wednesday."

John agreed, "Dr.Ravi, I will set that meeting up on Wednesday at 1pm. May I join you in your meeting with Dr.Chang?"

Dr.Ravi replied," Of course, John, That would be wonderful."

With that, they said goodbye to each other.

John, Steve, Harrish and Veena got together in the conference room. John called Mr.Williams to find out whether he completed reading Steve's report.

Mr. Williams answered, "Yes, John. It is an excellent report-very convincing – very well written. Let me now call Jack Daman, another member of Board. He is a very inquisitive type and will, I am sure, ask you guys a lot of questions."

John Williams, next called Jack Daman and apprised him of all that had taken place in Saturn Computing. Jack, in turn, called Gigabit and talked at length with John Viterbi, Steve Roberts, Harrish and Veena— each separately. Jack got convinced and agreed to support John Williams. Jack Daman very much wanted to call Jack Taylor but John dissuaded him to wait till Wednesday 1pm where he could ask all the questions he wanted to. Jack agreed fearing that an early call would tip Jack Taylor to come up with an ingenius counter plan.

John Williams called the two other Board members and all the calls ended around midnight Newyork time and 9pm San Francisco time. John, Steve, Harrish and Veena were all tired and exhausted but reasonbly happy that the Board of Directors had agreed to meet on Wednesday and to take action. They were also worried what Jack Taylor might do on Wednesday.

Chapter - 39

At exactly 1pm., on Wednesday, the Saturn Computing Boardroom was full of business executives. The room was charged with an atmosphere of extreme gravity; no one smiled and everyone was too serious. There was a long Mahagony table and John Williams was seated at the center.

To his right was Jack Daman. On his left were two of his friendly members of the Board of Directors. Opposite to John Williams, on the other side, was Jack Taylor flanked by his two buddy Board members. At the other far end of the table were special invitees Dr.Ravi and other investors; behind them were John Viterbi, Steve Roberts, Harrish and Veena as special guests. At the near end, Dr.Chang and the other Directors were present.

Dr.Chang had a long conversation with John Williams and Dr.Ravi that morning. Dr.Chang was startled and pained by the turn of events. He promised total support to John Williams. Thus, John had majority votes in his hands as he opened the meeting.

It was customary for Jack Taylor to open the Board of Director's meeting as its Chairman. Today, however, John Williams started the meeting with the following comments; "Thank you all for coming to this emergency meeting on such a short notice. We have a serious problem to discuss."

A Tender Melody

Jack Taylor angrily interrupted John.

"John, you did not tell all of us what this meeting was all about. You have informed some of the members but others including myself don't know what the heck is this emergency meeting for."

John answered softly,

"Jack, you and others would know shortly all there is to know."

Jack said in an angry, disgruntled voice,

"John, let us move forward quickly. I don't have much time."

John answered,

"That suits me fine, Jack. As you know, a few months ago, we agreed in our Board meeting that we need proper substantiation of the profits of the subsidiaries by a top accounting company"

Jack interjected angrily,

"Yes, I have appointed a top accounting company and I have their first report on the first subsidiary."

John observed politely,

"Yes, Jack. As you know, they subcontractred it to Roberts & company"

Jack again interrupted,

"That was my idea, John. I have taken Steve Roberts personally to the first subsidiary."

"Yes, Jack. Everything is fine with the first subsidiary— the revenue, profit etc tally nicely."

"Then, what the hell is the problem, John?" asked Jack in angry frustration pounding on the table.

John Williams now raised his voice to a very firm, authoritative tone;

"Jack, the problem is Steve Roberts could not get any proper records on the second company. Moreover, when he visited the company at the address given, all he saw was a guard. There was no one else— no operation and no information available."

John raised his voice even more;

"Jack, this is damn serious to justify this emergency meeting. Not only was this the case for the second subsidiary but his report here summarizes all the same for the third, fourth, fifth, sixth, seventh and eighth subsidiary. Little company, little revenue and no profitt. Steve has spent considerable time and effort to explore these."

John showed everyone the report and gave all a copy.

Jack defiantly said, " Steve should have come to me and I would have given the right answer"

John got angry and said,

"Jack, give us the answer now."

Jack replied,

"John, I need time to prepare. You cannot expect me to answer immediately. You did not even tell me what this meeting was all about."

John was totally frustrated and said in a deliberate, firm, no nonsense but rich voice,

"Jack, either you cooperate with us fully now or we would not hesitate to prosecute you in the criminal court."

Jack was totally taken aback—— he was stunned— the matter had gotten out of hand——

"Criminal court"— he never thought of that— he did just an accounting gimmicry——he just wanted to enchance the company's bottom line— he looked around –all the Board of Directors including his buddys were very serious—no one came to his rescue including Dr.Chang or his friends. The investors seemed angry and furious.

Jack never thought this would come to this——he thought no one would notice—almost no one did——the main company was running fine—he wanted to quickly grow the company on paper. Who would care to check the small subsidiaries? Now, he was facing a calamitous choice.

Jack felt he probably had no choice but to resign. But, being a clever lawyer, he wanted to leverage his resignation for other benefits. So, he issued a bravado statement.

"John, I am a top lawyer here in LosAngeles. I can fight your guys in the court forever— criminal or otherwise. But it might not be in the best interests of "Saturn Computing."

John Williams quickly seized the opportunity and then lowered his voice. He spoke in a calm, conciliatory manner.

"Jack, we don't want to go court either. We want to settle this amicably. We recognize that you have worked hard for "Saturn Computing". We want a smooth seperation."

"John, then I don't want my stock options cut back and insist on my severance package that we have negotiated."

John answered,

"Jack, we will try to be as fair as possible under the legal framework. We would recognize your dedicated effort."

Jack, then in a big surprise move, wrote out his resignation letter and gave it to John Williams and John said,

"Jack, thanks for your cooperation. You know the company could be investigated if this leaks out and hence we need to secure all the papers. Please wait in the adjacent room and some of us would meet you shortly."

Jack quickly left the room without looking at anyone. There was a sigh of relief in the room but everyone was too worried about the immediate future to rejoice.

John Williams sensed that everyone was concerned about the future and decided to quickly address that challenge.

"Outstanding concern now is the appointment of the next Chairman. Jack Taylor is a well-known leading lawyer in LosAngeles and California and hence, his resignation would be bad publicity for "Saturn Computing", unless we appoint immediately another Chairman better in stature, reputation and character. That task is not easy. I and some of the Board members spent considerable time yesterday mulling over this challenge. Our consensus was to request Dr.Ravi to be an interim Chairman. He has the stature and respect of the business community and is well known as a technology leader. The more we talked, the more we loved the solution."

"But, Dr.Ravi is extremely busy running a billion dollar company. Hence, it is not fair to ask him to chair this company. So, my proposal is that I am willing to be Vice Chairman and I will come every two weeks to Los Angeles. Jack Daman has agreed to come every week. Moreover, let me tell all of you present here, utmost impressed am I with two of Gigabit's employees, namely Dr.Harrish Sridhar and Ms.Veena Ravi, daughter of Dr.Ravi."

"It was Dr.Harrish Sridhar, who first suspected, that something was worng about the subsidiary income in the annual report.. Harrish informed Veena who in turn alerted Dr.Ravi immediately. In Singapore, he checked out two of them and found one a small company and another no operation. Thus, the ball got rolling. They both pursued it vigorously and diligently and got Steve Roberts involved. Let us now give them a hand".

Both Harrish and Veena stood up and the Directors and investors gave them a vigorous applause.

"Let us now give a hand to Steve Roberts who did a phenomenal job in preparing this report". Next, Steve stood up and got a warm hand.

"Finally, I want to thank John Viterbi for his able and wise guidance of this team."

Everyone clapped their hands when John stood up.

John Williams continued,

"Dr.Ravi, what I would request you is to keep this great team together to watch "Saturn Computing". We would provide offices here for Harrish and Veena and they could come every week. Young as they are, this small company, would give them incredible training. Steve and John could help them. This would reduce your load as the Chairman."

Dr.Ravi thought for a moment. Everyone was silent and expecting. Dr.Ravi felt that John was right. This would give excellent training for Harrish and Veena. Steve and John Viterbi would give them guidance. Moreover, John Williams was taking charge and Jack Daman would be here every week. He felt "Saturn Computing" badly needed a Chairman now and above all, Gigabit had invested in Saturn.

Therefore, Dr.Ravi said, "John, I see your desparate need and hence I agree to be Chairman temporarily, though I have little time to spare. I could agree to have Veena and Harrish work here every week and let John Viterbi, Steve Roberts guide them. But, John, you have to watch the store diligently."

John Williams agreed heartily. The entire Board and investors clapped their hands cheerfully and now there was a positive, hopeful mood in the room.

John Williams continued, "We have four unfinished items. First, we need to prepare a press release and I would work on it tonight and issue it tomorow. Second, we should contact our key customers; Dr.Chang and I would work on it tomorow— may be, we would visit a few of them either with Dr.Ravi or John Viterbi participating on the telephone. Third, we must inform the other investors immediately; I request Dr.Chang and Jack Daman to call tonight. Finally, we need to tell the employees."

Dr.Chang interrupted,

"John, during lunch time, the employees noticed a number of Board members. Hence, big rumors are floating around."

John answered,

"Dr.Chang, why don't you set up an all employee meeting in the auditorium at four thirty, half hour from now? Let us introduce the new Chairman."

The board meeting concluded shortly and key directors including John Williams proceeded to the auditorium.

The atmosphere in the auditorium was very tense and everyone seemed very very anxious. John Williams quickly took to the podium and said,

"Ladies & Gentleman, let me be quick and direct. Due to differences of opinion with the Board of Directors, Jack Taylor resigned today. The Board is extremely pleased to tell you that Dr.Ravi, whom most of you know, the Founder-Chairman of Gigabit inc has agreed to be our Chairman. Here is Dr.Ravi."

As Dr.Ravi was alighting the steps of the podium, the entire audience stood up and broke into cheerful applause. They gave Dr.Ravi a standing ovation. John Williams was ecstatic seeing the spontaneous enthusiasm of the employees. Utmost touching was the tumultuous welcome to Dr.Ravi.

Dr.Ravi spoke briefly, "Thank you, thank you for your confidence. As you know, I came here last year and was impressed by your products. So Gigabit invested in Saturn Computing. Unfortunately, Jack Taylor resigned today and I have agreed to be your interim Chairman. Dr.Chang, your president, would continue in his post. As I am very busy, two of my esteemed employees would be here every week. One is Dr.Harrish Sridhar. We just promoted him to be Gigabit Vice President last night. We have been so busy that I have not told him till now."

Everyone clapped their hands as Harrish stood up smilingly.

"Second, is Ms.Veena Ravi, again newly appointed Vice President."

Veena was also cheered.

"Ably asisting them would be Steve Roberts, President Roberts & Co and John Viterbi, my senior counsel. John Williams had agreed to be Vice Chairman and would play an active role. He would be here every other week. Jack Daman, another important Director, would work here every week. We are determined to take Saturn Computing to a new level of achievement and we want your dedicated continued support."

The employees felt charged and again gave Dr.Ravi a standing ovation. The atmosphere in the auditorium became wildly cheerful. Dr.Chang then outlined some of the immediate projects and challenges. The meeting was adjourned around 6pm.

Dr.Ravi took Harrish and Veena aside for a moment and smilingly shook Harrish's hand and said, "Congratulations, Harrish, wonderful job."

Then he said, "Great job, Veena". He gave the both their new Gigabit cards with their designations as Vice President. "These cards would be useful to you tomorrow as you meet Saturn Computing management. Please stay here a few days and keep me posted."

John Williams stopped by and said, "Dr.Ravi, it is getting late for your flight"and he escorted Dr.Ravi to the car. Some of the Board members followed them.

John Viterbi, Steve Roberts, Harrish and Veena were walking behind. Steve said to Harrish smilingly, "Harrish, I have to go home now and take my wife to dinner. I have been extremely busy and away too long."

Harrish replied with a laugh, "Steve, that is the most important job for you now."

Veena and John joined the laughter. Dr.Ravi and John Viterbi left. Steve said to Harrish and Veena,.

"Will see you guys, Friday. Tomorrow, I have to catch up on other things. At 10am.on Friday, we would meet with Jack Daman to go over the new financial statements—will see you then." Steve waved goodbye and literally ran to his car.

When almost everyone was gone, John Williams came to Veena and Harrish and said,

"I cannot thank you both enough. A malignant cancer was spreading in Saturn and thanks for detecting and helping us to remove it. I have your bags secured in Dr.Chang's office. We will arrange for the company car and please go and have a nice dinner."

Veena looked at Harrish and said with a smile, "Harrish, I am so famished. I was so nervous that I could not eat lunch. I did not know what stunt Jack Taylor might pull."

"Me, too Venna "replied Harrish with a grin.

Together, tired but happy, they left for dinner.

Chapter - 40

Around 5pm next week, Latha called Kumar and said anxiously,

"Kumar, I want to talk to you immediately. Could we meet on the banks of Charles River opposite Sloan school?"

Kumar replied, "Yes, Latha, I will join you in five minutes."

Latha was standing, watching the beautiful Charles River when Kumar came, and asked "Latha, what is up? Why is the alarm in your voice?"

Latha answered,

"Kumar, my mom just called. The Senator's office just called her and said that the Senator cannot come to the book function on that day. Utmost sad are we."

"Oh! That is terrible. What happened?"

"Well, the Senator has to go to Europe on an emergency NATO issue; he is the Chairman of the Senate Armed Services Committee. That trip cannot be changed."

"Latha, that is awful. What are you going to do? Change the date or find another distinguished chief guest on the same day."

"Kumar, it is impossible to get a chief guest of that stature in three weeks- — it is impossible to get such a guest on that specific day. Therefore, we have to postpone the function."

"Oh! That is horrible, Latha –but when?"

"Almost two and a half months away."

"Latha, have you informed everyone?"

"No, Kumar, I just got the call. My mom is calling all the speakers."

"Okay, Latha, I can call a few people. I have my cell phone here –whom do you want me to call?"

"Kumar, please inform Harrish and request him to tell Geetha before she departs."

"Okay, I will call my mom also. Why don't you call Veena?" said Kumar.

"Okay" said Latha

Kumar called Harrish,

"Harrish, an unfortunate thing happened. The Senator cannot make the book function and hence the function is postponed. Please inform Geetha before she leaves".

Harrish was stunned and agreed to call Geetha immediately. Kumar called his mom who decided instantly to go to Syracuse to help Chitra. Latha called Veena who agreed to tell her parents.

Kumar asked, "Latha, don't we need to cancel the auditorium? Do we know the new date? Could we try to book the hall for that date?"

Latha answered, "Kumar, let me call my mom now to find the answer."

Latha's mom said on the phone, "Latha, I got three dates from the Senator's office. The other speakers can make two of those dates. Please call the auditorium."

Kumar called the hall front office and quickly he booked it for one of those dates. Latha called her mom and informed her of the new date. Next Kumar and Latha discussed further the implications of the date change. After half hour, Latha said to Kumar, "Kumar, thanks a lot for responding so quickly. I feel so much better after talking to you. Now, I am late for a seminar——will see you soon."

Saying this, she ran across the Memorial drive. Kumar called out to Latha and said, "Latha please wait; I will come with you." And he dashed across the Memorial drive.

As Latha tried to turn, she heard a loud thundering noise of the car brakes. She saw a car coming to a fullstop with screeching brakes and Kumar was lying in front of the car. There was blood all over. Latha ran towards Kumar. "Oh Kumar, are you alive? " Gone was her usual composure. Tears were rolling down her cheeks. She came close to him and he was in a pool of blood. She knelt down and holding Kumar's hands said, "Kumar, how badly are you hurt?"

Kumar was conscious but he could not speak. Gone was his winning smile—his face showed intense pain. He was slowly losing consciousness.

Latha pleaded with tears. "Kumar, Kumar, don't leave me, don't leave me—please—don't leave me. Please stay awake."

Kumar tried to be awake but the pain was intense and he slowly closed his eyes. A small crowd gathered around and some one had called "911". Latha heard the sound of the distant siren, squeezed Kumar's hand, and begged, "Kumar, Kumar, the ambulance is coming. We would be in the hospital in a minute – please be awake, Kumar."

Every second seemed like an hour——finally, the ambulance arrived and the paramedicals rushed to Kumar. They examined his wounds, bandaged, and said to Latha, "Madam, his bodily injuries are not that severe –he has no broken bones – but he may have a head injury. The hospital would do a CATSCAN. Let us rush him to the hospital."

They hurriedly transported him to the ambulance and with Latha seated next to him drove fast to the emergency ward of the Mass General Hospital across the river. They wheeled Kumar to the emergency ward and then after a brief examination hurried him to the "CATSCAN" room.

Latha sat alone in the emergency ward –with tears in her eyes, she thought of Kumar –she liked him immensely –his sweet and cheerful smile and spirit was so full of support and strength. So far, she had taken him for granted – "Oh, my God! Am I going to lose him?"

She prayed fervently for his survival.

Suddenly, she thought she should call his parents. But she did not have their telephone numbers handy. Hence, she called Harrish. With quivering voice she said, "Harrish, this is Latha."

"Hi Latha –what is up? You sound so anxious. I just called Geetha."

"Harrish, this call is not about the Book Function. But, this is very very serious ——Kumar was hit by a car."

"Oh, my God!! Is he alive?"

Latha cried a little;

"Harrish, he is in the hospital now; they suspect head injury."

"Oh, my God! Latha, Kumar is my most dear friend –I cannot lose him –oh my God! What a tragedy! I am leaving right now and catching the next flight."

"Harrish, Please –we need to call his parents. I don't have their numbers here."

"No problem, Latha –I will call them now."

"Thanks, Harish –Tell them they are doing CATSCAN now."

"Okay, Latha, please call me every half hour."

Harrish was in a state of shock. He literally adored Kumar. "Such a dear friend. It is incredible that he is hit by a car –Oh my God."

Tears rolled down his cheeks. –He started praying for Kumar.

He immediately remembered that he should call Mrs.Ram on her cell phone.

He composed himself as Kumar had warned him about his mother. She could be very emotional. Of course, anyone would be now.

"Mrs.Ram, this is Harrish" said Harrish calmly, controlling his emotions.

Mrs.Ram was cheerful and said,

"Harrish, how are you? I am on my way to the airport to go to Syracuse. By the way, have you heard about the date change for the Book Function?"

Harrish replied, " Yes, I know about the Book Function date change. Mrs..Ram, by the way, are you driving or going by a cab?"

"By cab. Harrish, why are you asking that question? You sound very very serious. Harrish, what is going on?" asked Mrs.Ram alarmingly.

Harrish decided to be slow and deliberate and not shock her.

"Well, Mrs.Ram; please don't panic. Talking to Latha, I just found out that Kumar is not well."

"Harrish, what is wrong? Is he sick or does he have stomach cramps?"

"No, Mrs.Ram. He fell down and has no broken bones; all his bodily injuries are minor. He is in the hospital being bandaged."

Mrs.Ram asked, "Harrish, could I call him now?"

"Not really, Mrs.Ram. When he fell down, he hit his head and there is a head injury. They are doing CATSCAN now."

Mrs.Ram hit the roof.

"CATSCAN!! Harrish, tell me the truth. Remember I know all about "CATSCAN"——my husband is a neurologist. What is going on, Harrish?"

She screamed. Harrish now told her everything.

Mrs.Ram asked, "Harrish, please give me Latha's number and I will call her now. I am going to Boston now."

Harrish gave her Latha's number and got from her Dr.Ram's number –the best number to reach him. Harrish also assured her that he would change her ticket.

Before reaching Dr.Ram, Harrish quickly called Veena and informed her. Veena was stunned but she agreed to book Harrish's ticket and also Dr.& Mrs.Ram's through her secretarial help. Veena also decided to go to Boston. She called her mom who also wanted to accompany her to Boston to comfort Radha.

A Tender Melody

Harrish instantly phoned Dr.Ram and informed him of all the details. Dr.Ram called quickly the head of the emergency department, Dr.Sam swift, to get all the medical details.

Dr.Swift told Dr.Ram, "The CATSCAN has just been completed and it looks like "Epidural Himatoma" –an artery is bleeding in the brain. Hence, Kumar is being wheeled into the Neurosurgery Operation Theater now."

Dr.Ram urgently called his friend, the Chairman of the Neurosurgery Dept at Mass General, Dr.Gary Snowden. They did residency together in Mass General.

Dr.Ram said," Gary, Hi, this is Ram."

"Hi, Ram, how are you?"

"Gary, I need a favor from you right now. As you may recall, my son, Kumar, is a Phd student at MIT. Tragically, he got hit by a car half hour ago. He is in your hospital now and after CATSCAN, they suspect "Epidural Himatoma". He is in your Operation Theater. Could you please examine him and let me know? I am on my way to Boston."

Dr.Snowden replied, "Oh my God! Ram, Iam so sorry to hear this. I assure you, I, myself will go to the Operation Theater and give personal care to your son. Please call me in two hours. Please stop by my office when you come here. I will be working late tonight"

Dr.Ram immediately called Radha –"Radha"

As soon soon as Radha heard his voice, she broke down,

"Ram, what will happen to my dear dear Kumar?"

Dr.Ram had a tear or two,

"Radha, don't worry. I just called the Chairman of the Neurosurgery Department in Mass General, Dr.Snowden. He is one of the top Neurosurgerons in the world. He will personally take over Kumar's case. We know each other for thirty years –I was a Neurology resident and he was a Neurosurgery resident at Mass General."

"Radha, he is in the Operation Theater now. One of his blood vessels in the brain is bleeding and they will stop it now. Hopefully, there is no further damage."

"Ram, how do we know that?"

"Radha, we don't know for sure. But his other bodily injuries are minor. So, we suspect no big injury to the brain."

"Ram, when would we know that for sure?"

"Radha, when Dr.Snowden looks into the brain, he would know the extent of the damage. But, even he would not know how the functions like speech are affected. We might have to wait for a few days."

"Oh God, would Kumar become speechless?"

"Radha, please don't panick now. It is too early to worry. We simply have to wait. But, it does not seem like a big accident"

Radha screamed with tears, "Ram, what do you mean –not a big accident – he is in the Neurosurgery Operation Theater –how bigger can it get –except death?"

"True, Radha. It is not small –but remember, I have been in this business for thirty years –please believe me –it may not be that bad. But, I cannot give you hundred percent guarantee now."

"Ram, what can you be sure of now?"

"Radha, numer one –he would be alive. Number two –many of his functions would be normal. But, there could be some damage."

"Okay I am so so sad about my dear dear Kumar –let me pray –Ram, where are you now?"

"Radha, I am on the way to the airport."

Veena had arranged quickly, as was her habit, all the tickets and conveyed to everyone their flight details. They were all converging towards Boston—— Dr & Mrs.Ram from Atlanta, Mrs.Aruna Ravi and Veena from San Francisco, Harrish from Los Angeles and Mrs.Chitra Gangadharan (whom Veena had called) from Syracuse –all extremely worried and concerned about Kumar.

Chapter - 41

Latha was pacing up and down outside the Operation Theater waiting room. She was all alone and extremely worried, "Would Kumar be alright? Would he survive this? Would there be permanent damage? What would he lose—speech, coordination, thinking capacity, memory———? "

She was extremely anxious. As she was pacing this, she saw Dr.Ram and Mrs.Ram coming to the Operation Theater. She ran towards them and hugged Mrs.Ram. They were both in tears. Utmost sad were they! "What would happen to Kumar?" was their common grief.

"Latha, tell me everything "said Mrs.Ram and held Latha's hands. As they sat down, Dr.Ram said, "Radha, Latha; I am going to the Operation Theater and I have already prearranged everything with Dr.Snowden. I want to see the operation."

Saying this, Dr.Ram went into the Operation Theater. After being properly scrubbed and dressed, he entered the Operating room. Though Dr.Ram had witnessed hundreds of operations, when he saw his dear son, Kumar, lying there on the operation table, he was totally overwhelmed. Tears started gushing. He stood still for a few minutes to control his emotions. Then slowly, he walked towards the operation table and Dr.Snowden said, "Ram, we have stopped the bleeding of this particular artery. There does not appear to be any severe damage. Most of the functions should recover soon. But, as you know, this is on the left side and speech may be affected. However, it might recover also."

Dr.Ram looked at Kumar's brain. He did not see severe damage. It looked almost normal. He felt quite hopeful. But, he knew that nothing could be predicted with certainty now. They just had to wait for a few days. Soon, Dr.Ram left the Operation Theater and the operation team started to close the brain.

Dr.Ram hurried to Radha and Latha to convey the news, "Radha, Latha I was in the Operation Theater at the right time. I saw Kumar's brain.........they have stopped the bleeding. There does not seem to be much damage. It looks almost normal. So most of the functions should resume. But being on the left side, speech may be impeded but may become okay later. High on your worry list is his recovery. I am very hopeful that he would be almost normal."

Radha hugged him,"Ram, thanks a lot for this good news. I will keep praying for his total recovery." Latha hugged Dr. & Mrs.Ram. Latha also felt much relieved but they could not be too sure now.

An hour and a half later, Kumar was wheeled into the Intensive Care Unit. He was still unconscious and Latha, Radha and Dr.Ram stood around his bed. They were waiting for him to regain his consciousness——they were very worried and afraid. Gone was their cool; they were tense and anxious.

At this time, Chitra Gangadharan arrived; Latha ran to her mother and hugged her and cried saying "mom". Radha turned around and said "Chitra". They hugged each other with tears in their eyes. Only a mother could feel the anguish of the other mother.

Kumar was still unconscious and they did a "CATSCAN" again. Gone was his blood clot and there was no further bleeding in the brain.

An hour passed and it was like a day. The anxiety level was intense. Kumar slowly opened his eyes and everyone said "Kumar". Kumar seemed to recognise his mom and there was a smile when he saw Latha. The doctor-in-care asked Kumar to wiggle his toes and move his fingers. Kumar wiggled his toes and moved his fingers. Dr.Ram was thrilled.

He said to Radha, "Radha, this means that he can hear, understand, process the information, give command to his bodily organs and they obey. This is indeed huge!"

Radha was relieved but she asked, "Ram, would he talk?"

"Radha, we have to wait and see. We all take for granted the basic functions of the brain. But it is indeed miraculous. On the otherhand, when something goes wrong, it is indeed so tough to bring it back to normalcy."

Latha asked anxiously, "Dr.Ram, how long would it take to get back speech?"

"Latha, we would know in a few days how deeply speech is affected. We have to wait patiently."

Kumar closed his eyes and went back to sleep.

Dr.Ram turned to Latha and said, "Latha, you have been facing this ordeal, mostly alone for six hours. Please go and eat something. May be, Radha and Chitra, you can accompany her. I will watch Kumar –he would probably sleep for some more time. We all need to plan for the longhaul."

Radha looked at Latha, and she looked so tired and worn out. Radha saw the logic of Dr.Ram's comment and entreated Latha to go with her for some food. Chitra, Radha and Latha left for the cafeteria.

After two hours, while the four of them were sitting around Kumar, they heard footsteps. It was Harrish. When Harrish saw Kumar lying down with all the tubes around him, he became emotional and tears flowed. Dr.Ram hugged him and informed him of all the details. Harrish went close to Kumar, held his hands and said,"Kumar, dear Kumar – this is your dear Harrish- How are you?" A few minutes later, Kumar opened his eyes and seemed to smile. He also put a little pressure on Harrish's hand. But Kumar was too tired and went back to sleep.

Within half-hour, late in the night, Veena and Aruna Ravi arrived.

Latha embraced Veena and was happy to see her. Aruna hugged Radha and Chitra. Both Veena and Mrs. Aruna Ravi were sad to see Kumar with bandages and with monitors all around him.

Dr.Ram said encouraging words. Kumar was still sleeping.

Dr.Ram said, " Kumar would not wake up for a while. Why don't you all go to your hotel and get some sleep. I will stay here."

Harrish said," Dr.Ram, I slept on the flight a little. I am on West Coast time. I could stay here. You must be totally exhausted after such an excruciating day. You also need to take care of yourself and plan for the longterm." Radha saw Harrish's point. Dr.Ram looked rather tired. She wanted Dr.Ram to stay healthy during this long ordeal. So she persuaded him to take rest. Dr. Ram then instructed Harrish as to what to expect.

Venna said," I will keep company to Harrish. I am not sleepy either."

Aruna Ravi also decided to stay. With the three of them near Kumar'side, Radha felt much better in leaving Kumar. After they left, at Veena's request, Harrish narrated all he knew to Veena and Aruna Ravi.

Kumar did not wake up till early morning. He groaned a little and slowly opened his eyes. He saw Veena and gently squeezed her hand. He was still very weak and was groggy. A doctor came and gave him some neurological tests. Kumar did quite well. Only speech did not come yet; no word would come out.

Kumar was taken for another CATSCAN. At this time, Dr & Mrs. Ram arrived. They thanked Harrish, Veena and Aruna who brought Dr.Ram up to date. Dr. Ram felt good that Kumar recognized Veena.

When Kumar came back from CATSCAN, the doctor- in- charge told Dr. Ram, " Kumar is responding very well. But, there is a small contusion in his left temporal lobe which may make him drowsy and may explain his loss of speech. This may go away in a few days."

Latha and Chitra Gangadharan arrived soon. Latha looked rested; Radha and Dr. Ram derived strength from their presence. Radha was touched by the affection Latha had for Kumar. Dr. Ram explained the current status of Kumar. Latha asked, " What is the prognosis?"

Dr.Ram replied, "Kumar will definitely walk, eat and may write— but speech may not recover soon."

Latha was so sad. Kumar would talk mile a minute and he gave her so much strength and cheer with his smiling talk. Oh! Would she miss his speech!!

Chapter - 42

Geetha was preparing seriously her music for the Newyork Book Function when she received a call early in the morning from Harrish," Geetha, this is Harrish, I have not-so-good news, The Book Function has been postponed because the Senator could not make it."

"Harrish, this is not so bad for me. I could stay here with my mom."said Geetha.

Geetha was happy. But, this was shortlived as she received another call from Harrish informing her of Kumar's accident. Geetha was sad as she liked Kumar. She immediately called Dr.Natchikethas. They both talked about Kumar and especially the hard blow this would be for Dr.Ram and Mrs.Ram.

Later in the evening, Dr.Natchikethas, Geetha, Parvathi and Lakshmi discussed Kumar's injury. Dr.Natchikethas was worried because brain injury was unpredictable. He wondered whether Geetha should go immediately. Soon, the consensus emerged that Geetha should leave the next day. They all felt that Dr. Ram and Mrs. Ram had been so supportive of Geetha's music that she should visit them in their hour of crisis. Moreover, they all loved Kumar.

Back in Boston, Kumar was still asleep. Dr. Ram, Radha, Latha and Chitra were seated around him. They were anxious but less than yesterday. Kumar had been responding well. The whole day and night passed like this with everyone taking turns. Kumar would wake up for a few minutes and perform a few neurological functions and then go back to sleep.

Next day around three in the afternoon, all of them were together. Harrish, Veena, Latha, Chitra, Aruna, Radha and Dr.Ram were around Kumar. Harrish went near Kumar, held his hands and said,"Kumar, Kumar please wake up. We all want to talk to you".

Kumar slowly opened his eyes and he looked around. He seemed less sleepy.

Radha asked," Kumar dear-would you like a cup of tea?" Kumar nodded his head. They got him a cup of tea. Kumar was able to hold the tea cup and saucer and drink tea slowly. He looked normal and they were all thrilled.

Then, Kumar wanted to say something. No word would come out. He could talk in his mind but nothing came out. Dr.Ram said, " Kumar, let us see whether you could write."

A Tender Melody

He got a slate and a small chalk piece. Kumar tried to write. To the surprise of everyone, he was able to write slowly. He wrote," Harrish, how are you?"

Harrish was excited that Kumar could write and replied, "Kumar, I am fine. The real question is how are you? How do you feel? Are you aware of what happened?"

Kumar wrote slowly," I feel less sleepy. Yesterday I was drowsy all day. Dad, why can't I talk?"

"Kumar dear, you had a head injury. It is on the left side where speech functions are located. It would take sometime before speech recovers."

Kumar wrote, "All I remember, is talking to Latha. .Latha, what happened?"

Latha said almost with tears, "Kumar, so much happened so quickly. I am still overwhelmed. The toughest moment was when I saw you lying down on the road in a pool of blood. I didn't know whether you were alive or dead." Then slowly controlling her emotions, she narrated all that happened.

Kumar listened intently and was so surprised. Kumar wrote, "Oh, my God! Latha, you really went through hell."

"May be – but, Kumar, you actually went to hell and came back! We were so scared for the last three days."

Kumar wrote, "Dad, what is the prognosis?"

Dr. Ram replied," Kumar, it is excellent so far. You have recovered so many functions that it is absolutely thrilling. Kumar, you could even write."

Kumar felt rather tired and wrote that he wants to rest. He closed his eyes and soon went to sleep.

Next day, Kumar got up in the morning but was awake only for a short time. Around noon, he was really active. He saw his mom and wrote," Mom, could I have a cup of coffee?"

As Kumar was sipping his coffee, Veena, Aruna Ravi and Harrish arrived. Kumar had a big smile for Veena. He wrote, " Veena, How are you?"

Veena smiled back, went near him and held his hand and said, " I am fine Kumar. How are you, today?"

Kumar wrote slowly," I am feeling much better. The pain from bodily injuries are less; I only feel a little pain in the shoulder and the leg. I think Iam going to be alright except for speech. For speech, we have to wait and see."

Veena said, "Kumar, you do look great. You look almost normal today. We were so worried about you – You look so good. It is indeed a miracle."

Kumar had a big smile. Kumar then asked on slate, " Hey, you guys, Veena, Harrish; what happened to Jack Taylor? You guys didn't call me."

Dr. Ram signalled to Harrish and Veena to engage Kumar in a long conversation. Harrish said, " Kumar, we would love to bring you upto date. Please tell us what you remember."

Kumar told on the slate," Harrish, you got Steve Roberts to write the report on the subsidaries of Saturn Computing."

Harrish was totally astounded. " Kumar, you remember very well."

Dr.Ram was mightily pleased. This meant Kumar's memory was intact – he could recall perfectly. This augured well for Kumar resuming his studies and career.

For the next two hours, Veena and Harrish, fresh from their triumph, related the entire episode with enthusiasm, humor and gusto. Kumar cheerd them on laughing heartily at the jokes and sighing at the tough parrt of the story. Radha and Latha were touched by Kumar's emotional response. He was back as the cheerful, jolly Kumar. Dr. Ram was watching Kumar intensely. He was happy that Kumar was responding well emotionally.

Kumar wrote," John williams has handled superbly Jack Taylor in the Board meeting."

Veena and Harrish heartily agreed.

Kumar looked at Mrs.Ravi and wrote, "Mrs.Ravi, I am so proud of Dr.Ravi."

Aruna came close to Kumar and said with emotion," Kumar, right now, I am so proud of you. You are battling bravely this injury."

Kumar held her hands for a minute and thanked her with a smile. Then, Kumar looked at Veena and Harrish and wrote with a twinkling smile, " Hey, you guys are great partners in victory—may, be, you would be great partners in life."

Then he laughed.

Veena colored a little and said with a smile," Kumar, your mischief is back in full swing!!"

In fact, Kumar might have been closer to truth than either Harrish or Veena would acknowledge. This point was not lost on Aruna Ravi who wondered whether Harrish or Veena realized how close they were.

A Tender Melody

Kumar looked at Mrs.Gangadharan and wrote, "Are you having the function on that new date?"

Chitra said,"Yes, Kumar. The invitations would go out tomorrow. Two days ago when you did not wake up I thought of cancelling it."

"Please don't cancel. I will be alright. It is almost two and a half months away. It means so much to Dr.Gangadharan. By the way, the book looks so great—Latha showed it to me. Now, I have to read it!"

The conversation took its toll on Kumar; he bcame rather tired and went back to sleep. Everyone was happy about his progress.

Harrish went to the airport to meet Geetha. When Geetha saw Harrish, she enquired anxiously, "Harrish, how is Kumar?"

"Geetha, he is recovering well. He is able to write slowly. He cannot talk yet—he has not walked either. But his functions are becoming normal."

After a quick shower in her hotel, she rushed to the hospital to see Kumar. When Kumar saw Geetha, he was stunned since no one had told him about her visit. With a huge surprised smile, he wrote,"Geetha, what a surprise!"

"Kumar, when we heard about your accident, we were so worried. I had to come and see you. Dr.Natchikethas promised to take care of mom. You look good; actually, you look great!"

Kumar wrote, "Geetha, you look beautiful"

Geetha smiled, "Kumar, you are normal enough to comment on my beauty—Thanks!"

They talked a while about Kumar's health. Then Kumar asked, "How is your mom?"

" She has recovered so well that I could leave her and come and see you."

"Your mother is dear to you."

"Yes, she is very very dear to me."

"How is Dr.Natchikethas?"

" He is fine and really taking good care of my mom."

Kumar then wrote,"Is he still sitting in front row and listening to your music? Sometimes, I wonder whether he is appreciating your beauty or listening to your music?"

As he gave her the slate, he had a big mischievous smile.

When Geetha read it, she blushed. How true it was! Kumar did not know—he had already proposed and she had not accepted it. She could not answer Kumar for a second. Kumar quickly realized that he had touched a very sensitive nerve.

He wrote apologetically, "Geetha, I was just joking!"

Geetha quickly recovered and smiled.

Chapter - 43

Kumar got up rather early in the morning *i.e.,* around 8 am, and he asked his mom for a cup of coffee. Latha came as he was sipping his coffee. Latha was surprised to see Kumar get up so early and asked with cheer, "Kumar you are up early. How are you?"

Kumar wrote with a smile, "Latha , I am feeling great. Even my pain in the leg has subsided."

Dr.Ram then said with anxiety, "Kumar, you can then try walking."

Kumar was excited and wrote "Dad, that is a great idea!"

Dr.Ram came near Kumar and holding his dad, Kumar put his left leg down. Then he slowly brought his right leg down and started to exert some preassure. He felt some pain but he persisted. He was able to take a few steps limping on his dad's shoulders. Soon, gone was his pain; he was able to walk slowly after some effort. Latha could not believe it. Kumar was walking!!

Chitra looked at Kumar and said with admiration and joy, "Kumar, you are walking. One by one, your functions are becoming normal. You can walk, eat, write and read. Only speech needs some work. I am sure your speech would recover soon."

Turning to Radha, she said, "Radha I have to get back. Dr.Gangadharan needs me."

Radha hugged Chitra and thanked her for coming. Chitra hugged Kumar and was in tears.

Kumar wrote, "Mrs Gangadharan thanks a million for coming. I will definetly come for the Book Function."Kumar held her hands with emotion. Latha embraced her mom and Chitra left soon.

Radha became a bit emotional after her dear friend left. She turned to Dr.Ram and said "Ram ,could we leave for Atlanta with Kumar? He is becoming almost normal."

Dr. Ram agreed, "Radha that is a wonderful thought! Let me check with the doctors. I have tons of contacts at Emory University-especially speech therapists." Dr. Ram left to consult the doctors.

Then Geetha came. Kumar was delighted to see Geetha. Kumar wrote with a big grin, "Geetha how are you?" Kumar proudly wrote "Geetha, I can walk. Let me show you." Kumar started to walk with a cane. Geetha exclaimed, "Kumar, you are walking almost normally!" Kumar smiled with pride.

Dr. Ram came and said excitedly, "Radha, the doctors said we could leave tomorrow." Radha was thrilled "Great! Let us leave in the afternoon." Geetha was happy to hear that and said, "That is wonderful. I also want to get back to my mom. I am so happy to see Kumar recovering well."

While Kumar, Geetha and Latha were chit chatting, Harrish, Veena and Aruna Ravi came and were exuberant to see Kumar walk with a cane.

Harrish said with awe, "Kumar, that is superb, you are almost normal."

Radha said, "We are planning to take Kumar to Atlanta tomorrow."

They all exclaimed with joy, "Tomorrow!"

Kumar wrote to Veena, "Where are you both going? Los Angeles or San Francisco?"

Veena replied, "We are going to Saturn Computing in Los Angeles. We have lots of work there."

Kumar asked on slate, "What work?"

Veena replied, "You know that Jack Taylor was trying to make the company profitable using fraudulent subsidianes. But the basic problem remains. The company's expenses are high. Expense increases as fast as the revenue. So, the company is not that profitable. We are investigating several ways to reduce the expenses."

Kumar wrote, "Such as?"

Veena answered, "For example, Harrish found out that software expenses are increasing astronomically. Therefore, we are investigating whether we could do the high speed processor software in V-digitronics in Chennai. This would reduce our expenses."

Kumar said on paper, "That is an excellent idea!" Kumar, Veena and Harrish talked for a while about Saturn Computing and V-digitronics. At the end, Aruna Ravi came close to Radha held her hands and said with feeling, "Radha, I am so glad that Kumar is recovering so well. I hope his speech resumes soon. Radha I am thinking of leaving this evening."

Kumar wrote, "Mrs Ravi, Thanks a lot for coming. It meant a lot to me. I am feeling much better. By the way, could you record your lessons to Veena and Harrish on Carnatic music and send it to me. I also want to learn carnatic music. I would have some time now."

Geetha exclaimed, "Is Veena learning music?"

Harrish answered, " Yes, she could sing very well. Music comes so naturally to her."

Geetha said, "That is marvelous."

Mrs Ravi said to Kumar, "I would definitely do that, Kumar. Moreover, I would come to Atlanta and spend a week with you and teach you music."

"That would be lovely, Mrs. Ravi" wrote Kumar.

At the Logan airport, Kumar, Dr.Ram and Radha were all set to go through the security to their gate. They said "good bye" to Harrish, Veena and Latha. Harrish hugged Kumar and they had a tear or two in their eyes. Kumar held Veena's hand with a lot of emotion. Finally, he came close to Latha and clasped her hands first and then wrote "Latha, I can't thank you enough for what you have done!" Latha was a bit overwhelmed as she saw Kumar almost normal. A few tears rolled down her cheeks. They hugged and Kumar left.

Veena, Harrish and Latha chitchatted for some time about Kumar and then Veena and Harrish moved towards the security gate saying that they should meet in Atlanta in two weeks to cheer up Kumar.

After Harrish and Veena left for Los Angeles, Latha returned to her room in MIT. But she could not stay there for a minute. It was too confining; she needed space for moving around. So she decided to take a long walk along the Charles River. It was a beautiful evening.

During her walk,she came near the Sloan school. All the painful memories of Kumar's accident came gushing down in her mind. She could hear the screeching brakes and she could see Kumar lying down on the road in a pool of blood. Tears came unsolicited, "Oh God! Kumar could have died! Life and death are so close, so near each other, so scary! Death can take every thing away in a second. Life is so precious. Each day is so precious."

"Thank God, the ambulance came so quickly and Kumar was saved. The neurosurgury went well. Kumar now can walk, eat, read and write. It is indeed miraculous. Above all, Kumar's personality is coming back; he is jovial, lively, fun loving and cheerful."

"Boy, I am already missing Kumar. The hospital was so lively and cheerful the last two days though he was not well. I have to think more why am I missing him so much? I do not know. I need time to ponder over this issue. The accident has opened my eyes – life is so short. I can't wait for ever for the Phd to be over. I need to make important life decisions now."

Thinking thus, she reached her room but she soon got caught up in her work that were in arrears.

Chapter - 45

Geetha boarded the plane in Boston for London and then on to Chennai. While she was flying, she had some time to think. When flying into Boston, she was too worried about Kumar. Now, she was more relaxed because Kumar was recovering fast. Her mind drifted to her mom. "Thank God, she is also recovering beautifully." She thought of the night when her mom had intense chest pain. "What a nightmare! But, it was really God's blessings that Dr.Natchikethas arrived so quickly and took charge. Oh ! what a nightmare it was! The whole night, Dr.Natchiketas operated on her and was indeed successful." A feeling of gratitude overwhelmed her. Now he was again in charge of her mom. She decided that she would thank him personally for his care of her mom.

Then, the comment of Kumar flashed through her mind. "Was Dr.Natchikethas enjoying her music or was he appreciating her beauty?" She could not help smiling. "Boy! Isn't Kumar's comment sharp? Oh! I need to think about Dr.Natchikethas' proposal. I have to be ready with an answer if he were ask to again."

Then, she listed a few of the pressing questions. "Am I ready for marriage? How would that affect my career? Music is a tough field and self-made. It is not like going to office from 9 to 5. It demands total dedication."

"Would marrying a surgeon give us time together? My career would take me to different cities. He would spend a lot of time in the hospital, in the Operation Theater."

"Do I really like Dr.Natchikethas well enough to marry him?"

"Above all, does Dr.Natchikethas still want to marry me?"

This last question bothered her quite a bit. "Is he still interested after her refusal?" She decided to ignore that question for now, as it was not in her hands. However, since Dr.Natchikethas had served her mom so effectively, she had to give a thoughtful answer if he were to propose again.

She spent considerable time on the flight pondering over these weighty questions. When she landed in Chennai, Pavitran, her brother, came to the airport to pick her up. The first question she asked anxiously was " Pavitran, how is mom?"

"Geetha, she is recovering so well that we could go home in another week."

"Pavitran, that is fabulous."

Pavitran continued, "Dr.Natchikethas has gone to Bombay to attend a medical conference and would be back in two days, Saturday evening. His assistant comes every day to check mom."

Geetha was happy to hear that. Dr.Natchikethas was indeed keeping his promise to her that he would watch her mom. She was also very glad that she did not have to face Dr.Natchikethas now. She simply was not ready.

Next two days passed happily for Geetha. Her mom was progressing wonderfully. She was thrilled.

Later, on Saturday evening, Dr.Natchikethas arrived. It was his custom to examine Parvathi, Geetha's mom, on Sunday morning and spend some relaxed time with her. Therefore, on Sunday morning, he came to Parvathi's room to examine her. Geetha was not there; just Parvathi and Dr.Natchikethas. Usually after the examination, they both chitchatted relaxedly – they both enjoyed it.

Today after the medical check up, Parvathi asked, "Dr.Natchikethas, may I ask you a question?"

Dr.Natchikethas simply said, " Of course, Aunty- you always ask good questions"

Parvathi asked, "Dr.Natchikethas lately, I have been wondering about this topic. You are a surgeon in good standing. You have sold V- digitronics and hence somewhat relaxed. Have you thought about your marriage?"

Geetha was in the kitchen helping with the breakfast preperation when she heard from Vimala that Dr.Natchikethas was with her mom. She hurried to ask Dr.Natchikethas a few questions about her mom's health. She entered the side room, the music room, by another door. Then she heard this question from her mom to Dr.Natchikethas "Have you thought about your marriage?" Neither

Dr.Natchikethas nor her mom could see her. The question stunned her and could not move for a few minutes.

She heard Dr.Natchikethas' answer, "Yes, aunty, I have thought long and hard about my marriage. Actually, I have proposed to a beautiful and talented woman."

Parvathi asked anxiously, "What did she say?"

Dr.Natchikethas answered seriously, "That she was very much into her career, she did not want marriage. She was also worried about my profession— surgery."

Geetha was sweating profusely. She could not move a step. She also did not want to embarrass Dr.Natchikethas either by going in.

Parvathi asked curiously, "What is the problem with your surgery?"

Dr.Natchikethas replied with a touch of sadness; "She felt that a surgeon is extremely busy. She thought the two careers would not mix properly; she would not be able to pursue her career effectively."

Parvathi asked with great concern, "Dr.Natchikethas, who is that girl? What is her name? I would like to talk to her. She is simply looking at her career – she is not evaluating life as a whole."

Geetha was very startled, "My mom wants to talk to that girl- oh my God! That is I! Mom is too sharp. She already knows that I did not want to marry. She knows that Dr.Natchikethas loves my music. Now, if she ever catches Dr.Natchikethas looking at me admiringly, she would know. Oh my God! What should I do? I do not want her to find out –it would pain her immensely. She has just recovered from a surgery."

She quickly made up her mind and simply went into their room.

Dr.Natchikethas saw Geetha coming in and was amazed, he exclaimed "Geetha!"

Geetha walked fast and came near them. As she said "Mom," her voice faltered. She said in a faint, almost whispering voice, " Mom, that girl is me!"

She saw the pain in her mom's face.

Gathering all the courage she had, she whispered gently, "Mom, if Dr.Natchikethas still wants to marry me, I will marry him,"

She simply sat on the bed with almost no energy left.

Dr.Natchikethas with an astonished but jubilant voice said, " Geetha!"

Parvathi was thrilled but she saw that Dr.Natchikethas had million things to say and million questions to ask; therefore, she quietly left the room with joy.

Dr.Natchikethas went near Geetha, held her hands and said softly, endearingly; "Geetha, I am so ecstatic with joy. My dear Geetha, of course, I want to marry you and spend the rest of my life with you. Would you marry me?"

Geetha became very shy; things happened so quickly. Nevertheless, she also felt as if a big burden had been lifted from her shoulders. She murmured with a soft, shy smile, "Yes!"

Dr.Natchikethas was exuberant and his joy and cheer were contagious- Geetha slowly relaxed.

Dr.Natchikethas said, " Geetha you have made me so joyous today. It is the happiest day of my life." Geetha smiled. Dr.Natchiketas continued with curiosity "Geetha, when did you find time to resolve all those tough questions?"

Geetha answered quietly; "Dr.Natchiketas, I found time during my trip to USA. I thought I should give you a thoughtful answer if you were to raise the topic."

Dr.Natchikethas proceeded with cheer, " Geetha, I am so glad that you took the time to think. Please tell me how you looked at these challenging issues."

Geetha slowly started, " The first issue was you career, your profession- surgery. The day my mom had a heart attack, God opened my eyes to another facet of surgery. Outstanding was your dedication in saving my mom. Outstanding was your care of my mom after surgery. Your love for surgery kept you awake all night to perform the operation meticulously. My heart softened towards surgery. The only remaining question regarding your career was whether you had enough free time."

Dr.Natchikethas asked with concern, " Geetha, how did you resolve that question?"

"Well, Dr.Natchikethas, the fact that I stayed here for a while helped me to observe your time. You had free time on Sunday. You made sure that you were not busy on Sunday. You indeed were totally relaxed on Sunday. You were also home one weekday morning. You had time on some evening. You did not perform surgery every night. I compared your time to Pavitran's. You were only a little bit busier. Therefore, free time would not be a problem. The next question was how would marriage affect my music career."

"Yes, that is indeed a very difficult question!" commented Dr.Natchikethas sympathetically.

A Tender Melody

"True, that was indeed the toughest challenge. I have dedicated my life to music. I really had to wrestle with that issue. Obviously, marriage would give me less time for music. However, I had to look at life as a whole. My mom just had a heart surgery. I suddenly realized that I had assumed that my mom would live forever. Suddenly, her frailty was brought home to me vividly. My mom wanted me to marry long time ago and I was resisting. Would that be fair to her? She was worried sick about my future."

Geetha became very emotional talking about her mom and her eyes became teary. She was silent for a moment. Dr.Natchikethas could feel her love for her mom. He gently pressed her hand.

Geetha continued in a low voice," The more I thought about my mom, the more my resistance to marriage crumbled. Dr.Natchikethas, I realized that I have to manage my music carrer in and through marriage. I have to watch my time carefully. Moreover, you love music and you have supported my music these four weeks. So, I was finally left with two key questions."

"What were they?" asked Dr.Natchikethas inquisitively.

Geetha answered, "Whether you were still interested? Whether, I really like you?"

Dr.Natchikethas prodded her saying "Well ....."

Geetha with a shy smile said, "Dr.Natchikethas, we just answered these two questions."

Dr.Natchikethas kiddingly said, "Geetha! I want to hear more details."

Geetha with a mischievous smile replied, "Later- there will be time later—now it is time for breakfast."

Around that time, Lakshmi was looking for Geetha and Dr.Natchikethas and wanted to chide them for being late for breakfast. She was totally flabbergasted when she saw Geetha and Dr.Natchikethas sitting closely and smilingly chitchatting. Dr.Natchikethas, seeing mom, said, " Mom, please come. I have a wonderful news for you. I just now proposed to Geetha and she agreed to marry me."

Lakshmi was so ecstatic and she hugged Geetha and Dr.Natchikethas. Lakshmi exclaimed "Parvathi, please come here."

Parvathi came quickly, though she knew, she had no time to hug them which she did now to her heart's content. Pavitran and Vimala came running to witness the commotion and Vimala hugged Geetha saying "Oh! Geetha, I am so happy to have you as my sister-in-law. I have been praying for this day!"

Pavitran was simply overwhelmed and hugged Geetha and Dr.Natchikethas. The whole family was shedding tears of joy!

Chapter - 46

For Latha, after Kumar left, the next three days were hectic. Four days later, on Saturday evening, she received a call;

"Latha, Hi! – This Veena."

"Veena, Hi – How are you?"

"Fine, Latha. How are you holding up?"

"Okay, I guess, Veena- I was down on the first day but now I am very busy with my work."

"Me too, Latha- but I shudder whenever I think of the accident."

"True Veena. On the day you guys left, I was very lonely; I went for a long walk along the Charles River and I cried when I came near the Sloan School."

"Well, Latha – it must have been very hard on you. You were there alone – you were there from the beginning."

"Yes – alone—all too alone, Veena. But, I am glad that Kumar is almost back to normal."

"Agreed, Latha. I talked to Mrs. Ram; Kumar is walking fast – back to normalcy. He is writing fast. Only speech remains and he has started his speech lessons."

"Yes, Veena. I called too – all of that makes me feel so much better."

" Latha, by the way, have you heard the news?"

" Well, what news, Veena?"

" So, you have not heard, Latha, I just learned from Harrish that Geetha is going to marry Dr.Natchikethas."

"Veena, really! That is indeed a big surprise! I thought Geetha was very much into her career."

"Me too, Latha – Actually I talked to her at length about her marriage when she was in San Francisco a few months ago. She wanted to devote her time to music – I talked to her just now – She said her mom's heart attack changed all that."

" What else did she say, Veena?"

"Well, Latha, actually, Dr.Natchikethas proposed to her few months ago and she declined. When he brought it back again today, she agreed. Her mom's desire for her to be married was the chief motivating factor."

"That might well be true, Veena. But I think there is another critical factor."

"Really, what, Latha?"

"I think, Veena, she must have fallen in love with Dr.Natchikethas in these couple of months. They have been so close recently. Dr.Natchikethas performed the operation on her mom and she is living in his house. They also have a common interest- Music."

Veena was quiet for a moment.

Latha asked, " Veena, you are silent."

Veena answered, " Latha, I really don't know how this love comes."

Latha did not answer that question. They drifted to another topic. When Veena put the phone down, she was amazed by Latha's assertion.

Veena immediately called Geetha. Geetha politely said, "Veena, you just called me!"

"Yes, Geetha but I have a burning question to ask you."

"Okay, Veena- What?"

"Geetha, this is very personal-could I ask you such a question?"

"Veena, you are indeed a very close friend. I will try to answer."

"Geetha, I just talked to Latha and told her everything. She asserted that there is another pressing reason why you agreed to marry Dr.Natchikethas."

"Veena, what is that?"

Veena said softly "Geetha, she felt that deep down you must have fallen in love with Dr.Natchikethas."

Geetha was quiet and pensive; she said in a low voice, "Well, Veena, I cannot deny that my liking for him has grown a lot. On that night, when he performed that operation successfully— that early morning, when he walked slowly and tiredly after the operation is when my heart went out to him. Slowly, he has indeed won my heart."

Veena thanked Geetha for her openness.

Geetha said thoughtfully, "Actually, Veena, this has been a revelation for me too. True, I do indeed love him deeply now."

Veena asked with curiosity, "How does it happen, Geetha?"

Geetha thought for a moment. "Why is Veena asking this question? She never asked me such a question. Does she like Harrish? Harrish oh! My dear Harrish – That would be lovely- Veena is adorable-But I do not know what Harrish wants- Is Latha out of his system. May be, I should talk to him."

Thinking thus, Geetha answered slowly, "Veena, I really don't know——so many things have to come together for it to happen—— it is almost an act of providence! However, if two people like each other, then it blossoms over time if the environment is favorable."

Then, Geetha added very softly with a personal touch, "Veena, you may feel it sooner than you think."

Veena, then, was not too comfortable to talk about that topic and so she ended the conversation quickly, thanking Geetha again for her openness.

Veena then thought, "How did Latha know so well? I have to find it out."

Therefore, she called Latha "Latha, I just called Geetha. Even Geetha had to think deeply and then she agreed. Latha how did you guess so well?"

Latha did not answer-

Veena continued, " Latha, could I ask you a question?"

Latha replied, "Veena, no-no-no: please don't ask me that question."

"Latha, then, is that true?"

"Veena- Please- may be- I am all confused now."

"Is it that confusing?"

"I really don't know how deep these feeling are."

"Really "

"Veena, I really don't know. It is all new feelings. I don't know how deep these feeling are."

"Really"

"May be, only time would tell."

"Okay, Latha, I will not bother you."

"You are my closest friend. I will definitely confide in you—— please give me time."

"Okay- Good night –Latha."

"Good night- Veena."

Latha thought quietly for a moment; "Oh boy – this Veena is sharp! I make an innocent comment on Geetha and she turns it around on me! I need to probe into my own feelings. Love is so mysterious!"

Chapter - 47

Next day, on Sunday, Veena got up rather early in the morning, around 5am. She thought a little bit about the last night's conversation with Latha but quickly decided to focus on music. Music relaxed her in the morning. Every Sunday morning, Harrish, Veena and Mrs. Ravi spent a relaxed two hours on carnatic music lesson from 6am to 8am. Today, Veena decided to go to the music room and practice the songs that her mom had taught her. After shower, she wore an elegant saree and went to the music room. With reverence, she prostrated before the pictures of the music masters Thyagaraja, Shyama Shastri and Dikshithar and then, started her music. Today, she was in the mood for music and was soon very absorbed in the songs.

Soon, Harrish and Mrs. Ravi joined her but they quietly sat and listened in deference to the music mood of Veena. The devotion of Veena to music touched Harrish. At the end, Harrish commented, "Veena, today you are singing beautifully."

Veena with a shy smile said, "Thanks."

Turning to Mrs Ravi, Harrish said, "Mrs. Ravi, may be, Veena should learn first. She is grasping quickly and moving fast."

Veena asked " Why? Harrish"

Harrish replied, "Veena, I don't want to hold you up, you can go faster. Moreover, you can use your time more effectively when I learn slowly."

"Harrish, you ask good technical questions – I do learn then."

After the music lesson, Harrish usually joined them for breakfast on Sunday. Dr. Ravi made sure that he was free on Sunday morning and they never talked business during breakfast; but, after breakfast, Veena, Harrish and Dr.Ravi discussed a few pressing business issues. Dr.Ravi could be relaxed and very open during this session and it was a great learning experience for Veena and Harrish.

During breakfast, Veena asked her dad, "Dad, do you know Geetha and Dr. Natchikethas are getting married?"

"No- Veena – I came rather late last night – That news is wonderful; I like both Dr. Natchikethas and Geetha – That is indeed great. I will call them after breakfast. By the way, how is Kumar doing? Harrish, you are close to him."

Harrish replied, "Dr.Ravi, Kumar has recovered fast. He is almost normal. Only speech has not come yet. He is taking speech lessons."

Veena added, "Dad; Latha, Harrish and I plan to go to Atlanta two weeks from now. We want to cheer up Kumar."

Mrs Ravi commented "I may go a few days earlier. Kumar wants to learn the basics of music."

Dr.Ravi encouraged the plan – "That is great! Kumar has gone through hell. All of this would certainly cheer him up."

About two weeks from then, one by one every one arrived in Dr.Ram's house in Atlanta – Mrs. Ravi on Wednesday, Latha, Chitra and Dr. Gangadhran on Friday evening, Harrish and Veena on Saturday morning. Saturday noontime, they all got together for a simple brunch with Idly, samber, salad and curd rice. The mood was lively and cheerful; everyone was relieved that Kumar escaped severe tragedy. However, Latha was somewhat introspective and solemn. Veena and Harrish noticed it but did not bother her.

After brunch, Harrish looked for Veena and found her in the front porch admiring the beautiful garden. Harrish said, "Veena, I want to discuss something with you."

"What? Harrish."

"I thought Latha was reflective and sober. Normally, she is jolly and fun loving in these functions. Do you know why?"

Veena was surprised at this question and she did not know how to answer. She sort of knew, but, not quite. Veena thought, "Even, Latha is not fully sure – what could I tell Harrish?"

Harish saw the delicate reticence of Veena. Harrish gently told Veena, "I see that the matter is subtle, private and tentative. Hence, let me withdraw the question."

Soon, Harrish went to a quiet place in the garden and paced back and forth thinking about the issue. "What is bothering Latha?" He thought about Kumar's hospital stay. "Is Kumar's lack of speech worrying her? No, she was very happy about his recovery." Then the airport send off flashed in his memory.

"Latha was very much in tears. She was quite emotional. Why?"

Harrish was not sure. Then, something triggered in his mind. "Oh! Was she missing Kumar? May be, does Latha love Kumar?" He thought of Veena's face. It was a little embarrassed, delicate and uncertain – she suspected it but not sure. "Oh, Latha might have loved Kumar along. Probably, it was in her subconscious mind. That is the reason she did not encourage me. I should have talked to her at length"

He thought "Past is past – no point in wasting the time on the past – let us move forward." He wondered "why is Latha so serious? – She should have been merry and lively." He remembered that Kumar hardly talked to Latha. Usually, they chit chatted and kidded around jovially. He could not figure out why. The more he thought, the less he could understand it. "Why? Why? Why?" Then, he decided to talk to Kumar.

He went around looking for Kumar but could not locate him. Therefore, he decided to ask Mrs. Ram about Kumar's whereabouts. He found Mrs. Ram on the side porch talking with Aruna and Chitra. Harrish went near them and asked Mrs. Ram "Mrs. Ram, where is Kumar? I cannot find him."

"Oh Harish, Kumar has gone for a speech lesson. He is very serious about speech. As you know, when Kumar is serious, he is intense. He does not want to miss a single class. He would be back by tea time."

"Mrs. Ram, that is indeed great. By the way, how is his speech? I did not get a chance to talk to him about it."

" It is getting better everyday. He is able to say one word. However, you have to ask a question. For example, early in the morning, if I ask, "What do you want, Kumar?" He would say " coffee." If I ask him in the afternoon, "where do you want to go?" He would say "movie."

Chitra said, "Radha that is great. That means he can articulate his basic needs."

Radha agreed, " Chitra, life is much better now. He could answer the entire question with one word, but is not yet spontaneous. He cannot yet come out with phrases."

Aruna asked, "How does he practice?"

Radha answered, "Aruna, it is an all day process. We have to ask him questions all day."

Harrish commented, "Mrs. Ram, then, I could call him every day and ask questions."

"Harrish, that would be lovely."

Harrish waited for Kumar and after tea, they walked in the garden.

Harrish asked, " Kumar, now that you could say one word, how do you feel?"

"Great!" said Kumar.

"I will call you every day and ask you questions."

"Thanks."

"I have a question to ask you."

"Okay."

"During lunch, Latha was subdued and contemplative. You hardly talked to her. What is going on, Kumar? Could you write please?"

Kumar became thoughtful and then paused for a while. Then he wrote, " Harrish, this is a delicate subject. I really do not know every thing fully. I suspect that Latha likes me. However, I do not want to encourage her. I cannot talk fluently yet. Latha could do better."

After he wrote that, Kumar hurried into the house. He did not want to discuss that subject.

Harrish was surprised at Kumar's decision. " I will talk to Kumar later. Too much is happening in his life now."

Harrish looked for Veena so that she could convey this information to Latha. He did not want Latha to misunderstand Kumar. When Harrish informed Veena, she was amazed and asked, " How could Kumar make such a decision?"

Harrish replied, " Veena, Kumar has just recovered from a severe accident. So much is going on in his life now. We need to give him time."

Veena agreed.

In the evening, Dr and Mrs. Ram arranged a gala dinner with several local and out of town guests to celebrate Kumar's recovery. Every one was well dressed and was in a jovial, jubilant sprit. When Kumar entered the living room in a blue suit and a colourful red tie, he looked handsome. Every one gave him a warm, spontaneous applause. Kumar gave a big beaming smile and shook hands with every one. The gourmet dinner was delicious; it was fitting to the sunny, lively, sparkling spirit.

Next day morning, Veena and Latha went for a walk. Veena gently informed Latha the conversation between Harrish and Kumar. Latha became meditative and then remarked softly, " Veena, I could appreciate the noble sentiments expressed by Kumar. However, I have my own feelings too. Kumar has to respect that. I have made up my mind. Speech, of course, would be great. However, it is not paramount for me. He is able to communicate well by writing. There are many speech processors in the market today. Utmost important to me is compatibility and respect for each other."

"Anyhow, Veena, I'm going to be busy with the Book Release Function. Kumar is also working hard on his speech. May be, I would talk to him after the Book Function."

Chapter - 48

On the Book Release Function day, on Sunday, everyone started arriving in New York City. Dr.Gangadharan, Mrs. Gangadharan and Latha came on Saturday evening so that they could rest well. Because of the time difference, the west coast residents, Mrs Ravi, Veena and Harrish, came also on Saturday evening. The rest came on Sunday morning and Dr.Ravi flew on Sunday afternoon from London.

The function was to start at 5 pm with informal tea at 4:15pm. The key organizers came in early at 3:00 pm. Harrish was in charge of the podium and mike arrangements. Veena and Latha were responsible for welcoming the guests. Dr.Ram managed the seating arrangements. Dr. Gangadharan and Mrs. Gangadharan were to welcome the special guests. Kumar was not given any assignment due to his recovery and was to come late. Dr Ravi was arriving late around 4:30pm directly from the airport.

Mrs. Gangadharan asked Latha to stand in front of the hall fifteen minutes before 4pm, just in case, a guest were to arrive early. Latha was dressed in a gorgeous blue saree and looked fabulous and charming. Lo and Behold! Two persons who looked like guests did arrive early. Their car pulled up in the front and a young couple alighted from the car. Latha wondered who could it be – the closer she looked, it was none other than Geetha and Dr.Natchikethas. Dr.Natchikethas had flown from Houston that morning. She ran towards Geetha hugged her and congratulated Dr.Natchikethas and Geetha. Spotting Geetha, Veena came and hugged her. Harrish was thrilled to see them. Soon, everyone came and congratulated the newly engaged couple. The mood became lively and jubilant.

Soon, Geetha excused herself; never did she talk much before the concert. She focused all her attention on music. By her serious face, everyone understood that she wanted to be alone to focus on her music. Harrish helped her with the mike arrangements.

Dr.Ravi arrived on time, which was a big relief to Dr and Mrs.Gangadharan. Aruna Ravi rushed from the tearoom to greet him and Veena seated him in the front dignitary row. Senator Tom Brooks entered the hall five minutes before the function and Dr, and Mrs.Gangadharan escorted him and his wife to the distinguished guest row in the front.

Latha was looking for Kumar. He did not arrive yet. The function was about start in two minutes. Latha was supposed to sit in the front row. Not wanting to dissappoint her parents, she rushed to the front row still wondering about Kumar. "Is he mad? Why? Is he mad at me? A jolly guy – what is going on? He loves my dad and mom. He would not do this to them." Then it struck her. " Oh I see – he cannot talk – so he did not want to embarrass himself – he cannot respond to questions. Why should he think that way? He could write; true, it is a bit slow – so what?" She was wondering thus.

The function started exactly at five. Geetha sang melodiously with all her heart. Latha forgot Kumar for a while. Geetha started with a touching song about India "Vande Matharam." Next, she sang with great devotion "Nagendrahara", paying homage to Lord Shiva. She followed with a popular piece from "Meera Bhajan" on Lord Krishna and her emotional rendering of that song touched everyone. She ended with a beautiful piece from Poet Bharathiar. Geetha received a standing ovation from everyone.

Prof. William H.Malcolm, professor of Economics at Harvard University, gave the keynote address. "The book – "Gone a golden moment – is it?" - is a deep, erudite masterpiece work on the tough subject of India – US trade. The book probes deeply into the central question – why is the Indo – US trade in doldrums compared to that of China or Far East? – It not only asks that question and answers it comprehensively – moreover, it delves deep into ideas to improve the situation." Prof. Malcolm discussed at length one chapter and every one gave him a warm applause appreciating his thoughtful speech in a sonorous voice.

Latha was wondering about Kumar. When the audiences were clapping for Prof. Malcolm, she quickly almost ran to the back to look for Kumar. Kumar was nowhere to be seen. Latha quickly got back to her seat so that her parents would not look for her. However, she worried a little "Is Kumar in any accident?" This thought gripped her as she had just witnessed an accident of Kumar. "But his parents would have known. They are participating cheerfully." Latha decided that there was no point in worrying and she would ask Mrs. Ram and Harrish at the end of the function.

As planned, Prof. Malcolm's speech was long where as Honorable Joseph Gore made it crisp and to the point. Senator Tom Brooks gave a stirring speech; he praised the book illustrating it with real life examples from his tenure as Ambassador to India. The audience enthusiastically clapped his speech.

Dr.Gangadharan marched to the podium amidst thunderous applause. Latha was very proud of her father. Chitra Gangadharan was overwhelmed. She had tears in her eyes. What a struggle it had been ever since his heart attack! She was so proud of him as he had successfully chosen a second career. It was a telling moment for the family. Dr.Gangadharan briefly recalled the challenges in creating the book. He thanked Chitra Gangadhran for her infinite support. He cited the help of Dr.Ram's family and of Harrish. He thanked the audience for their generous support. He was given a standing ovation.

Once the function was over, Latha and Veena had pre-assigned task to taking care of key guests; they were both extremely busy thanking those guests and saying "goodbye" to them. Latha had zero time to look for Kumar or Mrs Ram; actually, all the organizers were extremely busy attending to guests. Almost all the guest had departed; the spacious hall was sparsely populated. Latha had just completed her task and she started to proceed towards Mrs.Ram to enquire about Kumar.

As she was walking towards Mrs.Ram, she felt a tap on her shoulder and a familiar voice saying, "Latha." She turned around and there was Kumar standing in front of her with a big smile. He was dressed in a dark gray suit and an arresting maroon tie. He held something at the back of him. She thought it might be his writing slate.

Latha had not seen Kumar for two months; neither did they correspond with each other. They had avoided each other though Latha kept in touch with his mom. She did not how Kumar was going to behave today. He was disregarding her in Atlanta. He did not show up early in this function either.

Latha was stunned to see his smile. He had not smiled like that for a long time. Now, Kumar came closer and put his one arm on her shoulder. Latha's heart started to pound. What was he planning? She was too nervous to reply to his calling "Latha." She knew that he could say one word but now it was spontaneous.

Now Kumar looked into her eyes and softly asked, "Latha, will you marry me?".

Latha was astounded and speechless. "Kumar is talking! Kumar is talking! He is asking me to marry him!" However, she was totally numb for a moment.

Kumar lovingly and emotionally said, "Latha, just four days ago – words came out spontaneously – next day phrases and then two days later sentences - I could not believe it. It was indeed a miracle! I thought I would keep it a top secret and surprise you. Even my parent's do not know- no one except my speech therapist and I had her promise to secrecy. I wanted my first words to the outside world to be " Latha, will you marry me?"

Latha was totally overwhelmed. She simply put her arms on his shoulders and hid her face on his chest. Tears of joy started to flow.

"Latha, I brought you these beautiful roses from Atlanta. "saying this, he gave her the roses and gently hugged her.

A little later ,Kumar impishly and teasingly reminded her, "Latha, you have not answered my question!"

Latha lovingly pinched his cheek and said, " Kumar, I have and you know I have!"

Dr Gangadharan and Mrs. Gangadharan saw Kumar near Latha and they hurried to Kumar to ask him when he came. When they were near, Kumar said, "Oh, Dr Gangadharan and Mrs. Gangadharan—— surprise, surprise – I can talk now!"

They were astonished and hugged him saying 'Kumar!'". They were thrilled to hear his voice; then Kumar continued, " I have another big surprise for you . I just asked Latha for her hand in marriage and she accepted. May we have your permission?—"

Before he could finish, Dr Gangadharan hugged him ,"of course, Kumar, you have my heart felt blessings!! What a day this is!!"

Chitra was simply ecstatic and with tears she embraced Kumar and Latha. Dr.Ram and Radha seeing the commotion with Kumar and Latha came fast towards them. Kumar ran to his mother and hugged her, "Mom, I can talk now. I just asked Latha to marry me and she agreed"

Radha was so overjoyed that Kumar could talk. Now Kumar was going to be married!! She could not believe it!

Dr Ram and Radha embraced Kumar and Latha— also Dr and Mrs. Gangadharan.

Seeing the tumultuous scene, Harrish rushed towards Kumar. When he found out that his dear friend, Kumar could talk, he was flabbergasted. "Kumar, it is great that you can talk. I missed your speech so much. I am also thrilled that Latha and you are getting married—congratulations!!" He hugged them both and congratulated them with all his heart. Veena embraced her dear dear friend Latha and then congratulated Kumar.

Truly, the Book Release Function became a small Engagement party!!!

Later, Dr and Mrs.Gangadharan had arranged a thank-you dinner for their closest friends and organizers— Dr and Mrs Ravi, Veena, Dr. and Mrs Ram , Kumar, Harrish, Geetha and Dr. Natchikethas.

It became a jubilant, colorful engagement dinner for both the newly engaged couples - Kumar and Latha, Geetha and Dr Natchikethas!!!

Chapter - 49

After the Book Function dinner in NewYork, Harrish went to his hotel room to get some sleep so that he could catch the flight to Los Angeles at 6 am the next day. He had to attend an important meeting between V –Digitronics and Saturn Computing executives at 11 am in Los Angles on Monday morning. Since Harrish had arranged the meeting, he had to be there positively. Veena was arriving the next day for the technical meeting .There would be intense technical discussion on Tuesday and Wednesday and the whole business and technical deal between V-Digitronics and Saturn would be wrapped up on or before Friday.

Harrish prepared well for the meeting on the flight and once all the key issues were thought through and written down, he had some time to reflect. He was extremely happy about Kumar's and Latha's engagment. Kumar was his dear dear friend and Latha his close friend. It was wonderful to see them happy—Boy, Kumar was talking! It was superb!! Utmost great was seeing Geetha and Dr Natchikethas. Together they were laughing during the whole dinner.

Harrish's mind then thought of Veena. " She was so lively and resplendent during the dinner; she was so beautiful! I need to talk to her soon, to keep the dialog going. As Geetha said, communication is the key. I have to talk to her wherever it may lead." He jotted down the points he wanted to talk to her over the weekend.

On Saturday morning, right after the music lesson, Harrish spent an hour thinking through the issues. One thought bothered him. "Am I ready for another rejection? But one cannot be afraid. Life has to move on. Moreover, Veena is worth the extra pain. I don't want to lose her by not putting forth the needed effort."

Once determined, he called Veena on her cell phone,

"Hi! Veena, this is Harrish."

"Hi! Harrish, what a surprise call."

"Yes, I want to talk to you. Would you have time in the morning?"

"Yes, Harrish ,when?"

"In ten or fifteen minutes"

"Okay, where?"

"Veena ,why not here in my place?"

"Fine, will see you soon."

Veena knew Harrish was serious by nature and hence, this must be quite important. She also knew Harrish to be kind and gentlemanly. So she was not too worried about the topic. She dressed simply and tastefully and walked over and rang the doorbell. Harrish opened the door and smiled.

"Veena, thanks a lot for coming:"

Veena smiled and came in and Harrish offered, "Veena, I have some tea ready. Would you like a cup?"

Veena said, "Ok thanks, I see this would be a long conversation."

Harrish smilingly said, "Yes, I guess you are right."

After pouring the tea, Harrish started, "Well, Veena, as you know the V-Digitronics and Saturn Computing meetings went extremely well. I feel the project would go outstandingly great."

Veena cheerfully agreed. "Yes, Harrish,they went beyond my expectations too."

Harrish added warmly, "I am happy about Kumar's speech and excited about his engagement to Latha. I was thrilled to see Geetha and Dr Natchikethas happy together."

Veena laughingly said, "Harrish, you are in a good mood today."

Harrish replied with a grin, "Yes, Veena, I want to fully utilize that mood today. Hence, I want to start the dialog with you now. As I told you before, communication is very important."

A Tender Melody

As soon as Harrish said "communication", Veena knew instantly what he wanted to talk about. She was not sure whether she was ready to discuss that issue now.

Seeing the cloud on her face, Harrish said in a soft, entreating tone,

"Veena, this is important—— no big decisions today—— just a dialog—— you will have plenty of time to think about it."

Veena looked at Harrish. She felt that he was very very anxious to talk about the issue. She felt calmer as she remembered "no big decision today."

Veena said quietly, "Okay, Harrish, as long as it is just a dialog."

Harrish responded with emotion, "You know, Veena, the engagement fever is contagious. I saw so many happy faces—they have inspired me —otherwise, I also would have postponed the discussion."

Veena looked at Harrish and replied softly, "Harrish, I see that you have given a lot of thought to this issue. Please express your thoughts and feelings. I will listen carefully and respectfully. I might need some time to respond properly."

Harrish opened his thoughts and feelings on the subject; "Veena, I feel two things are necessary for two people to be married happily— first, is compatibility and second is certain "positive chemistry". We are indeed very compatible—— both of us are deep and thoughtful—— we get along famously in the business world—we worked superbly well in V-digitronics and Saturn Computing".

Veena said, "I agree, Harrish."

"Moreover, recently we have been taking music lessons together . You sing melodiously and I love music—so there is wonderful compatibility there also."

Veena murmured, "True".

"The topic of chemistry is, of course, subjective; I have given a lot of thought to that challenging mystery. Utmost attracted am I to you. I cannot define it – I just feel it, Veena".

So saying Harrish looked at Veena. Veena was touched by his sincere feelings.

She paused for a few minutes and then replied with a touch of softness and feelings, "Harrish – I really— really respect your feelings. Please give me some time to think about the chemistry." and then she quietly left.

Veena rang the doorbell and her mom opened the door. Veena looked serious. Veena said "Mom, I have something deep to think about. Please, I don't want to take any phone calls." Her mom knew that Veena needed time alone when she was introspective and hence agreed readily.

Veena went up, closed the door of her room and sat on her sofa. She was surprised by Harrish's proposal. She had thought that he might take a long time— if ever. So she had not spent much time recently thinking about the issue.

"Harrish had been honest—— the engagement fever was on." Veena smiled thinking of Latha and Geetha.

"Am I ready?" worried Veena.

"Let me go through the points Harrish enumerated. First, is compatibility- yes, we work extremely well together in the business world—nay—we just click- my dad thinks very highly of him –actually, he could be a great asset in Gigabit. He has already saved $ 5 million investment and turned around Saturn Computing from disaster. He has outstanding business savvy. What he lacks is deep technical knowledge. That is where I could help him. We indeed form a great fabulous team there."

"Music is a surprise area of compatibility. I thought he was way above me in music – surprise, surprise – I sing much better than him." Veena smiled at this victory !

"The next question is a tough one –chemistry— Boy !—— How do I define it? Harrish says he is attracted to me—he is indeed very sincere." She smiled and was very happy to hear that.

"But am I attracted to him? Yes—I do like him a lot – is that love? —I am not sure"

Then, from nowhere, a most troubling thought penetrated her mind.

"Latha——he liked Latha first——why?—he has openly talked about it . Why am I troubled? What is wrong with me? Is it my ego? Latha told me "not to hold that against him"—I told her bravely "he had a wonderful taste—it just did not work out"—of course, at that time, Harrish and I were just getting to know each other. Now, it is way different. Kumar had said "it would have fallen apart" but why didn't Harrish see it then?"

"I need to talk to someone openly. Kumar is too partial to Harrish . Latha is an involved party. Could I talk to my mom? No—she adores Harrish – she would totally forgive him"

While mulling over this topic, her cell phone rang. She did not want to take the call but she was curious to see "who" and she looked at the number. It was Geetha's number –Geetha had a cell phone to enable people to contact her as she traveled in the USA—Veena quickly decided to take the call.

"Geetha, this is Veena, what a surprise call".

"Yes Veena –I am in Chicago and giving a concert tomorrow here. I am flying to Phoenix, Arizona on Monday for a concert on Tuesday. Suddenly a group is arranging my concert in San Francisco."

"Geetha, that's wonderful –when?"

" Thursday evening"

"Geetha, I will pick you up at the airport. Please tell me when and what airlines. Of course , you are staying with us."

"What is convenient for you?"

" Wednesday morning would be perfect. I have a meeting in the afternoon. If you could come in the morning, we can have breakfast and then chit-chat. You could practice your music in the afternoon."

"Okay, Veena –I will take the seven thirty am flight and would be there early."

"Great, Geetha—will see you then""

Veena decided to talk to Geetha. She knew Harrish very well but was also very level headed.

Chapter - 50

On Wednesday morning after breakfast, Veena and Geetha sat together on the sofa and Veena opened the conversation.

"Geetha, I have something important to talk to you"

"Veena, I am all ears for you"

"Geetha, Harrish proposed to me a few days ago"

Geetha was thrilled within to hear this, but she felt Veena had some concerns and so did not show her emotion. Instead said, "Veena, it seems you have some worries. Please tell me."

Hearing Geetha's sympathetic voice, Veena poured her heart out including the Latha issue.

Then, Veena asked,

"Geetha, why am I not jumping up and down with happiness? Why do I have all these concerns?"

Geetha smilingly said, "Veena could you believe it? When Dr.Natchikethas proposed to me, I was mad at him."

Veena laughed.

Geetha continued seriously,

" I was not ready then. Please give it some time. If it is destined, it would happen."

Veena said gently, " Geetha, I do like Harrish a lot. Why am I troubled by this Latha issue?"

Geetha became contemplative for a moment – then said, "Veena, let me tell you an episode. One day, you and Dr. Natchikethas were sitting in our living room discussing "V—digitronics". I came down the stairs and saw you both sitting close and intimately discussing. Dr Natchikethas had not even proposed then. I felt very jealous."

Veena laughed heartily—— "Me and Dr.Natchikethas! ha! ha!"

Now Geetha caught her, "Now you see Veena – you laugh heartily at my expense but it is the same between Latha and Harrish – even worse – at least Dr.Natchikethas and you had common interest in V- digitronics – moreover, Dr.Natchikethas' mother liked you a lot—it is not as far fetched as you think."

"But, in Latha's case, she had zero interest in Harrish from the beginning and Harrish's interest had waned quickly to zero long time ago. As you know, Harrish had felt for sometime that it was a naïve mistake on his part. You saw how happy he was when Kumar proposed to Latha and how warmly he congratulated them. Yet, you are troubled—why ?—please think deeply- you will find the answer."

Geetha paused for this point to sink in. Veena became quite thoughtful—she asked herself "Why? Why ? Why was Geetha jealous? Was I jealous? Am I jealous? Why?"

Then the truth hit her ———

"I really, do love Harrish! I have loved him all the time! I was jealous when he showed interest in Latha. I did not like it— his liking for Latha bothered me for a long time—— even now ——— I have loved him all along! He is very very dear to me!!."

Veena sat there speechless but there was a warm glow on her face. Geetha saw that halo and felt that her work was done. Veena looked at Geetha and knew that she understood .She just hugged Geetha and thanked her.

A Tender Melody

Geetha was ecstatic. Harrish was extremely dear to her and she adored Veena. It would be wonderful ! Geetha felt that Veena would need some time to sit and think; so she quietly left the room.

Veena reflected on her new found knowledge, "When did I start liking Harrish? –maybe in the fourth meeting— when did I get mad at him? When I found out that Latha was not keen – I found that out at M. I. T but Harrish did not see it –that's when I was upset with him."

" When Latha told Harrish bluntly her feelings, my anger subsided and I was sympathetic—I offered him the apartment in our house and got Geetha to talk to him. Did I move to San Francisco to be near him? —— May be —in a way, that was the best move—— everyday, we were getting closer together—we have spent a lot of time together——finally, Harrish proposed – "utmost attracted to you"— —at some level, he must have sensed my love—he has been so cautious and yet he proposed — what has been my problem? —I had not fathomed my own feelings— it took a Geetha to point it out to me."

Then, she thought of Harrish,"Poor Harrish; he must be wondering —I have not said a word—four days have passed—is it another rejection? – but he told me that I had plenty of time to think – just a dialog—but, still he must be worried".

Her heart melted for him. Then Veena thought, "I need to act fast". Once Veena decided on something, she always moved quickly.

Veena called her office and postponed all her meetings.

Next she called Harrish on his cell, "Harrish, this is Veena"

Harrish was astounded — "Veena?"

"Harrish, yes it is me— I need to talk to you—are you in a meeting?"

"Yes Veena—but it will be over in half an hour"

"Harrish, could you postpone your afternoon meetings? I have postponed mine –could we meet at Gaylord's restaurant in one hour?"

Harrish knew Veena had something critical to discuss; so he said quietly "Of-course, Veena— will meet you in one hour."

"Thanks, Harrish"

"Veena, will see you soon"

Veena dressed simply but beautifully with a colorful salwar, which Harrish had liked before. Then she quickly rushed to the restaurant – she wanted to be there a few minutes before Harrish.

As she stood near the entrance, Harrish arrived in a few minutes. Harrish always dressed stylishly with taste for the office as he had business meetings every day. He was in a dark blue suit with a matching attractive tie. He looked handsome and he walked briskly to meet Veena. She looked gorgeous to him.

As he alighted the steps, she walked fast towards him – a startled Harrish stopped.

Veena placed her hands on his shoulders and said almost in a whisper, "Harrish, I have so much to tell you."

Harrish anxiously looked at her face. She had a shy, cheerful smile with sparkling, glowing eyes. That gave him the answer that he was desperately seeking for the last few days.

He put his arms around her and said, "Oh! Veena, I really love you—— I found out how deeply in the last few days fervently waiting for your answer"

"Harrish, I just found the answer——I had loved you all along——just did not know my own feelings —— utmost confused was I with small issues —it all became clear to me just now—thanks to Geetha — Harrish, you have always been very precious and dear to me".

Harrish hugged her and said lovingly, "Veena, I am indeed very happy now!"

She could feel his warm and affectionate love. In a few minutes, they entered the restaurant joyfully holding hands.

Around lunchtime, Mrs. Ravi looked for Veena, not knowing that she had left. Then, she searched for her car and it was not there either. Mrs. Ravi then called her office and they told her that Veena had taken the afternoon off. She was puzzled, "Where is Veena? She always informs me". Geetha just came out of her room.

Mrs. Ravi asked anxiously, "Do you know where Veena is?"

Geetha replied, "No, Mrs. Ravi, she said she had a meeting at the office"

Mrs Ravi said, "She had cancelled her meeting and taken the afternoon off, she has even turned off her cell phone"

Geetha mused, "Strange! Have you called Harrish ? They work on so many projects together."

Mrs. Ravi agreed, "Good idea—let me call Harrish in the office."

Harrish was not there either and had taken the afternoon off. Geetha could not help a flicker of a smile for she guessed "why." She told Mrs. Ravi to try

Harrish on his cell. Harrish picked up the phone and said, "Mrs. Ravi, hi! what a surprise call"

"Harrish, is Veena with you?" asked Mrs. Ravi with concern.

"Yes Mrs. Ravi – here she is" and gave the phone to Veena.

Veena said apologetically, "Mom, I am so sorry— I was in a hurry and rush – I always leave a message—but, mom, to soothe your feelings, let me give a wonderful news."

Startled Mrs. Ravi asked, " Veena, what?"

Veena said with excitement, "Mom, just now Harrish and I agreed to marry – we are engaged!"

Mrs. Ravi shrieked in joy, "No kidding—I can't believe it. Now you are forgiven! Is that why you were so solemn the last four days?".

"Yes mom—Harrish proposed on Saturday and it took me four days to decide—I had lot of thinking to do"

" I understand now, Veena — I really do"

"Mom, is Geetha there?"

"Veena, she is right here" saying that Mrs. Ravi gave the phone to Geetha.

"Geetha, thanks a million—it is all set now"

"Veena, congratulations a thousand times. May I talk to Harrish?"

"Harrish, congratulations!! You have a wonderful life partner. Please take good care of her "

Harrish agreed enthusiastically, "Geetha, of course, I will—thanks a lot Geetha – Veena told me all about it" Geetha gave the phone to Mrs. Ravi.

"When will you guys be home? Veena, we will have some of your favorite desserts and coffee here – please don't eat sweets there"

"No, mom – we are just having soup and pakoda snack, we are so busy talking; will be there in two hours."

Mrs. Ravi was all excited and called Dr Ravi on his cell. She rarely called him.

"Aruna, what a surprise!!"

"Yes dear – a wonderful news have I, Veena and Harrish are engaged"

Dr. Ravi who is calm usually, jumped, "Can't believe it, Aruna! What a great news! Two of my most promising young Vice Presidents are getting engaged !".

Mrs. Ravi kiddingly said, "Ravi dear, it is always Gigabit –isn't it? Please remember they are my students too!"

Dr Ravi smiled and asked, "When are they coming home?"

"Three pm"

"Okay Aruna – I have to come in person to congratulate my young executives!"

Geetha and Mrs. Ravi planned the evening and came up with a great idea. They arranged for sweets and went upstairs to get dressed.

Exactly at three, the door bell rang. Mrs. Ravi, well dressed, opened the door, smiled cheerfully at the newly engaged couple and lovingly said,

"Veena dear, Harrish dear – please wait for one minute."

Veena and Harrish looked gorgeous and radiant together and stood patiently.

They watched Geetha, resplendently dressed, and Mrs. Ravi bring a decorated deep brass plate with saffron-colored water (Arathi). They saw Dr Ravi smilingly standing a little bit away.

Mrs. Ravi and Geetha holding the Arathi together waved it artfully in front of the couple, singing the soul-touching song "Jaya jaya mangala_____"in the melodious "Bhairavi" ragam. The song pleaded for Victory and Auspiciousness to the Goddess of Learning.

Why Goddess of Learning? — Because, Knowledge is needed for victory.

But way beyond Knowledge is the Soul. As the melody moved deeper and deeper, Veena and Harrish were touched—the song touched their hearts—they held their hands softly and lovingly—the depth of the melody touched their souls – a tear or two appeared in their eyes.

When a divine Melody touches the Soul, blessed Peace descends that takes you beyond the cares!!